BEST SERVED COLD

A Monika Paniatowski Mystery

Sally Spencer

This first world edition published 2015
in Great Britain and the USA by
SEVERN HOUSE PUBLISHERS LTD of
19 Cedar Road, Sutton, Surrey, England, SM2 5DA.
Trade paperback edition first published
in Great Britain and the USA 2015 by
SEVERN HOUSE PUBLISHERS LTD.

British Library Cataloguing in Publication Data

Spencer, Sally author.
  Best served cold. – (The Monika Paniatowski mysteries)
  1. Paniatowski, Monika (Fictitious character)–Fiction.
  2. Police–England–Fiction. 3. Theatrical companies–
  Fiction. 4. Murder–Investigation–Fiction. 5. Detective
  and mystery stories.
  I. Title II. Series
  823.9'2-dc23

ISBN-13: 978-0-7278-8507-4 (cased)
ISBN-13: 978-1-84751-611-4 (trade paper)
ISBN-13: 978-1-78010-662-5 (e-book)

All Severn House titles are printed on acid-free paper.

Severn House Publishers support the Forest Stewardship Council™ [FSC™],
the leading international forest certification organisation. All our titles that
are printed on FSC certified paper carry the FSC logo.

Typeset by Palimpsest Book Production Ltd.,
Falkirk, Stirlingshire, Scotland.
Printed and bound in Great Britain by
TJ International, Padstow, Cornwall.

Revenge is a dish best served cold.

PROLOGUE

30th March 1957

H e stands at the centre of a small, transient world – alone, save for the stink of violent death. He looks down at the three corpses – the girl, her brother and the man who would have been her husband – then holds up his bloodstained hand, in which he clutches his dagger, to the light.

There is silence all around.

Silence from the king, the duke and the viceroy, who are all standing further downstage.

Silence from those who have paid their money to sit in the darkness and watch the tragedy unfold.

It is the king who breaks this silence.

'But now what follows for Hieronimo?' he asks the viceroy.

He is talking about the man at the centre of the stage, and he still clearly believes that he has been watching a play in which the actors have only *pretended* to die.

He is about to learn otherwise.

Hieronimo walks to the back of the stage, and pulls away a curtain to reveal the fourth corpse – that of his son, Horatio.

Horatio – as the audience already knows – was murdered by Lorenzo and Balthazar, and now that they are dead, too, Hieronimo is avenged.

The king, looking down at the fallen Lorenzo and Balthazar, finally realizes that what he has just seen has been no pretence, and is stricken with grief.

Watching the performance from the wings, Geoff Turnbull was feeling a grief of his own.

He took a letter – already well-worn through usage – out of his pocket, and held it up to catch what light was available, though, in truth, the light was not necessary because he had already memorized the missive's contents.

Dear Mr Turnbull,

We would like to thank you for all your work at the Whitebridge Theatre in the last twelve years. However, we must regretfully inform you that, in the current economic climate, the theatre gives a poor return on investment, and since we have received a very fair offer from . . .

It had been a gutsy decision to choose this play as the company's last production, he told himself. Most manager-directors would have selected something safer – something easily accessible to an audience more familiar with Christmas pantomimes than with high tragedy. But he had decided to go out with a bang – and that took real balls.

Or did it? asked a nagging voice at the back of his head.

After all, whatever play he had chosen, it would have made no difference to the outcome – the theatre would have closed down anyway – so where was the courage in that?

He pulled his hip flask out of his pocket, and took a generous swig.

God, he really hated the theatrical world, he told himself.

Hieronimo – who, in real life, is an actor called Mark Cotton – is still very much centre stage.

'And gentles, thus I end my play, urge no more words, I have no more to say,' he tells both the audience and his fellow characters.

He exits, stage left, noticing, as he passes Geoff Turnbull, that the theatre manager seems rather unsteady on his feet.

He mounts the stairs behind the stage, conscious of the fact that if he wants to maintain the atmosphere he has worked so hard to create, he must make his next entrance on time.

And he has so little time to prepare, because the dramatist, Thomas Kyd has – in his wisdom – only written four lines of dialogue to cover his absence.

He reaches the platform, clicks on the harness and reaches for the noose which is hanging from an overhead beam. He takes a step forward and the spotlight hits him.

He moves closer to the edge of the platform – and hears the audience below gasp.

They don't actually think he will jump.

Of course they don't!

But he is close enough to the edge of the platform to make them feel uncomfortable.

He steps out into empty air.

There are some in the audience who actually scream!

The harness tightens immediately, under his arms and around his chest. He can feel the rope pressing against his throat, but it is only a minor discomfort, because the harness is taking all the strain.

Hands grab his arms and heave him back on to the platform. There are groans of relief from down below.

The cleaners have been complaining all week that some of the audience have actually wet themselves, he thinks, but then what is live theatre – after all – if it isn't thrilling?

His hip flask empty, Geoff Turnbull had retreated to the bar. By rights, there should have been no one there except the barman, but there were always some philistines who preferred drink to culture, and that night – a night on which they had reduced bar prices in order to get rid of stock – it was fuller than usual.

'Give me a whisky, Arthur,' he said. 'Make it a double.'

Two middle-aged women were sitting on stools a little further down the bar. They were wearing dresses which were cheap and hurried copies of the sort of dresses theatregoers in London might well be wearing that evening.

'So what do you think of the play, Cynthia?' one of the women asked the other.

'Well, I don't really know,' the second woman confessed. 'All that killing – it seems a bit unnecessary, doesn't it?'

'It's a revenge tragedy, madam,' Turnbull said, realizing how drunk he sounded, and not really giving a damn. 'People are supposed to get killed in revenge tragedies.'

'Aren't you the manager?' the first woman asked.

'Indeed I am,' Turnbull affirmed.

'Well, since this was your last show, I thought you might at least have put on a nice musical,' the woman said.

It makes you want to weep, Turnbull thought – it just makes you want to bloody weep.

The bloody play reaches its bloody climax. The soldiers, having prevented Hieronimo hanging himself, drag him back to centre stage, where the king demands he confess who else was involved in the conspiracy. Hieronimo refuses to speak, and when the king threatens him with torture, he bites out his own tongue and spits it on to the stage, which – while not quite as dramatic as the attempted hanging – is dramatic enough.

There is more bloodletting as Hieronimo manages to get his hands on a knife, which he uses to kill first the Duke of Castile and then himself. And then the chorus – in the form of a ghost and the spirit of Revenge, make a final comment on the events, and the curtain comes down.

The applause, when the curtain was raised again, could not have been called ecstatic, though only the harshest and bitterest of critics would have described it as rather lukewarm.

It was a mixed audience, Mark Cotton thought, as he took his bow. There were those who genuinely appreciated top quality acting when they saw it, those who rather liked the gore, those who would have preferred a nice cosy comedy, and those who wished they'd stayed at home and watched the television.

Well, sod those last three groups!

And sod Whitebridge as a whole, for not appreciating just how lucky it had been!

The curtain went down for the last time, and there were the inevitable sounds of seats being raised and people scrambling for the exits.

As the noise faded, the King of Spain turned to the Viceroy of Portugal and said, 'Let's go and get rat-arsed drunk.'

Joan Turnbull – always a keen observer of the human condition – came to a halt at the entrance to the Green Man's saloon bar and took a moment to study the group of young people who, until an hour earlier, had all been members of the Whitebridge Players. She was particularly fascinated by the way they had arranged themselves – or had *been* arranged, perhaps – around the long oblong table. The placement – whether voluntary or gently coerced – would have been no accident. Actors – even young inexperienced ones – were always acutely aware of how they positioned themselves, both on and off the stage.

Mark Cotton was sitting at the head of the table. That was only to be expected. He was, after all, the leading light of the company. And that was fair enough, because he was a good actor, though not as good as he thought he was, since nobody – in the entire history of the theatre – had ever been *that* good.

The interesting thing, however, was where Sarah Audley had chosen to park her pert little behind. For weeks, Sarah had been hanging on to Cotton like a limpet, but now she was sitting at the other end of the table, with her elder sister, Ruth, who had herself made the bed springs squeak with Mark, before – very wisely, in Joan's opinion – giving him the elbow.

So what had happened?

Had Sarah rejected Mark, too?

It didn't seem likely, given the mournful glances she was shooting at him when she thought no one was watching.

And if Mark *had* been jilted, he was showing no signs of it. In fact, he seemed to be more than happy that the space Sarah had vacated had been filled by Lucy Cavendish, who was pretty enough but rather vacuous.

'Hey, everybody, Joan's arrived,' she heard a voice say, and realized that she had been spotted by Tony Brown, who was probably the nicest person in the entire company.

The rest of them looked and waved at her. She waved back.

'So where's Geoff?' Mark Cotton demanded.

'I . . . err . . . thought it best to drive him home,' Joan said. 'He wasn't feeling well.'

Mark snickered. 'I'm not surprised,' he said.

Joan felt a sudden burst of rage.

'Yes, he's been drinking,' she admitted. 'But isn't that understandable? He's worked very hard for you – you've no idea *how* hard – and he's bitterly disappointed at the way things have worked out.'

The whole cast – with the predictable exception of Mark Cotton – looked slightly embarrassed.

They blame Geoff for all this, she thought. They believe it's his fault.

'He *has* worked hard,' she persisted. 'He's not to blame for the fact that fewer people are going to the theatre these days.'

'Of course he isn't,' Tony Brown agreed. 'Why don't you come and sit down, Joan?'

But she couldn't.

Not now.

Not once she'd realized what they were thinking.

'I'd better go back and see how Geoff is getting on,' she said.

And no one tried to dissuade her.

*   *   *

It was not until almost closing time that the subject of Joan Turnbull came up again, though it was obvious, when he spoke, that Tony Brown had been brooding about it since the moment she left.

'You should never have spoken to Joan like that,' he said, as another tray of pints arrived at the table.

'Are you talking to me?' Mark Cotton asked, aggressively.

'Well, of course he was talking to you,' said Ruth Audley. 'Who else was bloody rude to Joan?'

'I wasn't rude to her,' Cotton said, slightly more defensive now he felt he might be losing the support of the room. 'I hardly spoke to her.'

'You didn't need to speak,' said Bradley Quirk, who fancied himself as the company's expert on Oscar Wilde and Noel Coward. 'You're an actor, dear boy – you can convey your contempt with the slightest twitch of your eyebrow.'

It could have been a compliment or the opening salvo in an attack. Cotton didn't know which, and decided that, rather than risk being blindsided, he would go on the attack himself.

'Well, I was right, wasn't I?' he demanded. 'Geoff *did* let us down. We're a bloody good company – an excellent company – and now we're all out of work. Who else is to blame?'

'As Joan said, times are hard . . .' Tony Brown said.

'Then why haven't other companies gone under as well?'

'Perhaps because their leads weren't two beats too late on a hanging scene,' said Jerry Talbot, who had been Cotton's understudy in *The Spanish Tragedy*, and was bitterly disappointed that Cotton had not been infected by the flu that was going around.

'I was *not* late,' Cotton said hotly. 'I was—'

'Please, please,' said Phil McCann, who was generally acknowledged to be the company's diplomat and smoother of ruffled egos. 'We're not here to attack each other. We've gathered together to mourn the passing of the Whitebridge Players, but at the same time to celebrate the life of what was an excellent theatre company. Isn't that right?'

The others nodded. Phil was so reasonable that it was always difficult to disagree with him openly – even when you did privately. And anyway, on this occasion, he was dead right.

'If we failed, we failed because the public wasn't ready for us,' Phil continued. 'If they did not appreciate our *Spanish Tragedy*, it is because it was ahead of its time.'

'Ahead of its time, dear boy!' Bradley Quirk repeated. 'The bloody play is four hundred years old!'

'Our production – our interpretation – was ahead of its time,' Phil said levelly. 'If we were to put it on again twenty years from now, it would be an absolute sensation.'

'Then why don't we?' Ruth Audley asked, out of the blue.

'Why don't we what?'

'Why don't we put it on twenty years from now?'

'Me thinks my lady has lost her marbles,' Bradley Quirk said.

'No, listen,' Ruth insisted. 'We're all agreed that we were an excellent company, aren't we?'

The others nodded, though some of them were thinking that although that might be stretching the truth a little, the company did have at least *one* excellent player.

'So why don't we all come back here in twenty years' time and put on the play again? It would be sort of like a memorial service for the Whitebridge Players.'

'The theatre will be gone by then,' Bradley Quirk said. 'They're probably knocking it down even as we speak.'

'This is Lancashire, where they know the value of a shilling,' Ruth argued. 'They don't knock buildings down – they convert them for other uses. And we could convert it back – if only for a little while. Besides, if the old building's gone, there are others we could use – it's the spirit of the thing, not the bricks and mortar, which matters.'

'It would cost a small fortune,' Phil McCann said dubiously.

Ruth smiled. 'Anyone who doesn't think he or she will be a huge success in twenty years' time, put your hand up now,' she said.

Nobody did.

'You see?' Ruth asked. 'We'll all be rolling in money by then, and the odd couple of thousand will seem like small change to us. And if a couple of us aren't quite the success we expected to be, well, I'm sure the rest will be more than willing to subsidize them.'

The others thought about it. Their time in Whitebridge was over, and they were already re-imagining it – editing out the quarrels, frustrations and pettiness as they went – as a golden time in which a group of idealistic young people had striven to make a real cultural difference. So it would be nice to come back. It would be living proof that success had not changed them – that they were humble enough not to have forgotten their roots. It would be nice too, to treat the other members of the company as if they were all still equals – just a bunch of jobbing actors getting together for old times' sake – though there would be a certain amount of satisfaction in seeing the others, who had not had quite the same success, pretending that they really thought nothing had changed.

'So what do you all think?' Ruth asked.

'It sounds like a really great idea,' Tony Brown – good old Tony Brown! – said.

'I think it would be fun,' Ruth's sister Sarah agreed.

'Provided my contractual obligations will permit it, then I'm in favour,' Mark Cotton said.

'I'm in, though – of course – it will never happen,' Bradley Quirk told the rest of the company.

But that was where he was wrong. It *would* happen. The button on the time clock had been hit, the countdown had already begun. And at the end of that countdown – in nineteen years and three hundred and sixty-three days – one of the assembled company would die rather horribly.

ONE

14th March 1977

Apart from the odd attack of morning sickness, Monika Paniatowski had hardly noticed the first stages of her pregnancy at all. But now, as time relentlessly moved on (whether she willed it or not), she was counting in weeks rather than months and was becoming more and more aware of the small, demanding life which was growing inside her.

She was not sleeping well – although that might have been as much for psychological as physical reasons – and simple tasks such as getting out of bed in the morning were becoming a real challenge.

That particular morning, descending the stairs seemed a more formidable task than ever, and for one brief, mad moment, a demon in her head suggested that if she were to 'accidentally' lose her footing, the problem of a child she had never sought might be instantly solved.

She gripped the banister rail more tightly.

She *could have* aborted the baby in the early months. Indeed, her close friend, Dr Shastri, had urged her to do just that – and not just because of her age. But she had decided not to get rid of the child – or rather, her newly rediscovered Catholic faith had forbidden her to – and now she was stuck with the consequences. She would, she had promised herself, bring the child up carefully and responsibly, and if she could not love it, then she would at least do her best to fake that love.

She found her adopted daughter – for whom she had no need to *fake* love – sitting at the dining table, already wearing her smart school uniform and eating a thoroughly sensible breakfast of Shredded Wheat.

'Did you sleep any better last night, Mum?' Louisa asked, concerned.

Paniatowski was tempted to lie, if only to ease her daughter's anxiety, but she had never lied to Louisa about anything, and so she said, 'Not really, no.'

'Then are you sure you're up to tracking down cold-blooded killers today?' Louisa asked innocently.

'Just at the moment, there are no cold-blooded killers to track down,' Paniatowski replied, not realizing until almost the end of the sentence that she had walked into a trap.

'In that case,' Louisa said, 'you can afford to take the day off. Do it for the baby.'

She had been delighted when Paniatowski had announced that she was pregnant, but had never once asked who the father was, perhaps because she thought – wrongly – she already knew the answer, or perhaps because she sensed her mother's reluctance to tell her.

'Did you hear what I said?' Louisa asked, a little sharply.

'First of all, the doctor has assured me that my going into work for another week or so will do the baby absolutely no harm at all,' Paniatowski countered. 'And secondly, just because there have been no murders doesn't mean there's no work to do. As a matter of fact, Chief Superintendent Holmes has called all senior officers in this morning for a briefing session.'

'What about?'

Paniatowski sighed. 'Nothing much. Apparently, there's this actor called Mark Cotton who will be in Whitebridge for a couple of weeks and—'

'Mark Cotton!' Louisa exploded. 'In Whitebridge!'

'Oh, you've heard of him, have you?'

Louisa shook her head in despair. 'Mark Cotton,' she said slowly. 'Vic Prince.'

'It still means nothing to me,' Paniatowski admitted.

'DCI Prince,' Louisa said, as if she was still hoping to find some small corner of her mother's brain that showed just a glimmering of intelligence. 'From the television!'

'Ah, he's a television cop!' Paniatowski said.

'He's *the* television cop,' Louisa told her, 'and he's the sexiest thing on two legs.'

Paniatowski was seized by conflicting emotions. On the one hand, she was pleased that she and her daughter had such an open relationship that Louisa felt free to make such a comment. On the other, she was not entirely happy that a sixteen-year-old should *have* such thoughts at all – even in the privacy of her own head.

'How old is this Mark Cotton?' she asked.

Louisa shrugged, as if she thought that, of all the irrelevant questions asked since the beginning of time, this was the most pointless.

'Forty-two or forty-three,' she suggested.

'I thought girls of your age were supposed to fancy young pop singers,' Paniatowski said, slightly worriedly.

'I do,' Louisa agreed. 'And I wouldn't give most men of his advanced age a second glance. But Mark is different. He has a certain magic about him that very few people ever have.' She paused. 'It's not just me, you know.'

'What isn't?'

'It's not just me that goes weak at the knees at the very thought of him. Nearly all the girls in my class feel the same way. And women who are even older than you go wild for him, too. *Prince* is the most popular series on television. It has over *twenty million* viewers.'

'Even so, I still don't quite see what all the fuss is about,' Paniatowski confessed.

'Last week, he was due to sign his autobiography at Foyles on Charing Cross Road,' Louisa said. 'That's a book shop – in London.'

Paniatowski grinned. 'Thank you, my darling, but your explanation was totally unnecessary. I may well be an uncultivated barbarian, as you seem to think, but I'm not quite *that* uncultivated.'

Louisa grinned back. 'Oh really?' she asked. 'Anyway, as your carefully honed police officer's mind will have noted, I said he was *due* to sign his autobiography.'

'Yes, I did note that,' Paniatowski agreed.

'It never happened. It couldn't happen, because the crowd started building up at dawn, and it soon got so big that it was blocking all traffic within half a mile of the bookstore. People said it was like the heyday of the Beatles.' She grinned again, mischievously this time. 'Whoever they were. According to the reports, there were all kinds of people there – students, lawyers, *real* policemen, grannies waving their knickers above their heads—'

'Now I'm sure that's an exaggeration,' Paniatowski interrupted.

'Grannies waving their knickers above their heads,' Louisa repeated firmly. 'In the end, the police had to contact Mark's manager and ask if he'd be willing to postpone the book signing until they had enough men available to deal with the crowd.' She paused.

'What I don't see is why a superstar like Mark Cotton would ever think of coming to a dump like Whitebridge.'

'You shouldn't run down your home town,' Paniatowski said – rather guiltily, because she'd sometimes caught herself doing just that.

'Quite right, Mum. Sorry, Mum,' Louisa said contritely. 'But why *is* he coming here?'

'I believe he's going to be in a play,' Paniatowski said.

And then it suddenly occurred to her that if Louisa – who she now realized was a big fan of Mark Cotton – didn't know he was coming to Whitebridge, then possibly she wasn't *meant* to know – and neither was anyone else.

'You'll have to keep quiet about this until there's been an official announcement,' she added.

Louisa nodded her head solemnly.

'Of course,' she agreed. 'I'm good at keeping secrets. Can we get tickets for the play?'

'I don't know. If what you say about him is true, they won't be easy to get hold of.'

'Surely, a respected pillar of the community, a woman with considerable local influence could—' Louisa began.

'No, she couldn't,' Paniatowski interrupted.

'But I have to see the play,' Louisa protested. 'We're studying it for A level.'

Paniatowski smiled. 'Five minutes ago you didn't even know this Cotton feller was coming to Lancashire at all, and yet suddenly you know what play he's going to be in.'

'We are doing *three* plays, so there's a fair chance it will be one of them,' Louisa said sheepishly.

'Oh, absolutely,' Paniatowski agreed. 'I'll tell you what I'll do. I'll find out when the tickets go on sale, and then I'll ask one of the lads down at the station – as a personal favour – to be there when the box office opens.'

'In uniform?' Louisa asked hopefully. 'Because if he's in uniform—'

'Not in uniform.'

'Oh well,' Louisa replied with a shrug, 'I suppose that's better than nothing.' Then she smiled. 'You're a star, Mum. And it'll be good for the baby, you know – because a lot of experts believe that it's brilliant to expose them to culture, even before they're born.'

Now why did she have to go and destroy the cosy atmosphere by mentioning the baby, Paniatowski wondered.

It was the general opinion in the village that after so many years of debilitating illness, death must have come as a welcome release for Margaret Audley. And it was a welcome release for Ruth Audley, too, though you could see from the look of total misery on her face that she didn't think so herself. The way she'd cared for her mother for nearly ten years had been nothing short of saintly. But it had taken its toll – she'd been a young woman when she'd started nursing her, and now she was distinctly middle-aged.

Her younger sister – that Sarah – was hardly ever seen in the village. She probably helped support her mother and sister financially, and she could well afford that since she was on the television, but there was no substitute for the personal touch, now was there? Still, what could you expect – Sarah had been wild, wilful and overindulged when she was a kid, and there was no reason to think she was any different as an adult.

The weather had kept quiet for the whole week after Margaret Audley's death, but on the day of her funeral the skies opened, and, to make matters worse, a frenzied wind began to blow in from the sea. At the graveside, mourners struggled to prevent their umbrellas from turning inside out, and once the vicar had commended the departed soul to God, they had to undertake the messy and potentially dangerous journey back to the path over the quagmire that the churchyard had become.

It was a relief for Sarah and Ruth to reach the shelter of the funeral car, and yet, because they had not really had time to talk since Sarah's return, it was also a little awkward.

'How are you feeling?' Sarah asked, finally breaking the silence.

Ruth shrugged. 'Well, you know . . .'

'Yes, I do,' Sarah agreed. 'Look, I'm sorry I didn't arrive until it was all over. The producer asked me if I could put it off for a couple of days – just until we'd got the series in the can – and I said yes. But if I'd known she was dying, then, of course, I would have—'

'You shouldn't blame yourself,' Ruth said. 'If you'd come running every time it looked like Mother was about to breathe her last, you'd never have been away from the place.'

Sarah knocked on the glass partition with her gloved hand. 'You can go now,' she said.

The driver nodded gravely, and started the engine. He pulled away, and the vehicle made its way slowly down the tree-lined avenue with all the solemnity appropriate to the occasion.

'I know this might not seem like quite the right moment to ask you this,' Sarah said, 'but time's getting short, and I was wondering if you'd like to come to Whitebridge with me.'

'Whitebridge!' Ruth repeated, incredulously.

'The only reason you said you couldn't come when you were first asked was because of Mother, and now . . .'

Sarah waved her hand helplessly in the air.

'And now, Mother's dead,' Ruth supplied.

'Well, yes. So will you come?'

'I don't think so.'

'But I'd really like you to.'

'Would you?'

'Yes.'

It was true. Sarah considered that for someone in her profession, loyalty and affection were weaknesses, but she was prepared to make an exception for Ruth. She really *did* love her sister, though she was honest enough to admit to herself that when the love some-times became a little inconvenient, she would not hesitate to put it on hold.

'It's you I'm thinking of,' Sarah said. 'I'm absolutely convinced it would do you good to get away from the house for a while.'

And besides, she added mentally, Phil McCann almost begged me to try and persuade you – and it would be no bad thing to have him in my debt.

'It's such a long time since I've done anything like that,' Ruth said, wavering.

'I'll give you three reasons why you should come with me,' Sarah said. 'One: you need to get back in the saddle. Two: it might be good for your career, because the BBC is making a documentary about it. And three: since this was all your idea in the first place, it would be pretty poor form on your part not to turn up.'

'Is that why *you're* going to Whitebridge – because it might be good for your career?' Ruth asked.

'No. I'll be doing it just for fun.'

'Honestly?'

'Honestly.'

'You don't see it as a stepping stone to something else?'

'I don't *need* a stepping stone any more.'

'Why? Have you been cast in something good?'

'I've been cast in something very juicy indeed!'

'How wonderful! Tell me more!'

Sarah smiled enigmatically.

'I'll tell you later,' she promised.

She looked out of the window. It had stopped raining and – against all the odds – the sun had come out.

She turned to her sister again. 'It's funny that Mother died when she did, don't you think?'

'How do you mean?'

'Well, it's almost as if she chose to die then, so you'd be able to make it to Whitebridge after all. That would have been so like Mother – she never wanted to be any trouble to anyone.'

TWO

Monika Paniatowski's pregnancy had thrown the top floor of Whitebridge police headquarters into a panic. If George Baxter, the chief constable, had been in post at the time, the matter would have been dealt with immediately and decisively. Baxter, who unfairly held Paniatowski partly responsible for his wife's death, would have fired the DCI immediately, and then fought her reinstatement tooth and nail through the employment tribunals. But Baxter was *not* there. There were certain concerns over his health – no one had actually said out loud that he had had a nervous breakdown – and he was away on sick leave, which meant that the problem landed on the desk of Tom Pickering.

Pickering had examined it from all angles. There might be a case for dismissing Paniatowski on the grounds of moral turpitude, but he was only too well aware that there were male officers in his division who had had children with women who were not their wives, and was that really any different from an officer having a child with a man who was not her husband? This was, after all, the 1970s.

Plus, there were the internal and local politics to consider. Monika Paniatowski had her enemies in the force – what high-ranking officer didn't? – but she was rather popular with the lower ranks. And the general public – tired of grim, grey chief inspectors – loved her, so while there had been a few anonymous letters calling her a harlot (or worse), most of the people who read the *Evening Telegraph*, or saw her ever-burgeoning figure when she gave television press conferences, were firmly on her side.

So, taking it all-in-all, Pickering decided that a man occupying a temporary post – but one which he had some hopes would eventually become permanent – should not make more waves than he absolutely had to.

Jerry Talbot, who had once been Mark Cotton's understudy, and Phil McCann, who now had his own leather chair at the bank, were sitting in a pub overlooking the Thames. They had not seen each other for years, and were only meeting now because McCann had requested it.

McCann made his purpose clear the moment that the waiter had brought them their drinks.

'I hear you're having second thoughts about going up to Whitebridge for the reunion,' he said.

'That's not strictly accurate,' Talbot replied. 'What I'm having is my *first* thought for a second time.' He took a sip of his drink. 'None of us should go,' he continued. 'It will be a farce – and if it's not a farce, it will be a tragedy.'

McCann smiled. 'Well, it is *The Spanish Tragedy*,' he said. His expression grew more sombre. 'Seriously, why don't you tell me what you've got against a reunion?'

'Do you remember when Ruth Audley came up with the idea? The whole point of it was that we'd all get together, and it would be just like it had been that night in the Green Man.'

'Yes?'

'But it won't be like that at all, will it? Mark-bloody-Cotton's booked the theatre, he's paying for the lodgings . . .'

'I seem to remember that back then we also agreed that the more successful ones would subsidize the others,' McCann pointed out. He sighed. 'Except that back then, of course, each of us thought *he* would be the successful one.'

'That's the point,' Talbot said. 'I don't see why I should travel all the way up to Whitebridge simply to have Mark Cotton lord it over me.'

'He won't lord it over you,' McCann said.

'How can you possibly know that?'

'Because he needs you as much as you need him.'

'I don't need him,' Talbot said angrily.

'Don't you?' McCann asked. 'Are you telling me that you're perfectly happy as you are – playing bit parts in soap operas and appearing in the occasional advertisement?'

'There's nothing wrong with doing adverts,' Talbot mumbled. 'Some very big stars have done adverts.'

'Yes, but as themselves or the character they're best known for – not as whistling broccoli or a dancing coffee bean.'

'Listen . . .'

'I'm not denigrating what you've done, Jerry, I'm just pointing out all the advantages that being in the play and the BBC documentary will bring you. I'm right, aren't I? You could use the publicity.'

'I suppose so,' Talbot admitted.

'Then you *do* need Mark, because – don't kid yourself – without a big star like him, none of it would happen.'

'And because he's such a big star, he'll want to play Hieronimo every night, and the poor bloody understudy will never get a look-in.'

'That won't be the case at all. He'll let you play the lead on two of the six nights. I guarantee that.'

'Why would that selfish bastard—'

'Because he needs the play to be a success, and for that he has to have everybody's full cooperation. You see, he might have loads of money and the adoration of millions, but what he *hasn't* got is the respect of the traditional acting community – and I think he wants that more than anything. This is his shot at being taken seriously – at being spoken of as the new Olivier – and if to achieve that he has to be nice to you and help your career, then he's perfectly willing to do it.'

'How do you know all this?'

McCann smiled. 'Instinct and observation,' he said. 'And have you ever known me to be wrong about people?'

'No,' Talbot said, surprised to hear himself saying it, yet recognizing that what Phil McCann had said was true. 'No, I haven't.'

'Then come up to Whitebridge with the rest of us, and milk what you can out of it.'

'Why are you going?' Talbot asked, suspiciously.

'Me?' McCann answered evasively. 'I suppose it's because my kids would quite like to see me on the telly.'

'That isn't it,' Talbot said. 'Or, at least, it's not *all* of it.'

'Then maybe I just want to relive my glorious youth.'

That wasn't it either, Talbot thought. But while McCann might be lying about his own motives, what he had said earlier was undoubtedly correct.

'All right,' Talbot said, 'I'll do it.'

And though McCann did his best to hide his relief, it shone through like a spotlight hitting a darkened stage.

The meeting was held in the press briefing room, and every officer of chief inspector rank and above had been ordered to attend. Many of the attendees had chosen seats at the front of the room, just to show how keen they were to collaborate with the new order that had been established since George Baxter's departure, but Paniatowski – deciding that, when you were the size she was, you were entitled to a little more space – had selected a chair at the back.

When Chief Superintendent Holmes entered the room, he was looking grumpy, but that was hardly surprising since he was one of those men who fondly imagined that grumpiness was a clear indication of intelligence and efficiency.

Holmes stepped on to the podium and turned to face his audience.

'Has any of you people ever seen this DCI Prince television programme?' he asked.

No one moved. Not a hand was raised. Possibly some of them did watch it – and enjoyed it – but having read the expression on Holmes' face, they were certainly not going to admit it to him.

'I saw it for the first time last night,' Holmes said, 'and I consider it a disgrace. Most of the officers are portrayed as hapless idiots, and if it wasn't for the brilliance of DCI Prince, the cases would never get solved. But we all know it doesn't work like that, don't we?'

Paniatowski shifted position in a vain attempt to get more comfortable. The baby had started kicking recently, and not just in one spot, but – it seemed to her – all over her womb. Indeed, there were times when she thought she was about to give birth to an octopus rather than a child.

'Cotton wants to put on some sort of play in Whitebridge,' Holmes continued. 'If I had my way, we'd have nothing to do with him, but the powers-that-be have decided to extend the hand of friendship and cooperation. Their theory, you see, is that it will be good for Whitebridge's international image. Are there any questions before I go on?'

One of the CIs raised a hand.

'There is no theatre in Whitebridge. Where's he going to be putting this play on?'

'In the old Sunshine Bingo hall. It's being revamped with money from the government, the already-struggling ratepayers of Whitebridge, and Cotton himself. When he's finished his stupid little play, the theatre will be handed over to Whitebridge council.'

Louisa would like that, Paniatowski thought. Maybe if it had a theatre, she wouldn't consider Whitebridge such a dump.

'Now on to the practical details,' the chief superintendent continued. 'It will not be publicized that Mark Cotton will be in this particular play. In fact, all it will say on the posters is that it's being staged by the Whitebridge Players.'

'Why is that?' asked the CI who'd spoken earlier.

'Why is it?' Holmes said, and the exasperation was evident in his voice. 'It's because we're dealing with actors here, and actors simply aren't like normal decent people.'

'It won't work,' the CI said.

'Well, of course it won't work. On the first night, somebody in the audience will be bound to spot Cotton, and by the following morning it will be national news. I've told them that, but they won't listen.'

Word would get out well before then, Paniatowski thought, because all it would take would be for one of the officers present to tell his mate over a pint, and that mate to tell another mate . . .

'Once the shit hits the fan, there'll be absolute chaos,' Holmes said. 'We can say goodbye to smooth traffic flows in the centre of town for the whole week. But there's another problem, and the best person to talk about that is one of Mr Cotton's own team.' He nodded to the uniformed constable standing by the door. 'Ask Mr Gough to come in now.'

When Sunshine Bingo Ltd. bought the Whitebridge Theatre, its owners' main aim had been to rake in as much money as they possibly could from their customers, while spending as little of their own as they could get away with.

One basic economy they could make had been obvious from the start. Their customers, they knew from experience, would not give a hang about how the place looked. All that would matter to them would be their bingo cards – that magic collection of numbers which could bring them both excitement and cash. Thus, as long as the place conformed to the fire regulations, there was a very little that needed to be done to it.

Sunshine Bingo had not used the boxes in which the wealthier patrons of the theatre had once sat, but neither had it gone to the expense of having them removed. It had left the stage intact, even though only the very centre of it – where the caller and machine were located – had actually been utilized. It had ignored the overhead fly system, it had converted the dressing rooms into offices, and it had treated the prop room as a dumping ground for unwanted rubbish.

And that attitude, Geoff Turnbull thought, as he stood on the stage and looked out at the auditorium, had been the theatre's salvation.

It had not been too expensive to return the theatre to its former glory, but it had taken considerable time and effort. Geoff had agonized over how to re-cover the seats, before selecting a heavy green cotton cloth for the balcony seats and a rich violet one for the stalls. He had scoured the *Exchange and Mart* – and numerous junk yards – in the search for heavy chandeliers to replace Sunshine Bingo's more utilitarian lighting. He had had the garishly coloured walls overpainted in gentle pastels.

And now the results of his efforts lay spread out in front of him.

It was not a grand theatre, by any means. It could seat no more than four hundred-and-fifty people, and its boxes would never have been considered fit for royalty to plant their backsides in. But for all that, he loved it.

'It looks like it's going very well, Geoff,' he heard a voice say.

He turned, and saw his wife, Joan, who had brought him a flask of tea and some sandwiches.

'Yes, it is going well,' he agreed. 'They've nearly finished work on the platform. That's where Hieronimo tries to hang himself, if you remember.'

Joan smiled. 'I remember.'

'And do you also remember the moment when he steps off the platform – how it terrified the audience? I directed that perfectly, didn't I?'

'You directed so many scenes just perfectly,' Joan said.

It wasn't true, she thought. He had been a more-than-competent director back then, but he had never been a great one. Still, he had worked hard, and he had not deserved his fate – twenty years of plodding along in dead-end jobs, while trying to ignore the fact that he had the theatre in his blood. He looked happy now – for the first time since the Whitebridge Theatre closed its doors for the last time – and while she was glad of that, she also worried that he might be heading for another fall, and that this one would be even sharper than the first.

'You shouldn't set your heart on directing this time, you know,' she said cautiously.

'What do you mean by that?' Geoff asked, sounding genuinely mystified.

'Mark Cotton hasn't actually told you that you can direct, has he?'

'He's no need to tell me. It's my production – my overall concept – and he knows that better than most people. Besides, if he doesn't intend me to direct, why contact me in the first place?'

Because he needed someone to do the donkey work, Joan thought; he needed someone on the ground to handle all the tedious detail that had to be endured before a production could even begin.

'It's just that he might want to direct himself, especially with the television crew being here,' she said aloud.

Geoff laughed. 'Now that's hardly likely, is it?' he asked. 'Mark's an actor, not a director. He wouldn't have the first idea about how to put the play on. But if it will keep him happy, I'll make him assistant director. He might even manage to pick up a few tips.'

'You shouldn't . . .' Joan began.

'And after the play – after he's gone back to London – the council are bound to appoint me manager-director at the theatre,' Geoff enthused. 'After all, I'm the logical choice.'

'You mustn't let this mean too much to you,' Joan said, fighting back the tears.

'Mean too much to me?' Geoff repeated. 'What are you talking about? It means *everything* to me.'

* * *

Mr Gough – he didn't announce his first name, and nobody asked it – was around thirty-five years old, and though not particularly tall, he had massive shoulders and bulging muscles. Most men – even innocent ones – would have felt slightly uncomfortable about walking into a room of high-ranking police officers, but this one seemed not the least affected by the experience.

'I'm the head of Mr Cotton's security, and I'm here to tell you about the Cotton Buds,' he said from the podium.

'The what?' someone asked.

'The Cotton Buds,' Gough repeated. 'That's the name his fans have given themselves. It's a sort of play on words, see.'

Everybody did see.

'Now, we can divide them up into two groups,' Gough said. 'The Good Buds and the Bad Buds. The Good Buds are a real pain in the arse. Their whole reason for existing is to get close to Mark, and they'll do whatever that takes. Bribery, breaking and entering, jerking off the doorman – they've tried it all. But, like I said, they're just a nuisance. Now the Bad Buds are something else entirely. They start out as Good Buds, only they're even nuttier than the rest of the bunch. They're convinced that once Mark meets them, he'll realize what they've known all along – that him and her were meant to be together, sailing off into a golden sunset. Except that what Mark sees isn't his dream girl at all, but some mad little slag with revolving eyes – and, on occasion, he's not above telling them that. And that's when the trouble can start, because, as they see it, he's let them down, and he has to be punished for it.'

'What exactly do you mean by "punished"?' Superintendent Holmes asked.

'Some of the Bad Buds are happy just to slash his suits or scrape his car, but others want to really hurt him – and they're as fanatical about that as they once were about loving him. I had to take a knife off one of them once. I broke her arm in the process, and she was so charged up she didn't notice at first.'

So that was what this was really all about, Paniatowski thought – not traffic flow or damage to property, but the Bad Buds. The town council was hoping to get some very good publicity out of this visit, and the last thing it wanted was for Mark Cotton to be injured – or even killed – while he was in Whitebridge.

'How many of these . . . err . . . Bad Buds are there, Mr Gough?' CS Holmes asked.

'We don't know,' Gough admitted. 'Most of the Good Buds know each other, but the Bad Buds are loners. I'd guess there's around ten or fifteen, though there could be a few more or a few less. And the numbers will go up and down. One might get fed up of the whole thing and just give it up, and then, the very next day, Mark will find a way to piss a couple more off.'

'I see,' Holmes said thoughtfully.

Gough paused to light up a short thick cigar. Blue smoke rose from it, and instead of drifting, it chose to hover above his head, giving him an almost diabolical air.

'Now most of the time they're not *that* much of a problem,' he continued. 'They don't know where Mark lives – we've made sure of that – and usually, when he's not in his house, he's moving around. But he's going to be in Whitebridge for two whole weeks, and if it leaks out that he's here – and I'm pretty sure it will – that'll give the nutters plenty of time to organize themselves. Now, me and my team can pretty much guarantee security within the theatre, but we can't do the same for the hotel or any of the public spaces, and that's where you blokes come in.'

'Where will he be staying?' Holmes asked.

For a moment, Gough looked as if he were about to spin them a line, then – clearly deciding that honesty was not only the best policy but also the only practical one – he said, 'The story we'll be putting out to the press – if we need to put out any story at all – is that this is a grand reunion of old mates, and they'll all be staying in a theatrical boarding house together, just like they did in days gone by.'

'But, in point of fact, he won't be staying in the boarding house at all?' Holmes asked.

Gough shook his head.

'He'll go there at night, once the show is over, but it'll be a case of in through the front door and out through the back. Actually spending the night there would make our job much more difficult, and besides, Mark's already made it quite plain that his slumming days are over.'

'So where will he be staying?'

'We've booked him a suite at what seems, in this town, to pass as a grand hotel. I think it might be called the Royal Victoria.'

'It *is* called the Royal Victoria,' Holmes said, as several members of the audience bristled at the idea the Royal only *passed* as a grand hotel.

'He'll be registered under the name of Mather,' Gough said, indifferent to – or perhaps not even noticing – the hostility he'd managed to engender in the room. 'He'll enter it and leave it in disguise – he's an actor, remember – but we can't guarantee that one of the Bad Buds won't find out about it – and stopping them getting at him will be partly down to you.'

Paniatowski shifted position again, and thought about how glad she was that she was no longer in uniform and having to deal with this kind of shit.

THREE

16th March 1977

Maggie Maitland gazed into the mirror above the washbasin in the public toilet. She saw a lovely woman looking back at her – a stunningly *beautiful* woman – and because she sometimes found it hard to believe that nature had been so kind to her, she smiled at the woman and saw her smile back. Yes, that was her, all right.

She took a couple of steps backwards, so she could see most of her body reflected in the mirror, too. She liked what she saw, but then she'd known she would. Her breasts were well formed and firm. Her waist was slender. Her legs were sensational.

On top of all that, she was smart, she thought – so smart that she was at least a day ahead of the other Buds. And that wasn't because she'd had any unfair advantages over them. All the information that had been available to her had also been available to them – but they simply hadn't known how to use it.

It had started with an article in the Buds' newsletter which, strictly speaking, she should never even have seen.

'The *Good* Buds put me at the top of their banned list,' she told her reflection in the mirror. 'As if that would stop me – as if they thought I wouldn't find a way round it.'

Anyway, she'd seen this article in which several writers – several so-called experts on the subject – had been speculating about what Mark would do now that he'd finished filming the latest series of

DCI Prince. One of them thought he'd probably take a nice holiday somewhere. Another had suggested he was doing charity work under a false name.

Fools! Mark was too ambitious to rest. And as for doing charity work, the only charity Mark Cotton cared about was Mark Cotton.

She'd sat down and thought about what he might be really doing. And then it had come to her!

She was almost sure she was right, but she had to check through her files to be absolutely sure.

There it was – in a *Radio Times* interview from 1967.

'Even though I'm now doing a lot of work in television, I'm still very committed to theatre, which is where all good acting springs from,' Mark told me.

'All successful actors feel they have to say that, but they're really doing no more than paying lip service to the idea, aren't they?' I challenged him.

He seemed stung by the remark.

'That's certainly not true in my case,' he said.

'Then can you tell me when you'll be going back into live theatre?'

'I can't tell you exactly when it will be, no. But I can give you a time and place when I definitely will be back on the stage – March 1977, in Whitebridge.'

And then he told me a story which was too cute to have been made up, about how, in 1957, he and some other young actors had been working in provincial rep and . . .

Yes, this was where he'd be – right here in Whitebridge. They hadn't announced it yet, because the moment they did announce it, the place would be flooded with those crazy Buds. But the fact that the old theatre was being done up was all the proof that was necessary.

Maggie left the toilet, and looked up and down Whitebridge High Street. There was no sign of Mark's security people – they probably weren't even in the town yet – but you could never be too careful.

She opened her travelling bag and checked in the side pocket to see how much cash she had. Enough for a day or two, but then she would have to go to the bank.

She wondered how much money she actually still had in her

account. She'd got quite a good price for her father's house – though not as much as she would have done if she hadn't insisted on a quick sale – but that had been a while ago, and following Mark Cotton was an expensive business. Still, if things worked out as she planned, she wouldn't be needing money.

She walked down the High Street, passing the theatre on the other side of the road. It was flanked on either side by a bank.

That was bad luck, she thought. Banks were hard to break into – for obvious reasons.

The front of the theatre didn't look too promising, either. It had a canopy, projecting out over the pavement, which was held up by four slim pillars, and under that were two sets of double doors. Maggie guessed that on the night of a performance only one door in each set would be open, and that both doors would be manned by Mark's security people, so sneaking in would be almost impossible.

It had to be the back of the theatre, then.

She turned down a side alley.

When she reached the road paralleling the High Street, she saw that she was right. The back of the theatre was a good five yards from the road, and between that and the pavement there was a yard, protected by no more than a chain-link fence. It was being used, for the moment, as a store for the builders' materials. No doubt once the work was finished, they'd erect a wall, but walls could be scaled if you were determined enough.

And she was.

She checked quickly up and down the street to make sure that no one was watching, then walked over to the gate in the fence. It was padlocked, but the padlock was not a thick one, and presented no problems for a woman who always carried a small pair of bolt cutters with her.

She checked around once more, then snipped through the lock and pushed the gate open. Bricks were stacked high close to the road, which was good, because once she was on the other side of them, she had some cover.

She examined the back of the theatre with a practised eye. The door – or rather, the gap in which the door would be set – was in the dead centre of the wall. There were windows, but they were much higher up – above the level of the door – and even if there were no bars on them, entering that way would be difficult. Or maybe it wouldn't . . . not if . . .

'Can I ask you exactly what you're doing there, madam,' asked a voice behind her.

She swung round to find herself facing a man in a donkey jacket. 'Who are you?' she asked.

'I'm Bob Green, the site manager,' the man said. 'But more to the point, who are you?'

'Jill Thomas,' Maggie said. 'I'm from Moreton Village. I'm just in Whitebridge for the day, doing a bit of shopping.' She looked down at her travel bag. 'That's why I've got this thing with me.'

Oh, cunning Maggie, she congratulated herself.

Would any of those stupid Buds have thought to find out the name of a local village in case they were challenged?

Would they have thought of a way of explaining the travel bag?

No, they would not.

'So would you mind telling me, Miss Thomas . . . it is *Miss* Thomas, isn't it?'

'Yes, it is.'

'Would you mind telling what you're doing in this yard?'

'I didn't really know myself,' Maggie said. 'I saw the gate was open, and I suppose I was just curious.'

'It was open, you say?'

'That's right.'

Another man appeared, holding the padlock in his hand.

'Do you know anything about this?' Green asked, indicating the lock.

'No, I don't.'

Green seemed far from convinced. 'Would you mind opening that bag of yours, and letting me have a look inside.'

'I most certainly would mind.'

'Then maybe we'd better call the police.'

Maggie threw the bag at his feet.

'Go on then, paw through my personal possessions, if you feel you must,' she said.

Green unzipped the bag. Watching him examine her sexy underwear, she felt a shudder run through her. Then he closed the bag again, and she let out a sigh of relief.

'Well, did you find any bolt cutters?' she asked.

'Who said anything about bolt cutters?' Green asked suspiciously.

'Whoever cut through that lock didn't use a pair of nail scissors, now did they?' she countered.

'I thought you said you'd come to town to do some shopping,' Green said, 'but this isn't shopping – it's what you'd pack if you were going away on your holidays.'

'I don't have to explain myself to you,' she said, standing on her dignity.

'No,' the site manager agreed, 'but you will have to explain yourself to the police.'

Desperate times called for desperate measures. She favoured him with her sexiest, most radiant smile.

'Look,' she said, 'I've made a mistake. I admit it. But if you just overlook it this time, I promise you I won't bother you again.'

Green hesitated.

'Aye, all right then,' he said finally. 'Get yourself off quick, before I change my mind.'

She picked up her bag and hurried towards the gate. It had been a wise move to anticipate that something might go wrong and hide the bolt cutters behind the bricks, she thought. But it had been her smile, rather than a lack of physical evidence against her, which had been her salvation. That smile had dazzled him. You could see that it had. If the other man hadn't been there, he'd probably have begged her to go on a date with him.

The site manager and the workman watched her as she scurried off down the street.

'I'm surprised you let her off so easy, Mr Green,' the workman said. 'It was obvious she was up to something.'

Green shrugged, embarrassedly. 'Well, I felt sorry for her,' he admitted. 'Legs like a Shetland pony and a face like the back of a bus – she's got enough problems already without being in trouble with the police.'

'Aye, she's no oil painting, is she?' the workman agreed. 'If she was hung for being beautiful, she'd die innocent.'

Florrie Hodge had never expected to become a boarding house landlady.

'Your only job in life, my girl, is to look after me,' her husband Archie had told her, when they married in 1931.

And it had seemed reasonable at the time. Archie earned good money as a foreman at the rope works, and – much to the envy of Florrie's school friends – had bought (not rented!) a three-storey house a few doors down from the Whitebridge Theatre.

And so, for twenty years, she had cooked and cleaned for Archie – washed his clothes and darned his socks – and assumed she was perfectly happy.

Then there had been an accident at the rope works, and Archie had been killed.

Suddenly, she was all alone, living in a very big house on a very small pension.

She could have sold the house, but she couldn't bear the thought of it, so she reluctantly reached the inevitable conclusion that she would have to take in lodgers. And since the house was so close to the theatre, it had seemed logical that those lodgers should be theatricals, and so – despite her friends' warnings – she had gone to see the manager of the Whitebridge Rep.

It took her less than a week to decide she had made the right decision. Actors, it was true, were temperamental and unpredictable. They sometimes even did things she was not quite sure she should approve of.

But they were *interesting*!

She began to insert herself quietly into small corners of their lives. She ran errands for them. She tidied their rooms without being asked. She would even – on occasion – lend them money.

Now, looking back on her life with Archie, she began to see how boring and sterile it had been, and though she was not exactly glad that he had died, her new life certainly helped to ease the loss.

And then the Black Day came – the thirtieth of March 1957.

The theatre closed down. The actors moved on.

She'd taken in new boarders to fill the gap. They were mostly commercial travellers – vacuum cleaner salesmen and purveyors of ladies' surgical hose – and while she had nothing against them, they lacked the sparkle of the thespians who had preceded them.

But now – now! – she had been given her old life back, if only for two weeks. She would be a *theatrical* landlady again – and not just that, but the landlady to exactly the same company who had lodged with her in 1957.

She was over the moon!

The taxi driver who dropped them off at Euston station said Sarah looked familiar, and wondered if he'd seen her on the telly.

'No, it couldn't have been me,' Sarah said sweetly. 'I'm a vicar's wife, from Sidcup.'

Ruth waited until the taxi had driven off, then said, 'Why did you tell him that?'

'Because I didn't want to waste my time talking to someone who only vaguely recognizes me,' Sarah replied, with a slight edge of hardness to her voice. 'If he'd been a real fan, it would have been different.'

They met some 'real' fans on the station itself – a couple of small kids who had seen Sarah as the Kindly Witch on *Friday Corner*, and, after grabbing her with their sticky hands, shot a number of unanswerable questions at her while their parents looked fondly on.

'God, I hate kids,' Sarah said, as they climbed on to the train. 'I'm so glad I never had any of my own. I expect you feel the same way.'

'Not really,' Ruth said.

As the train pulled out of the station, Sarah looked at her watch and said, 'Twenty minutes late – as usual.'

'Why are you in such a hurry to get to Whitebridge?' Ruth asked. 'The rest of the cast won't be there for another two days.'

'I thought it would be good to get you away from Mother's house as soon as possible,' Sarah told her.

'That's not it,' Ruth said sharply. 'If you'd just wanted to get me away, you'd have suggested that we went to the seaside for a couple of days. So what's the real reason?'

'That *is* the real reason,' Sarah insisted, 'although,' she continued, reading the expression of disbelief on her sister's face, 'I will admit that I need to do some research before the rest of them arrive.'

'Research? How can you possibly research *The Spanish Tragedy* in Whitebridge?'

'It's not for the *Tragedy* – it's for that juicy job I've landed.'

'And you still haven't told me what that juicy job is.'

'I will – when the time is right.'

'You're being enigmatic again – and it's very annoying,' Ruth said.

Sarah smiled. 'Sorry about that.'

'So if you won't tell me about the research, will you answer another question that's been bothering me?'

'Perhaps.'

'You told me that you're going up to Whitebridge just for the fun of it. Is that right?'

'Maybe fun's not quite the right word. Maybe what I'm expecting is on an entirely different level to mere fun, but – for the sake of convenience – let's say that's why I'm going there.'

'So what I don't see is how being in close proximity to Mark Cotton for two weeks could possibly be your idea of fun.'

'I don't know what you mean.'

'After I chucked Mark, he started going out with you, didn't he?'

Sarah sniffed. 'Thanks for reminding me that he only picked me up on the rebound. That makes me feel just wonderful.'

'I'm sorry, I didn't mean to do that,' Ruth said. 'But you did start going out with him, didn't you?'

'You know I did.'

'And when he threw you over for Lucy Cavendish, a few weeks later, you were devastated.'

'I . . . I was a little upset.'

'You were devastated,' Ruth repeated firmly. 'He was your first love and you were only seventeen. So don't try to tell me you were just a little upset – because I sat up with you night after night, while you cried your eyes out. For heaven's sake, Sarah, you even talked about leaving the company – and if the company hadn't left us instead, I'm sure that's exactly what you would have done.'

'Perhaps I did take it badly at the time, but that's all water under the bridge, now.'

'The thing is, I don't think that's true,' Ruth persisted. 'I don't think you ever quite got over him. So here's my question. Why are you putting yourself through it all over again? Why are you so willing to spend two weeks with the man who broke your heart?'

The enigmatic smile was back on Sarah's face. 'We're playing in a revenge tragedy, aren't we?' she asked.

'Yes?'

'Well, that's why I'm going to Whitebridge – to get my revenge.'

Paniatowski put her mouth close to the grille and said, 'There are times when I hate my baby.'

'And do you think you're the first woman to feel that?' the priest on the other side of the grille asked. 'Many young women suddenly realize how much freedom they'll be giving up by having a child, and start to resent that child a little. But once your baby is born – once you hold him in your arms . . .'

'It's nothing to do with losing my freedom – and the feeling I get is nothing as petty as resentment,' Paniatowski said. 'But you already knew that, didn't you – because this is not the first conversation we've had on the subject. So why do you persist in playing the same old game – trotting out the same old line?'

'I'm your priest, Monika, not your suspect. And, in case you haven't noticed, this is not an interview room – it's a confessional.'

'I'm sorry, Father,' Paniatowski said.

'Your baby is a gift from God,' the priest told her.

'No, it isn't,' Paniatowski exploded. 'It's a gift from three drunken bikers who raped me in the woods.'

'A gift from God,' the priest repeated. 'And when he is born, you must remember that and forget the rest.'

'But what if I can't *love* him?' Paniatowski sobbed.

'You must never give up trying,' the priest told her. 'But if you can't – and there are some parents who, however hard they try, can find no love in their hearts – then you have the consolation of knowing that God will love the child, and that will be enough.'

'Will it?' Paniatowski asked. 'Are you sure of that?'

'Yes, I'm sure.'

'But how can you be so certain?'

'Because God loves me,' the priest said. 'I have no close relatives, no wife and no children – but God loves me, and that is all I need.

But was it? Paniatowski wondered. If the love of God was all that the priest needed to sustain him, then why could she smell his whisky-soaked breath even through the grille?

FOUR

18th March 1977

The room was in a private hotel close to Euston station. Mark Cotton had booked it, and Mark Cotton had paid for it, so when he'd asked the others to meet him there, prior to travelling up to Lancashire, most of them had come.

However, there were a couple of obvious absentees, Cotton noted, looking around the room.

'Does anyone know where Ruth and Sarah are?' he asked.

'Sarah phoned me at home,' Phil McCann told him. 'She said they'll meet us in Whitebridge.'

Cotton frowned. 'The plan was for us all to go together,' he said. 'But I suppose if they're not here, they're not here, so let's get on with it. Two things will be happening in the next fortnight. The first is that we will be rehearsing – and then performing – *The Spanish Tragedy*.'

'Really,' Bradley Quirk said. 'I didn't know that.'

'But the second thing,' continued Cotton, ignoring him, 'is that the BBC will be making a documentary about us. Now the hook on which this documentary will hang is that we're all mates who've got together after twenty years to try and recreate the magic we had back then. If we play things right, it will be good for all of us – and I do mean *all* of us, even those no longer in the business. For instance, it wouldn't do your prospects at the bank any harm to be seen in a favourable light on television, Phil. And as for you, Tony, your school governors will love it.'

'Interesting choice of words, that "play things right",' Jerry Talbot said. 'Are you suggesting we'll be *acting* in front of the cameras? Because I thought a documentary was supposed to be about life as it actually is.'

Cotton bit back an exasperated sigh. 'Either we can tell the story our way or we can allow the television crew to tell it their way – and, believe me, our way is better for us. But that involves us *managing* things.'

'Meaning what?' Talbot asked.

'That if we have any petty disagreements, we make sure we have them off camera.'

'So everything will be filmed as being all sweetness and light?' Phil McCann asked. 'Won't that make for a rather boring programme?'

'Everything won't be all sweetness and light,' Cotton said. 'We'll have disagreements – heated ones – but they won't be about whether you've eaten Bradley's sandwich, or Lucy has been using Sarah's make up.'

'In other words, you're not talking about the sort of stuff that really *does* go on,' Bradley Quirk said.

'That's right,' Cotton agreed. 'Our disagreements will be about artistic differences, as each of us strives to produce the best performance we possibly can. They'll be very dramatic while they're

going on – there'll be a great deal of storming about and screaming
in frustration, much as the public would expect from us – but eventually the arguments will end amicably, and everybody involved in
them will come away looking good.'

'I don't see that happening,' Jerry Talbot said, remembering the
arguments over 'artistic differences' that they'd had in the past.

'It will, if we plan it properly,' Cotton said. 'What we do is, we
sketch out the basic disagreement the night before, and then we act
it out when the cameras are rolling. We'll already have decided
how it will begin and end, so all we really have to do is improvise
in the middle.'

Bradley Quirk smiled sardonically. 'Let me see if I've got this
straight,' he said. 'We're performing in a play in which the central
point is that some of the characters, led by Hieronimo, pretend to
be actors and put on a play of their own. That's right, is it?'

'Of course it's right,' Cotton said, a little snappishly. 'It's the
play-within-the-play.'

'But what you're proposing isn't just that you play the part of
Hieronimo, who plays the part of Pasha in the play-within-a-play.
You're proposing that you play the part of an idealized – much nicer
– version of yourself, who plays the part of Hieronimo, who plays
the part of Pasha. In other words, the making of the play becomes
a play itself.'

'I wouldn't have put it quite like that,' Cotton said.

'I don't really think that there's any other way *to* put it,' Bradley
Quirk countered.

This time, Cotton did allow himself to sigh. 'Look, we're a
company of equals, just like we were in the old days,' he said.

Bradley Quirk sniggered, and Jerry Talbot pretended to be sick.

Cotton decided to ignore them both.

'You all know I've sunk considerably more of my money into
this project than all the rest of you put together, but that doesn't
give me the right to dictate how we do things.'

'No?' Bradley Quirk asked sceptically.

'No,' Cotton repeated. 'I happen to think – as I said at the beginning – that my way is the best way for all concerned, but if the
majority of you are against it, then I'm certainly not going to try
and force it through. However, my career is at a particularly complicated balancing point as this moment, and I don't want to put myself
into any situation which isn't at least partly scripted.'

'What does that mean, exactly?' Phil McCann asked.

'It means that I will continue to subsidize the company until the end of the production, but – though I wish you all the luck in the world – I won't be coming up to Whitebridge with you unless you agree to do things my way,' Cotton said.

He sat back and waited, and though he was seemingly oblivious to what was going on around him, he wasn't missing a thing.

He could see Jerry Talbot – his understudy for Hieronimo all those years ago – and could almost hear the way his mind was ticking over.

If Cotton isn't there, then I get to play Hieronimo, Talbot was thinking, and I'll do a great job – better than he could have done.

But then, who will come and see me doing that great job? he asked himself.

If Mark Cotton wasn't there, none of the London critics would make the trip up to Whitebridge to review the play – and neither would the London show business personalities make the effort. In fact, if Mark wasn't there, the BBC might well change their minds about making the documentary.

But what if Mark *was* there?

If he was there, there was a chance he could be persuaded to give his understudy the chance to play the lead on one or two of the less important nights midweek, just as Phil McCann had promised – especially if that understudy had gone out of his way to be amenable (i.e. sucked up for all he was worth). And even on those midweek nights, there was always the possibility that someone important in the world of theatre or television might just be there to see him perform.

Then, of course, there was the documentary itself. He would have to play the part assigned to him in that, but there would be every possibility he could play it in such a way as to upstage the rest of the cast.

'I think Mark's right,' he said. 'We would be better off doing a little preparation for the documentary.'

And once he – one of Mark's strongest antagonists – had given way, what choice did the others have but to follow suit?

It was Charlie Woodend who had started the tradition of holding team meetings at the corner table in the public bar of the Drum and Monkey. It was at this table that they had sat and discussed, over

pints of best bitter and shots of neat vodka, their most baffling
murder cases; here that the first faint glimmerings of light had begun
to shine in the corners of what had seemed dark, impenetrable
mysteries.

Now, Woodend was living in retirement in Spain, and, with
apparent success, was battling the cancer which had invaded his
body. But though Charlie had gone, the tradition endured, and for
both Monika Paniatowski (who had been a member of the original
team) and DI Colin Beresford (who had joined it later, as a fresh-
faced detective constable), the meetings had become almost a sacred
ritual.

The meeting that lunchtime was far from a typical one. Firstly,
there had been no murders recently, and the team were spending
most of their time catching up on mind-numbing paperwork. And
secondly, the leader of the team – who, it was wildly believed, could
drink the rest of them under the table – was neither drinking nor
smoking, and hadn't been since the day she discovered she was
pregnant. Still, it was an agreeable session in which four people
who liked and respected each other could chat about matters of
practically no consequence without feeling that they were wasting
their time.

It was Beresford who introduced a note of disharmony by asking
a question which DS Kate Meadows could cheerfully have killed
him for asking.

'So when are you going on maternity leave, boss?' he said.

'Another two weeks,' Paniatowski replied, in a tone which should
have warned him to leave the matter there.

'But you're owed weeks and weeks of ordinary leave,' Beresford
said, oblivious.

'We're *all* owed a lot of leave,' Paniatowski countered. 'We're a
hard-working team.'

'What I meant was, since there's nothing much happening at the
moment, you could go on leave now,' Beresford explained.

Paniatowski shuddered. The thought of being at home alone –
with nothing to distract her as the lump continued to grow in her
belly – was almost too horrible to contemplate.

She climbed clumsily to her feet. 'If you'll excuse me, nature
calls – and for only about the hundred-and-fourteenth time today.'

They watched her waddle awkwardly towards the corridor which
led to the ladies' toilet.

'I know women get big when they're pregnant, but the boss is the size of a house,' Beresford said. 'Who do you think the father is?'

'You mean she hasn't told you?' asked DC Jack Crane, MA, the youngest member of the team, who was tall and slim and looked like the poet that he actually secretly was. 'I thought she told *you* everything.'

'Well, she hasn't told me that,' Beresford replied, and there was a hint of hurt in his voice.

'Actually, there's a fair number of people back at the station who think you're the father,' Crane said.

'Me!' Beresford exploded. 'Me!'

'You have been close to her for a long time,' Crane pointed out. 'And you've got something of a reputation as a Don Juan.'

And so he had, but there was good reason for that. Though Beresford was good-looking in an unassuming sort of way, with thick dark hair, eyes which were intelligent (if not always sensitive) and a jaw which was reassuringly square, he had devoted much of his twenties to caring for his mother, who suffered from Alzheimer's disease, and as a result he had not lost his virginity until he'd turned thirty – and had been playing catch-up ever since.

But for anyone to assume he was the father of Monika's child . . .

They'd been friends for a long time. That was true. And he loved her. Perhaps he was even *in love* with her; he certainly had been when he was younger. But even so, the thought of them going to bed together was inconceivable – it would have put at risk so much of what they already had.

'The thing is, I'm not sure where she would have found the time to have a relationship,' he said hastily, in an attempt to cover his own shock and embarrassment. 'I mean, when she's not with us, she's with Louisa, and when she's not with Louisa, she's with us.' He turned to the third member of the team. 'What do you think, DS Meadows?'

Meadows didn't think, she *knew* – though Paniatowski was not aware that she knew. Dr Shastri, the police surgeon, had dropped enough hints for her to be able to work out what had happened to Paniatowski, and with the help of a motor cycle gang she had once ridden with, she had tracked down the rapists and extracted revenge. She still had the evidence of that revenge in a plastic bag in her deep freeze – and though she knew she should have thrown the frozen testicles out by now, she felt a strange reluctance to do so.

'I said, what do you think, Kate?' Beresford repeated.

'I think that, with the greatest possible respect, sir, you should try and keep your foot as far away from your mouth as is physically possible.'

'What have I said wrong now?' Beresford asked.

'You keep badgering the boss about taking leave, when it should be perfectly obvious to you that that's the last thing she wants to do.'

'Is that how *you* read the situation, Jack?' Beresford asked Crane.

'Pretty much, sir,' Crane admitted.

'I was only thinking about the baby,' Beresford said defensively.

'I know you were,' Meadows said, softening a little. 'Can we change the subject, sir?'

'If you like. To what?'

'There's a woman who's been watching the boss since she walked in, and I'm wondering why.'

'Are you sure it's Monika that she's watching?' Beresford asked. 'She could have her eye on Handsome Jack here – lots of girls do.'

'It's the boss she's studying,' Meadows said. 'Her eyes followed her to the corridor, and that's where they're still fixed, waiting for her to come back.'

'Where is this woman?' Crane asked.

'Far corner,' Meadows told him. 'Take a look at her yourself, but don't make it too obvious.'

Crane used the lighting of a cigarette as his excuse to shift position slightly. He saw the woman that Meadows had been talking about, and immediately agreed with her assessment of the situation.

The woman had auburn hair, and was in her middle to late thirties. She was very attractive – perhaps even beautiful – and her eyes were firmly fixed on the door to the corridor.

'There's something familiar about her,' Beresford said quietly, from the corner of his mouth.

'Do you think you know her, sir?' Crane asked.

'No, in fact, I'm certain I don't,' Beresford replied. 'But like I said, I do know the face.'

The woman turned, sensing their eyes were on her. When her suspicions were confirmed, she showed no sense of panic, but instead rose from her seat and exited in a calm – almost stately – manner.

'Maybe she's a reporter,' Crane speculated.

Meadows shook her head.

'Reporters don't move like that,' she said confidently.

'What do you mean?'

'With such easy grace and confidence – almost as if they were gliding. My guess would be she's in the performing arts – probably a dancer.'

'Do you know, I think you're probably right,' Crane said.

'I'm absolutely certain that I've seen that face somewhere before,' Beresford mused.

When the train pulled into Whitebridge railway station, no one got on it, and the only people who disembarked were the members of the newly re-formed Whitebridge Players.

It was unusual for Mark Cotton to arrive *anywhere* without there being hundreds of screaming fans already there waiting for him, and even though anonymity was part of the plan – which was why he was not accompanied by his usual minders – he still felt vaguely disappointed.

He looked across the platform at the pile of luggage which was being unloaded from the guards' van, and clicked his fingers to attract Phil McCann's attention.

'Get someone to transport all that stuff to the boarding house, will you, Phil?' he asked.

'You want your stuff taking there as well?' McCann asked.

'Yes.'

'But you won't really be staying at the boarding house, will you?'

'True,' Cotton agreed, looking down at the two battered suitcases which bore his name, 'but then, you see, that isn't my real luggage either, but merely part of the illusion.' He turned to the rest of the company. 'Come, children, let us march on the theatre.'

Geoff Turnbull had arranged a greeting committee for the company. He had intended it to be comprised of himself, Joan, and the four stagehands – two men and two women – who he had recruited. But then Joan – for some reason of her own – had not wanted to be there, so there was just the five of them.

Before they had assembled in the foyer, Geoff had given the stagehands a little talk.

'Actors can be very temperamental and need to be handled with care, so don't just go rushing up to them when they arrive, but wait until they approach you,' he had said to them.

The stagehands had looked a little disappointed, as he had expected them to. He'd smiled, understandingly.

'Look, I know the person you all most want to meet is the great Mark Cotton, and I promise you I'll introduce each and every one of you to him personally.'

He could see he had made them very happy, and he was pleased about that. They were a good bunch – stalwarts of local amateur dramatic societies. They all had other jobs, but had decided to take their annual holidays early that year, thus forfeiting their chance to roast on a warm Spanish beach in favour of two weeks' theatre work in cold, miserable March. Yes, he would certainly introduce them to Mark, and he would also make it quite clear to Cotton how much he – the director – depended on them.

The foyer door swung open, and the cast walked in. Mark Cotton was leading, of course – he was wearing a trilby hat and a woollen muffler, which was all the disguise that he needed on a freezing winter day – and the rest of the company trooped in behind him, like seagulls following an ocean liner.

For all his warnings that the stagehands should restrain themselves, Geoff Turnbull found it almost impossible to keep his own emotions in check.

'Mark,' he said. 'Mark Cotton! What a truly great pleasure it is to see you again.'

Cotton took off his muffler, stuffed it into the pocket of his overcoat, and favoured Turnbull with a puzzled frown.

'Do I know you?' he asked.

Turnbull heard one of his stagehands suppress a giggle, and felt his heart sink.

'It's me, Mark!' he said, almost desperately. 'It's Geoff Turnbull! The director.'

'Of course it is,' Cotton agreed, slipping out of his overcoat and handing it to Turnbull. 'It was stupid of me not to recognize you. Sorry about that.'

'That's all right, Mark,' Turnbull said, conscious that the stagehands were still watching the scene, and wondering what the bloody hell to do with Cotton's overcoat.

'Has all the work inside the actual theatre itself been completed?' Cotton asked. 'Is it safe for us to go inside?'

'Absolutely,' Turnbull assured him. 'It wasn't easy, but the reconstruction has been finished on schedule. I made sure of that.'

'Excellent! Well done!' Cotton said. He turned to the rest of the company. 'Well, people, what are we waiting for?' he asked, walking across to the door which led into the auditorium and pulling back the curtain. 'Let's go and see whether we've got the kind of theatre in which we can put on a play which will wow the critics and thrill the punters.'

The cast filed through the door with varying degrees of enthusiasm. Tony Brown and Phil McCann seemed interested, and perhaps even excited; Jerry Talbot stepped carefully, as if expecting an ambush; Bradley Quirk managed to convey the air of a man who had decided that since he was there, he might as well take a look; and Lucy Cavendish glided in like a star ready to take her bows.

Geoff Turnbull took the opportunity to walk over to where his stagehands were still standing.

'You'd better go into the auditorium,' he said. 'The cast may have questions they'll want to ask you.'

And as he was speaking, he was studying their faces, and saw that none of them was looking him in the eye.

They were disappointed in him, he thought. They'd listened to his tales of how the company used to be, and expected Mark Cotton to be pleased to see him as he'd been to see Mark – and Cotton hadn't even recognized him at first.

It was a tremendous loss of prestige, but he was sure that once they saw him working with the actors, they'd start to respect him again.

'Well, off you go then,' he said, attempting to replicate Cotton's jauntiness with the cast.

The stagehands did as he'd said, but he got the feeling that was more to do with getting away from him than it was about obeying his instructions.

He noticed he still had Mark Cotton's bloody overcoat in his hands, and felt a sudden urge to throw it to the ground and trample all over it. Then he saw that Cotton had not entered the auditorium himself, but was still standing in the doorway, watching him.

'I'll . . . err . . . put your coat on that, shall I?' he asked, indicating the usherette's chair. 'Is that all right?'

Cotton nodded.

Turnbull placed the coat carefully on the chair, and when he saw

that Cotton was miming a cigarette, he reached into his pocket for
his Players' No. 6.

'Oh, those cheap nasty little things!' Cotton said in disgust. 'You
don't happen to have a packet of Benson and Hedges Special Filter
about your person, do you?'

'No, sorry, only these.'

'Then I suppose they'll have to do,' Cotton said, extracting a
cigarette and putting it in his mouth.

'They're the only ones I smoke,' Turnbull explained, as he lit
Cotton's cigarette. 'Listen, Mark, I'd like us all to meet later, so I
can say a few proper words of welcome and hand out the rehearsal
schedules.'

The remark seemed to puzzle Cotton.

'Rehearsal schedules?' he repeated.

'Yes, don't you remember?' Turnbull asked. 'One of the things
I pride myself on when I direct a play is that the cast always knows
where it should be, and when it should be there.'

'Ah, we seem to have had a little bit of a misunderstanding,'
Cotton told him. 'I'll be directing.'

'But I'm the one who's overseen the entire restoration of the
theatre,' Turnbull said.

'Yes, and without even going into the auditorium, I can see, just
by looking around the foyer, what a splendid job you've done.'

'And I directed the play the last time that you performed it. I
made a good job of it.'

'Yes, you did, but times change and things move on.' Cotton put
a comforting hand on Turnbull's shoulder. 'Look, I don't *want* to
direct, Geoff,' he said. 'As far as I'm concerned, just acting the role
of Hieronimo is a big enough job for any man. But it's the backers,
you see – the money men. *They* want me to direct. In fact, they
insist I direct.'

'So where does that leave me?' Turnbull asked miserably.

'Oh, for heaven's sake, Geoff, don't look so down in the mouth.
You have bags of experience, and anyone who didn't take advantage
of it would be a complete bloody fool. You have a great deal to
contribute to this production.'

'Really?' Turnbull asked.

'Really,' Cotton assured him. He reached into his wallet and took
out two five-pound notes. 'The buffet car on the train was serving
food I wouldn't offer to a dog, and the whole company's teetering on

the verge of starvation.' He held out the notes to Turnbull. 'Take these and buy us a positive mountain of sandwiches, there's a good chap.'

There had been a time when the sound of approaching footsteps would have thrown Maggie Maitland into complete panic.

But that was in the old days.

Back then, she had been like a caterpillar – slow, wriggly and oh-so-squashable. Now, as a result of her raw courage and determination, she had pupated. Now, she was a Death's-head Hawkmoth.

The Hawkmoth did not run away from its enemies. Instead, it flew directly into the centre of their world – into the very jaws of their empire. The Hawkmoth would go right into the beehive – one frail creature taking on thousands of bees. And once inside, she would mimic their smell and steal some of their honey – take from them, in other words, a little of the one thing that the colony needed to survive.

'Now doesn't this place bring back loads of memories, Bradley?' she heard a man say.

'Indeed it does, Tony,' a second man agreed. 'It brings back memories of backbiting and egos as big as an elephant, memories of petty theft and even pettier betrayals.'

'There were good times, too,' the first man said. 'There were nights when we laughed so much we thought we would burst. There were times when one member of the company would do another a small, unexpected kindness, and you felt your faith in humanity had been restored.'

'Funnily enough, I don't remember any of those times at all,' the second man said.

'If you really feel like that, Bradley, then why – in God's name – are you here?' asked the first man exasperatedly.

'I'm here, Tony, to squeeze what I can out of the situation – to grab, for my own advantage, whatever Mark Cotton hasn't already nailed down.'

'It must be a very sad thing to look at the world through your eyes,' the first man said.

'At least it is the world – the real world – I'm seeing,' the second man countered.

They turned and walked away, their footfalls getting fainter and fainter with every step.

* * *

Florrie Hodge flung open the front door before Phil McCann had even had time to ring the bell.

'Welcome, welcome!' the old woman said. 'How wonderful to see you all again!'

'It's lovely to see you, too, Mrs Hodge,' Tony Brown said, and the rest of the cast – to a greater or lesser extent – agreed with him.

'Well, don't just stand there on the pavement,' Florrie Hodge said. 'Come inside before you all catch your deaths of cold.'

She led them into the hallway with a stag's antler coat rack and an elephant's foot umbrella stand.

'You'll find everything is pretty much as it was . . .' Florrie Hodge said.

'Oh God, how terrible!' Bradley Quirk muttered under his breath.

'. . . the dining room to your left, the lounge to the right. Your luggage is up in your rooms. I've already unpacked Mr Brown's and Mr Talbot's, hung their shirts and trousers up in their wardrobes, and put their socks, vests and underpants in their chest of drawers. I had hoped to do the same for the rest of you, but you arrived a bit earlier than I expected.'

'Which room is mine, Mrs Hodge?' Lucy Cavendish asked.

'Well, I know the ladies like to be near the bathroom, so I've put you in number three, on the first floor. The Misses Audley will be your neighbours, and also Mr Brown, because I know I can trust him to be around the fairer sex. The rest of the gentlemen will be on the second floor, which will suit Mr Cotton –' she flashed him a roguish grin – 'because that way I don't have to hear all the hanky-panky he gets up to.'

'Actually, Mrs H, I won't be staying here,' Cotton said.

The landlady looked devastated. 'But why won't you be? Don't you like it here?'

'I love it,' Cotton said smoothly, 'but I just couldn't bear the thought of your beautiful home being invaded by some of my half-crazed fans.'

Mrs Hodge was somewhat mollified, but enough of her disappointment and resentment was still bubbling under for her to say, 'Well, the least you could have done would have been to tell me you didn't want the room before I went to all the trouble of making it up.'

'But I did tell you,' Cotton protested. He clicked his fingers. 'No, I've got that wrong – I asked *Phil* to tell you.' He turned a reproachful gaze on McCann. 'Did you forget to tell our lovely Mrs H that I wouldn't be staying here?'

McCann – who had been asked to do no such thing – blinked uncertainly.

'No . . . err . . . I didn't forget,' he extemporized. 'The fact is, your security people didn't think it would be a good idea.'

'They probably don't trust you, Mrs H – but then they don't know you like I do,' Cotton said. 'I always say you can have absolute faith in Mrs H.' Cotton paused. 'There's one thing I need you to do for me, my lovely landlady – if any reporters come knocking on your door and ask if I'm staying here, and pray God that they won't, you're to say that I most certainly am.'

'Why?' Mrs Hodge asked, puzzled.

'Phil?' Cotton said.

'If the reporters find out that he's staying in the Royal Victoria, it might give them the wrong impression,' McCann told the landlady.

'I see,' Mrs Hodge said despondently – though it was perfectly plain that she didn't.

'Believe me, it's much better for all of us that I stay somewhere else,' Cotton said soothingly.

'If you say so,' Mrs Hodge conceded. For a moment, she looked really dropped on, then she brightened and said, 'Now who fancies a nice cup of strong hot tea?'

Maggie Maitland felt a pain shoot up her leg. That was because of the cramped conditions she was forced to endure, she realized.

It didn't matter. Later, when she was sure that the building was empty, she would walk around to relieve the stiffness. Later, she would survey the geography of the place, and work out her plan down to the last deadly detail.

She had supplies which, though they were monotonous, were sufficient to sustain her over a long wait. And she had the patience which that wait would demand of her.

'I am the Death's-head Hawkmoth,' she sang softly to herself. 'I will hold back until the time is right – and then I will suck the sweet-sickly life out of this place.'

FIVE

'Thomas Kyd was born in 1558, which made him six years older than William Shakespeare,' Mark Cotton said, looking into the camera with eyes that suggested both sincerity and scholarship. 'His father was a scrivener, which means that he knew how to read, and how to write letters, an important skill at a time when many people – including much of the aristocracy – were illiterate.'

The BBC team, consisting of two cameramen, a sound man and a director, had arrived that morning, and the moment they had set up the cameras, Cotton had insisted on them filming what he called his introduction.

'Kyd's father seems to have been very good at his job, since he was eventually appointed warden of the Worshipful Company of Scriveners of the City of London . . .' Cotton continued.

'Goodbye to the Whitebridge Theatre Company, and welcome to the Mark Cotton Show,' said Bradley Quirk, who was watching the interview from the wings with Jerry Talbot.

'You're spot on,' Talbot agreed.

'Of course, he's overplaying his hand right from the beginning,' Quirk said. 'There's no way that this pompous little lecture of his will go into the final documentary.'

'So why is the director even bothering to film it?'

'Because he's playing his own game – just like Cotton is playing his. He needs to get his teeth into something meaty, but he can't do that if he's already been kicked out of the dining room, so he's pretending to cooperate. He's a bit like Hieronimo in that way – all smiles and affability as long as it's necessary, but sticking the knife in as soon as he has the chance.'

'Kyd wrote *The Spanish Tragedy* sometime in the late 1580s, which means it was contemporaneous with – or even a little before – Shakespeare's first play,' Cotton told the camera. 'It was a great success, and – for a time at least – Kyd was considered one of England's pre-eminent dramatists.'

'I'm betting our Mark didn't actually know any of that stuff,' Quirk told Talbot. 'He'll have looked it up in the public library, and now he's trotting it all out in much the same way as a reasonably intelligent parrot might.'

'Don't you ever get tired of being so cynical about everything, Bradley?' Jerry Talbot wondered.

'Not at all,' Quirk replied. 'My cynicism is as necessary to me as a hunting knife is to an Eskimo, or a tin opener is to a modern mother – in other words, it is a survival tool.'

'As someone reminded me just the other day, without Mark this probably wouldn't have happened,' Talbot said.

'And that "somebody" was probably Phil McCann, the Henry Kissinger of assistant bank managers,' Quirk said.

'Yes, it was, as a matter of fact.'

'Would you mind if I were to ask you one simple little question?'

'It depends. What is it?'

'We have a six-night run here. On how many of those nights has Mark Cotton agreed to let you play Hieronimo?'

'Two.'

'That sounds fair, given that he's a major television star and you're dancing fruit,' Quirk conceded. 'But, of course, it will never happen. All actors are conceited – it's an essential part of their nature – but standing Mark Cotton's ego next to yours would be like placing a matchstick next to a giant oak tree.'

'What exactly are you saying?'

'I'm saying there's absolutely no way that he'll give you one third of the glory.'

'He better had do, or . . .'

'Or what?'

'Well, I don't exactly know – I haven't worked it out yet.'

'Get this into your head,' Bradley Quirk said. 'Mark Cotton is in charge. We may extract our petty revenges along the way – I certainly intend to – but mainly we have to roll with the punches and accept what crumbs Cotton sweeps off the table for us.' Quirk grinned. 'That's mixing my metaphors, but you know what I mean.'

'Yes,' Talbot said miserably, 'I do.'

'Thomas Kyd was arrested for heresy, and was probably tortured while he was in prison,' Mark Cotton was telling the camera.

The documentary director glanced down at his watch and sighed softly to himself. His surname was Sikes, and his parents had chosen to christen him William. He had never asked them whether they had done out of a complete ignorance of the major works of Charles Dickens, or because they had a particularly warped sense of humour, and since they had never volunteered the information themselves, they had taken their motivation to the grave with them. He had once thought of changing either his first name or his second, but had decided against it. He would tell his friends that it was a name which opened doors – well, after all, Bill Sikes had been a burglar, ha ha! – and it certainly insured that people he met at cocktail parties hadn't forgotten his name the following morning, when they sobered up.

'Kyd was eventually released without charge, but he was a broken man, and he died at the tragically early age of thirty-five,' Mark Cotton concluded. He looked across at Sikes. 'Was that all right?'

'It was perfect,' said the director, but – as Bradley Quirk had predicted – he had already decided to bin it.

The acting chief constable was still a bit of an unknown quantity, but, sitting opposite him, Paniatowski had already decided that he was a true political animal in a way that George Baxter could never have been.

'The town council is very much behind this play, Monika,' Pickering said.

'I gathered as much,' Paniatowski replied warily.

'And it's not just the BBC documentary or the restoration of the theatre that's got them worked up into a positive lather,' Pickering continued. 'They see before them a tremendous cultural renaissance in Whitebridge. In their minds' eyes, they're already picturing the Whitebridge Cultural Festival of the future, with famous dancers holding workshops, eminent painters displaying their newest pictures, and best-selling authors queuing up to sign their books.'

'Is that right?' Paniatowski asked, non-committally.

'It won't happen, of course,' Pickering told her. 'But when the council – several members of which sit on the police authority and allocate our budget – is excited, then we're excited, too. Isn't that right, Monika?'

'We're absolutely bursting with excitement, sir,' Paniatowski said.

Pickering smiled. 'I thought that might be the case – which is why you'll be only too delighted to meet the Kindly Witch from *Friday Corner.*'

'Who?'

'Sarah Audley. The actress.'

'Why should I want to meet her?'

'Because she wants to meet you.'

'Me *specifically*?'

'No, not you specifically, but apparently she's doing research for her next role and has asked to talk to a high-ranking woman police officer who works in our CID. Now which of the women who fulfil all her requirements do *you* think she should talk to, Monika?'

'There is only one – and that's me,' Paniatowski said.

'Exactly so.'

'I don't suppose I've any choice, have I?'

'Of course you have a choice. It's a private matter, totally unconnected with your duties, and you could – should you so wish – choose to disappoint both the town council and me.'

'Could you ask your secretary to set up the meeting?' Paniatowski said, resignedly.

'Yes, I could, and I'm sure she'll be delighted to do it, because she's just as excited about this whole thing as the rest of us are.'

When he'd been negotiating with the BBC over the documentary, Mark Cotton had promised that he would allow the camera crew completely open access, but even as the pledge was being made, he'd been adding the mental proviso that if they wanted the truth, then they were going to have to be much smarter and quicker on their feet than he was.

Thus it was that when he had his meeting with the three female members of the cast, it was in the bar, well away from the cameras.

'It's twenty years since we four last performed this play,' he said. He smiled his most winning wistful smile. 'Ah, time just flies by, doesn't it? It slips through your fingers like grains of sand.'

Ruth Audley returned the smile – and hers was wistful, too – but Sarah Audley and Lucy Cavendish showed by their expressions that they were not there to reminisce, but to do a deal.

'If I remember rightly, it was Ruth who played Bel-Imperia in that production,' Cotton said.

'And the maid, a watchman, several soldiers from both sides of the divide, and the messenger,' Ruth said.

'Yes, yes, we all know that in repertory theatre you have to play several characters, for God's sake, but we're here to talk about the leading roles,' Cotton said impatiently.

'Don't you dare speak to my sister in that tone of voice, Mark Cotton!' Sarah said.

Screw you, bitch! Cotton thought.

But he needed Sarah for the next few days, and so he allowed his face to become suffused with regret, and said, 'I'm sorry. I'm just nervous about the production. I do so want it to be a success – for all our sakes.'

'Just watch your step, that's all,' Sarah cautioned.

'I will,' Cotton promised. 'Now where was I? Oh, yes, Ruth played Bel-Imperia, Sarah played Isabella, and Lucy played Pedringano and understudied for Ruth. This time, I'd like Lucy to play Pedringano again – and of course, continue to understudy – but I'd like the lovely Audley sisters to exchange roles.'

'How do you feel about that, Ruth?' Sarah asked her sister.

Ruth shrugged. 'It's fine.'

'You're sure?

'Yes.'

It might be fine with Ruth but it clearly wasn't fine with Lucy, Cotton thought. But never mind, he had that in hand and would deal with it later.

Joan Turnbull had been looking for her husband and found him sitting disconsolately on the edge of the stage.

'What are you doing here, Geoff?' she asked. 'Rehearsals don't start until this afternoon.'

'I thought I might be useful,' Turnbull said, without much conviction. 'I thought a crisis might come up which only I could handle.'

'Nothing much is happening. Why don't you come home with me, and have a bit of lunch?' Joan suggested.

'I am *paid* to be here, you know,' Turnbull said, almost aggressively. 'I am earning a wage.'

'I know you are,' Joan said softly.

But it was a pittance – almost an insult.

Geoff looked around him.

'Two months ago, this was just a garish bingo hall,' he said, 'and now it's a real theatre again. And it wouldn't have happened without me.'

'It certainly wouldn't,' Joan agreed. 'You've worked miracles.'

'I thought they'd be bound to offer me the job of manager/ director once *The Spanish Tragedy* was over, because they'd have seen how well I directed that,' Turnbull mused. 'But I won't be directing it, will I? At best, all you could call me is an assistant stage manager.'

'You're vital to this production – even if some people don't realize it,' Joan said.

'Do you think I'll get the job anyway?' Geoff asked.

She wanted to say yes, but she couldn't lie to him.

'We'll see,' she said.

The last twenty years, since he'd lost the theatre, had been awful. But they had been nothing compared to what the next twenty years would be like – if Geoff even managed to survive for another twenty years. Mark Cotton had dangled the dream of a better future in front of him as long as he needed someone to do the donkey work, but the moment the work had been completed, he had snatched that future away. And now she hated Cotton more than she'd ever believed it possible to hate anybody.

Mark Cotton was walking at a brisk pace – as any man looking forward to a lunchtime of unfettered lust would – when he found his way suddenly blocked by a woman.

She was a dumpy little thing, with tight grey curls, thick glasses and a clipboard.

'Look, if this is some kind of survey you're conducting, I really haven't got time today,' he said.

He took a step to the side, with the intention of walking round the woman, but with remarkable alacrity for a person of her age and shape, she moved too, and successfully blocked him.

'It's not a survey,' she said. 'It's a petition. The council are poisoning pigeons in the corporation park, and we don't think it's right.'

For '*we* don't think it's right,' read '*I* don't think it's right,' thought Cotton, who knew a mad old bat when he saw one.

'I really am in a hurry,' he said, moving once more, and once more finding himself blocked.

The woman's mouth fell open in surprise.

'I know that voice,' she said. 'You're Vic Prince.'

Cotton made a quick calculation. He had written a role for himself and, so far, he considered he had been playing it to perfection.

In Act One, a successful actor tries – for love of his art – to stage a play anonymously, so that ordinary people can enjoy the drama *as* a drama, and not simply because of a famous name.

In Act Two, the secret is uncovered, and because of this, the play attracts even more attention than it would have done if he'd been open about it in the first place.

And then there is Act Three – the BBC documentary – in which he explains his original motivation, and everyone realizes that he is not just that cop from the telly but, in fact, a serious and dedicated artist.

The thing was, he was still in Act One, and was not entirely sure whether he wanted the second act to begin yet.

'You are him,' the woman said. 'I know you are.'

Even if he denied it, she'd still go off and tell anyone who'd listen that she'd seen him, he thought, and when it turned out she'd been telling the truth, that would reflect badly on him, because he always claimed to love his fans, and to spend as much time with them as he possibly could.

Besides, would it really matter if Act Two started a little earlier than anticipated?

He lowered his muffler, and gave the woman his widest smile.

'You're quite right,' he admitted. 'What a clever girl you really are.'

The compliment seemed to fluster her.

'Could I . . . would you mind if . . . that's to say, I'd like your autograph,' she gasped.

'Of course,' Cotton agreed.

The woman held the sheet on the clipboard, realized there were already the signatures of several other people she'd badgered into it, and pulled out a clean sheet from underneath.

'Shall I sign it DCI Vic Prince, or would you like me to put my real name?' he teased.

'Your real name, please, Mr Cotton.'

He took the clipboard from her.

'Call me Mark. And what's your name?'

'Vera.'

'So I'll make it out to Vera, shall I?'

'No,' she said, with sudden urgency. 'I just want your autograph. And could you put it at the bottom of the sheet, please?'

'Yes, I suppose so – if that's what you want. Is there any particular reason for it?'

'I want to put a picture of you above it, then have it framed and hang it on my bedroom wall.'

'I'm very flattered,' he said. He signed the piece of paper, and handed it back to her. 'Is that all right?' he asked.

'It's just perfect,' she said in a faraway voice.

'Now listen, Vera,' he cooed, 'it's a secret I'm here in Whitebridge, so you must promise me you'll not tell anyone you've seen me. Will you do that for me? Will you promise?'

'Of course,' she said. 'I'd do anything for you.'

He lent forward and pecked her lightly on the cheek, and this time when he stepped to the side, she did not try to stop him.

The best way to make sure a piece of news is spread is to swear someone to secrecy, he told himself. And then he banished all thoughts of Vera from his mind, and once more contemplated the hot, dirty sex that was awaiting him.

They had agreed to meet in the pub for lunch at one o'clock, but when Sarah got there – half an hour late – Ruth had still not arrived.

But maybe she was not just late – maybe she was not coming at all, Sarah thought.

She had seemed all right when Mark had announced that he was switching their parts around, but perhaps that was no more than an act, and she'd actually been so devastated by it that the idea of being in the same room as her sister was now almost unbearable.

The more Sarah considered it, the more likely it seemed that the demotion – coming on top of all the distress Ruth had been through with their mother's death – had been the straw which had finally broken the camel's back.

She hoped Ruth wasn't about to have some kind of nervous breakdown, because the last thing she needed, when she was coming to grips with the very difficult part of Bel-Imperia, was a loony sister.

The door opened, and Ruth walked in. She looked fine – in fact, better than fine.

So maybe, by not insisting she play the lead, I was actually doing her a favour, Sarah thought.

'Sorry I'm late,' Ruth said. 'I've been shopping – do you know, I haven't bought any new clothes for five years – and I didn't notice the time.'

'It's no problem,' Sarah assured her. 'It's nice to see you're taking an interest in things again.'

Ruth glanced around the public bar of the Drum and Monkey.

'Why did you choose this place?' she asked. 'It looks like a bit of a dump to me.'

'I'm doing research,' Sarah said. 'Remember that new part I said I'd landed – the one I didn't want you to talk about to anyone else?'

'Of course I remember.'

'Well, this is the pub the local coppers use, and I'm soaking up the ambience. So can you work out what that juicy part might be?'

For a moment, Ruth's face was a blank, and then it was flooded with sudden insight.

'You don't mean . . .' she began.

'I most certainly do.'

'And does . . .'

'Apart from you, me and the production company's inner circle, *nobody* knows.'

'Well, if that doesn't blow quite a few minds, I don't know what will,' Ruth said.

'How do you feel about playing Isabella rather than Bel-Imperia?' Sarah asked, more serious now.

'To be honest, I feel relieved,' Ruth said. 'Taking the part of Bel-Imperia would have been a bit like diving into the deep end of a swimming pool when you haven't swum for ten years. Isabella's more like getting in at the shallow end – I can paddle around for a while until I feel a bit more confident.'

'We haven't started rehearsals yet, so it's not too late for us to insist that it's you, and not me, who plays Bel-Imperia.'

'Thank you, but no,' Ruth said. 'But it really was very sweet of you to make the offer.'

And sweet it might well have been – but they both knew that she hadn't meant it.

Mark Cotton climbed out of bed and reached for his clothes, which he'd carefully draped over a conveniently close chair.

'Do you remember what you said to me when the Whitebridge Theatre closed down all those years ago?' asked a voice behind him.

'Probably,' he replied, slipping on his underpants. 'But why don't you remind me of it, to save me the trouble of having to think it through?'

'You said you'd ring me, and we'd talk about when we could get together. But you never did ring me, did you?'

Cotton pulled one of his socks up. 'I seem to recall that when I looked for it, I found that I'd lost your number.'

'There were thousands of ways you could have traced me – if you'd wanted to.'

Cotton examined himself in the mirror. Flat stomach, firm muscles – he looked as good now as he had when he'd first started acting.

'I said, there were thousands of ways you could have traced me if you'd wanted to,' said the voice from the bed.

'And *you* could have rung *me*, Lucy – if you'd really wanted to,' Cotton countered.

'It was the fifties,' Lucy Cavendish said. 'Women didn't do the chasing back then – they waited for the man to make the moves.'

'And then along came women's lib, and the golden age was gone forever,' Cotton said flippantly, as he reached for his shirt.

'You treated me very badly back then, and I think you should make up for it now,' Lucy said.

Mark threaded his tie through his collar. It was a nice tie, carefully chosen. It carried with it the suggestion that it might be the old-school tie from a very posh school, and if people chose to think that was what it was, then its owner – who had, in fact, attended a rundown secondary modern in a town much like Whitebridge – could hardly be blamed.

'How do you think I should make it up to you?' he asked.

'I think you should take the role of Bel-Imperia off Sarah and give it to me,' Lucy replied.

The knot he had tied was a half-Windsor – another hint that he came from a privileged background.

'I don't wish to seem rude, darling, but you have neither Sarah's modest fame nor her acting ability,' he said.

'But I've just been to bed with you!' Lucy whined.

Cotton turned round to face her.

It had been a mistake to screw her, he thought. True, she had an exceptionally good body for a woman pushing forty, but now that he was famous he could attract much fresher meat just by clicking his fingers.

'Are you saying that the only reason you went to bed with me was because you hoped I'd give you Sarah's part?' he asked sternly. 'In other words, my dear Lucy, are you saying that you're no better than a common whore?'

'Of course not.'

'Good,' Cotton said, 'because if that were the case, I'd lose all respect for you – and you wouldn't want that, would you?'

'No,' Lucy agreed, her dark eyes blazing simultaneously with anger and defeat.

'What you have to remember, my dear, is that there are no small parts, only small actors,' Cotton said.

'That's just a cliché,' Lucy complained.

'Cliché or not, Sarah plays Bel-Imperia,' Cotton said firmly.

SIX

25th March 1977

I t was Friday, the final day of rehearsals, and tempers – not least that of the director – were wearing thin.

They were rehearsing the final act, with Hieronimo and Bel-Imperia both being played by the understudies.

Hieronimo explains to the king and the viceroy what he has done, then turns and runs off-stage.

'*O hearken, Viceroy, Hold Hieronimo!*' the king says. '*Brother, my nephew and thy son are slain!*'

The viceroy is devastated. '*We are betrayed! My Balthazar is slain!*' he laments.

Hieronimo appears on the balcony, and then steps off it. He falls two feet before his harness restrains him.

'*Break ope the doors! Run, seize Hieronimo!*' the viceroy commands.

Two soldiers appear on the balcony, and reach down to pull Hieronimo back on to the platform—

'Hold it right there!' Mark Cotton shouted.

The two soldiers – who were, in fact, the male stagehands – had already got a grip on the harness straps, but now they froze.

'Are you saying that you don't want us to pull him back up yet?' one of them asked.

He sounded puzzled – and with reason.

'I know you're only bloody amateurs, but even *you* should see the importance of timing,' Cotton had raged at them in previous rehearsals. 'Pull him up too soon, and the audience doesn't have time to revel in the shock. Pull him up too *late*, and that same audience will be wondering why he hasn't bloody well blacked out.'

So what exactly had they done wrong now? the stagehand wondered.

'Leave him hanging where he is, and get back down here,' Cotton said harshly.

'You mean . . .?'

'I mean what I bloody say – leave him hanging there, and get back down here!'

The two stagehands hesitated for a second, before turning and descending the stairs.

Cotton strode angrily across the stage, twice, before looking up at Jerry Talbot again.

'You were three beats too late,' he said.

'I wasn't,' Talbot replied, without perhaps complete conviction.

'Don't tell me you weren't when everybody here knows you bloody well were,' Cotton said.

'I . . . I have such a short time to get into position,' Talbot said. 'The king and the viceroy only have two lines each, and even before the viceroy's last line, I'm supposed to be on the platform.'

'Good point,' Cotton said. 'I tell you what we'll do. We'll add a few more lines of dialogue, so you'll have all the time you need. Now what can we say? What words can we put into the king's mouth that Thomas Kyd wasn't bright enough to think of himself?'

'Mark, there's no need to—' Jerry Talbot began.

'Let me see – the king has just said that his nephew and the viceroy's son are dead,' Cotton interrupted him. 'Maybe after that, he'll change the subject – lighten the mood a little. Perhaps he could say, "Played any good rounds of golf recently, Viceroy?" And the viceroy, after expressing his deep anguish at his son's death, could say, "I went round the course at three under par last Sunday." What do you think of that?'

'This harness is starting to pinch,' Jerry Talbot said.

'Is it?' Cotton asked. 'Well, we all have to suffer for our art.

Listen, you useless prick, do you still want to play Hieronimo on Monday?'

'Yes.'

'Then you'll have to learn to get it right, won't you?' Cotton turned to the stagehand soldiers. 'Go back up there and haul him in.'

Cotton made Talbot practice it again – run off the stage, run up the steps, put on the harness, slip the noose around his neck, step off the platform.

And again – run off the stage, run up the steps, put on the harness, slip the noose around his neck, step off the platform.

And again – run off the stage, run up the steps, put on the harness, slip the noose around his neck, step off the platform.

The first time, he was possibly a beat too late, but on his other two attempts he was spot on.

'Again!' Cotton said.

'Oh, come on, Mark,' Geoff Turnbull protested. 'He's got it right twice, and it's bloody hard work. It's unreasonable to expect him to repeat it again, especially since he's so tired now that he'll probably miss it.'

Cotton swung round to face him.

'I think you've forgotten who *you* are and who *I* am,' he said angrily. 'I can have you thrown out of this theatre any time that I feel like it, Geoff. Is that what you want?'

Turnbull looked down at the stage.

'No, Mark,' he mumbled.

'I can't hear you,' Cotton told him. 'What was it you said?'

'I said, no, Mark,' Turnbull repeated, louder this time.

'Then I suggest you keep your mouth shut unless you've got something useful to say – and by that, I mean something that I want to hear,' Cotton said. He turned back to Talbot. 'Do it again, Jerry.'

Standing next to one of the cameramen, William Sikes emitted a quiet chuckle.

'Now this is more like it,' he said in a whisper. 'The beast unmasked. The bully-boy revealed. That's *real* television.'

There was only one woman in the public bar of the Drum and Monkey when Paniatowski walked in, and it was something of a surprise that, of all the places she could have chosen to sit, she had selected the team's usual table.

Paniatowski did not recognize the woman, but then she was not a great watcher of television, nor had she been at the table the previous Wednesday, when Meadows had spotted her and pointed her out to the others.

The woman stood up and held out her hand.

'Sarah Audley,' she said. 'It's a pleasure to meet you, Chief Inspector – though I don't imagine the feeling is reciprocated.'

'What makes you think that?' Paniatowski asked, lowering herself carefully into the chair opposite the other woman.

Sarah Audley laughed. 'I should have thought that was obvious. You're a hard-working police officer and must have a hundred important things you *could* be doing, but instead of that you're having to spend time with an actress who will probably misinterpret everything you say, and end up playing someone who shares a few superficial characteristics with you, but is, in fact, a gross travesty of everything you stand for. Have I got that about right?'

Paniatowski smiled. 'More or less.'

'I won't lie to you,' Sarah Audley said. 'I'll be working from a script which I won't have written, or even have had any say in. And that script will be unlikely to reflect real police work. But what I'd like to do is insert a small kernel of truth into my performance. I'd like to be able to *think* like a police officer, so that whatever my lines are, the viewers will get a glimmering of the pressure that front line officers are constantly under.'

'I see,' Paniatowski said.

Sarah Audley laughed again. 'No, you don't,' she said. 'To a practical woman like you, it just sounds like airy-fairy gobbledegook. But I hope that if you ever get to see my performance, you'll be able to recognize that there's at least a kernel of truth in it.'

'So what do you want to know?' Paniatowski asked.

'Everything from your childhood memories to where you buy your knickers,' Sarah Audley said, making an extravagant all-encompassing gesture in the air, with both hands.

'I buy my knickers from whatever department store I happen to be passing when I decide I need some new ones,' Paniatowski said.

Sarah Audley grinned. 'You needn't worry, you know,' she said. 'No one will see my performance and think, "That's Monika Paniatowski." It doesn't work that way.'

'Then how does it work?'

'I won't have your accent, I won't have your walk, I won't even imitate any of your facial expressions. But somewhere deep inside me, I'll be thinking, "What would Monika think about this?" – and that will add the slight edge of veracity to the performance that can make all the difference.' She paused. 'Please tell me some more, and – if you feel you can – please make it a little more personal.'

Paniatowski told her that her father had been a Polish cavalry officer who had been killed when leading a charge against the invading German tanks. She described the life she and her mother had led in war-torn Europe, constantly in danger of being arrested, constantly on the point of starvation. She talked about her early days in the police, when women officers were regarded as a dangerous experiment, and she had been generally known (after her first promotion) as Sergeant Pantyhose. She outlined her triumphs, too – some of the cases she had worked on with Charlie Woodend, and some of the ones she had handled alone, after he retired.

She did *not* tell Sarah Audley that her stepfather had started raping her before she'd even hit her teens, nor that she had once been in love with a married man who had killed himself to protect the reputation of the force. She kept well away from any discussion of that dead man's daughter, who she had brought up as her own, and loved with all her heart.

None of that, she'd decided, was any of the other woman's business.

When she had finally finished, Sarah Audley let out a gasp of admiration.

'I'm in awe of you,' she saw. 'I know that sounds as fake as hell, but it's true – I really am in awe of you.'

'Well, if you think it's helped . . .' Paniatowski said awkwardly.

'It's done more than help,' Sarah Audley told her. 'It's given me a whole new perspective on police work, and if I get a BAFTA award for the role – and I'm cocky enough to believe that I will – yours will be the first name I mention.'

Walking back to her car, Paniatowski quickly replayed the interview in her mind. She had talked more than she'd intended to, but then Sarah Audley had proved to be a very good listener. The one thing that troubled her was that she was not sure whether she did genuinely like Sarah, or had simply been charmed into *believing* that she liked her.

*   *   *

They had a full dress rehearsal that afternoon, and when it was all over, Mark Cotton addressed the whole cast.

'Well, children, what can I say? That was splendid, and I'm so proud of you all. To those of you who are going home to be with family for the weekend, I wish a really restful time. However, if you're staying in Whitebridge, I'd like to invite you to dinner in the Royal Victoria restaurant on Saturday night. You'll be able to gorge yourselves – and it won't cost you a penny.' He looked around him, and gave everyone a smile. 'That's it,' he continued, waving his hand in the air. 'Fly away, my pretty children.'

As the cast began to drift off stage, Cotton said, 'Can you spare me a minute, Sarah?'

'If I must,' Sarah Audley replied, with a lack of enthusiasm that was truly masterful in its projection.

'I . . . I think I might have gone a little over the top at the rehearsal this morning,' Cotton said, looking worried.

'A little over the top!' Sarah repeated. 'From what I've heard, you were more than *a little* over the top – you were a complete bloody prick.'

'It slipped my mind that the BBC was filming, you see,' Cotton said, chewing one of his fingernails. 'The cameras have become almost part of the furniture, and I was so wrapped up in directing—'

'In *directing*! Don't you mean in bullying the rest of the cast – especially Jerry Talbot?'

'In directing, that I forgot all about them. And now I'm afraid I might have ended up giving the wrong impression.'

'Or the *right* impression – for once.'

'Anyway, I'd like to show a little of the other side of myself – the gentler, more understanding side.'

'Is there such a side to you?' Sarah asked.

He must really be worried about his image if he was prepared to take this much shit, she thought. And it was such fun putting his balls through the ringer – though not anything like as much fun as she planned to be having in about another ten minutes.

'Anyway, I think that the television people want to show the other side of my character, too,' Mark Cotton said, ignoring the comment because he had no choice in the matter.

'What makes you reach that highly unlikely conclusion, Mark?' Sarah wondered.

'I suggested that they film the two of us having a natural conversation. We could give them that little scene we rehearsed together – although they won't know that it's rehearsed.'

'Of course they'll know,' Sarah said. 'They're not stupid.'

'Well, maybe they *will* know – but they'll include it in the documentary anyway, because nobody likes to get on the wrong side of an actor who's going places.'

'That scene was a stupid idea in the first place, and the more I think about it, the worse it's got.'

'Please, Sarah, do it for *me*,' Cotton said.

Sarah sighed. 'Oh Mark, I'd do anything for you.' She frowned. 'Those words sound familiar. When have I said them before?'

'It's like déjà vu all over again,' Cotton said, doing his best to divert her with an old joke.

But Sarah was not about to be diverted.

'Ah yes, I remember now,' she told him. 'I said exactly the same words, and in exactly the same tone, twenty years ago – about two days before you chucked me for Lucy Cavendish.'

'I may have behaved badly in the past, but I swear I'll make it up to you,' Cotton promised. 'Please, Sarah, do the scene.'

'Oh, I'll do it all right . . .'

'Thank you.'

'But not to help you get out of the hole you've dug yourself into. I'll do it for my own peculiar ends.'

'What does that mean?' Cotton asked.

'It's a quote. Iago says it in *Othello*.'

'I know that. But what does it mean when you say it?'

Sarah smiled. 'You'll soon find out,' she said enigmatically.

The camera panned in on Mark and Sarah, who were sitting on the edge of the stage and reading through the section of the play in which Bel-Imperia kills herself. Then, right *on* cue, Sarah deliberately *missed* her cue.

'Your mind seems to be somewhere else, this afternoon,' Mark said, in a kindly, understanding way.

Sarah sighed, wistfully. 'I suppose I was thinking back to the time when we first did this play – twenty years ago. I had quite a big crush on you in those days, you know.'

'Did you? I had no idea,' Cotton replied, sticking to the script. He laughed. 'But I'm assuming you've got over it by now.'

'Oh yes, I've quite got over it,' Sarah agreed. 'But I still enjoy working with you. In fact, I adore it.'

'Me too,' Cotton said. 'And with just a little bit of luck, we may get the chance to work together again.'

'Oh, there'll be no luck about it,' Sarah said.

That line had come completely out of the blue. What the hell was she playing at? Cotton wondered.

'No luck about it?' he repeated, to buy himself time.

'Well, we'll be co-starring in the next series of DCI Prince, won't we?' Sarah asked.

Cotton laughed.

'You're joking, of course,' he said.

But it was a pretty poor joke, he thought, and if she'd bothered to ask him, he could have provided her with a much better one.

A sudden look of concern came to Sarah's face – and *that* hadn't been rehearsed or discussed, either.

'Oh dear,' she said, 'I have rather put my foot in it, haven't I? But you see, I thought they would have told you by now.'

She was not making this up, he thought – she was not that good an actress. So it had to be horribly, horribly true.

He wanted to scream that it wasn't fair – that DCI Prince was his show, and he didn't want to share it with anybody – and especially not with one of his cast-offs from twenty years ago.

He wanted to run around smashing things up.

He wanted to slap Sarah – hard – across her stupid face.

But the camera was still rolling, and so none of those options were open to him.

So he reached over, and took her hands in this.

'That's wonderful news,' he said. 'And I'm glad the production company didn't tell me, because it's so much nicer hearing it from you.'

Sarah turned a little away from the camera, and he could see the gleam of malicious triumph in her eyes.

'I'm so glad you're pleased,' she said.

'Bloody great!' Bill Sikes whispered to his cameraman. 'You couldn't make this up.'

SEVEN

28th March 1977

The whispers he had sent out – including the one no doubt spread by the old bag who'd so willingly abandoned her poisoned pigeon petition the moment she'd recognized him – had done the trick. Now everyone knew that Mark Cotton – television star nonpareil – had turned his back on the glamour and glitz, and was performing in a humble repertory theatre for the sake of his art.

To the journalists and members of the theatrical world who had contacted him, he had managed to convey a feeling of bemusement, sprinkled with the slightest hint of outrage, and overlaid with ruefulness that he could ever have been so naive as to think he could get away with it.

'It's a bit of a disappointment nonetheless,' he'd said. 'I'd hoped that for just one week I might be able to get back to my roots and be no more than that backbone of the theatre – a simple jobbing actor.'

When they'd asked for tickets for the first night, he'd been most willing to supply them.

'I'm so glad you've chosen that night,' he said, 'because it will give you the opportunity to see my truly marvellous understudy, Jerry Talbot, in the role of Hieronimo.'

And suddenly, the first night hadn't been convenient for them at all, and they'd expressed a wish to come on the second or third night, when, unfortunately, they'd miss Talbot's performance. He'd tried to persuade them, because Jerry really was tremendous in the role, but, as he had expected, it had been to no avail.

He had his reasons for not playing Hieronimo on that first night. Opening nights had a certain magic about them – yes – but they also tested the cast in ways that even the most realistic dress rehearsal had not prepared them for.

Mistakes were made on the first night and timing was sometimes slightly off. Lessons were learned from the performance, adjustments were made after it, and – in his opinion – the second night was invariably better. And it was only when it was better – only when it was as good as it could be – that he wanted to put in an appearance.

The first night had finally arrived.

It had been stated very clearly that all the tickets had been sold, but there were still so many people calling in for returns that the ticket office had stopped picking up the phone.

The police had cleared the section of the street nearest the theatre early that afternoon, and had set up barriers immediately beyond that. Now, the only people allowed within fifty yards of the theatre were those who had tickets for the production or were on some other legitimate – and provable – business.

A dozen officers manned each barrier, and there were two police horses being held in reserve. There had been no trouble up to that point, but the crowd – which was mainly composed of women from their late teens to their early fifties – was growing by the hour.

Periodically, a sergeant with a large megaphone would read from a prepared script.

'You will not be allowed beyond this barrier until at least one o'clock tomorrow morning. There is nothing to see, and you would be well-advised to go home.'

The message was ignored by the Buds and the simply wannabe-Buds. They knew that there was only the slightest – most infinitesimal – chance that Mark Cotton would appear. But if he did appear, and they weren't there to see him, they would just die.

Inside the theatre, there was the usual controlled pandemonium and subdued hysteria. Cast members fussed over their make-up or paced out the stage, practising hitting their marks. Stagehands checked the props and tested the lighting. And Geoff Turnbull, who had expected to be at the centre of things, wandered about aimlessly, trying to look as if he was doing something important.

Jerry Talbot could see that something was wrong the moment Mark Cotton entered the dressing room.

'Why are you wearing make-up?' he asked.

'There's been a change of plan,' Cotton told him, with uncharacteristic nervousness. 'I'll be playing Hieronimo tonight.'

'But you said I could do it,' Talbot exploded.

'And now I've changed my mind.'

'You can't do that!' Talbot said, in a tone which was roughly halfway between extreme anger and abject begging. 'Not after what you put me through at Friday's rehearsal.'

'For Christ's sake, can't you see there's no point in arguing with me, Jerry?' Cotton asked exasperatedly, 'I simply *have* to do it tonight, and that's really all there is to it.'

'*Why* do you have to do it tonight? Don't you think I'm entitled to an explanation?'

'I've no time to discuss it with you now – I've got to get into the right frame of mind for my performance.'

'You *can't* do it,' Talbot whined.

'I'm the director and I'm also one of the principal backers – which means I can pretty well do what the bloody hell I like,' Cotton said. 'You'll probably get your chance to play Hieronimo sometime later in the week – but not if you continue to piss me off like this.'

He turned on his heel, and walked rapidly out of the dressing room.

'If you remember, I predicted that exactly this would happen,' said Bradley Quirk, who was sitting at the next make-up table. 'But even I didn't picture it quite like this. Our leader seemed rather rattled, don't you think. I would say he's very scared about going on tonight – yet, for some unfathomable reason, he feels compelled to.'

'He can't do this,' Talbot said.

'My assessment of the situation would be that not only can he, but he has,' Quirk replied.

'We shouldn't let him get away with bullying the company like this,' Talbot said. 'He depends on us as much as we depend on him. It's not too late to send a deputation to him now, and if he knows how the rest of us feel, he'll have to give way.'

'But how *do* the rest of us feel?' Quirk mused. 'Speaking for myself, whilst I strongly subscribe to the belief that no man is an island, ask not for whom the bell tolls, it tolls for thee, etc, etc, the simple truth is that I've still got my part, and I'd rather like to hold on to it.'

'You're an arsehole,' Talbot snarled.

'Granted,' Quirk agreed, 'but at least I'm an arsehole who still has a role to play.'

Talbot stood up, and stormed out of the dressing room.

But where do I go from here? he asked himself, once he was standing in the corridor.

He could always go back to the lodgings or slink into the nearest pub, but what if, at the last moment, Cotton sprained his ankle, and he was not there to replace him?

Cotton wouldn't sprain his ankle, he told himself angrily. Bastards like him always led a charmed life.

He reached the end of the corridor, and mounted the steps.

Once he was on the stage, he began pacing up and down.

But it was not random pacing, he suddenly realized, because though he wasn't consciously thinking about it, there was a part of his brain which was directing his legs to hit his marks.

Except that, as things had turned out, they weren't *his* marks any longer, he thought bitterly.

The last twenty years of his life flashed rapidly through his mind like a speeded-up film.

He saw the damp, dreary repertory theatres all over the country in which he'd worked.

He experienced anew the humiliation of having to dress up as a dancing banana, not to make an artistic statement, but to sell yogurt.

And worst of all, he recalled working as a barman or a cleaner, and having people laugh at him when he told them that this was only temporary, and that he was actually an actor.

Hieronimo had been his chance to finally break through, and Mark Cotton had stolen it from him at the last moment.

His soul – his very being – screamed out for revenge, and he swore he would have it.

The taxi had made slow progress along the one traffic lane which the police had managed to keep open, but at least it hadn't killed any of the Cotton Buds who, in their near-ecstasy, drifted into the lane and seemed totally unaware of both the approaching vehicle and their own mortality.

Now, finally, it pulled up outside the theatre, and two women and the girl alighted.

They made an incongruous trio. One of the women was blonde, in her early forties and heavily pregnant. The other was much younger, slim, and wore her dark hair so short that it was almost a fine piece of velvet balancing on her head. The girl had dark Iberian eyes. She was slim, too, but it was clear that it was only a teenage skinniness and that in two or three more years she would be turning men's heads when she walked down the street.

Meadows looked at the queue of ticket holders, stretching up the road almost to the police barrier.

'Can't have you standing out here in your condition, boss,' she said, and before Monika Paniatowski had a chance to reply, she was marching off towards the box office.

Tickets for *The Spanish Tragedy* had become like gold dust since it had leaked out that Mark Cotton would be playing the lead, but Meadows had told Paniatowski she could get her hands on some, and Paniatowski had believed her, because everything Meadows had ever promised – however impossible that promise might have seemed – had always been delivered.

It had seemed only polite, when Meadows had made the offer, to ask her to accompany them, but Paniatowski had been slightly surprised when the other woman had agreed.

'I like going to the theatre, but it's not the same on your own,' Meadows had explained.

And it occurred to Paniatowski, for the first time, that though Meadows always seemed so self-reliant, and had a very active – if rather bizarre – sex life, she was probably lonely.

Meadows returned.

'We can go in now,' she said.

'How did you manage that?' Paniatowski asked.

'I told them that you were pregnant.'

'And you didn't mention the fact that I was a chief inspector?' Paniatowski asked accusingly.

'Of course not,' Meadows replied. 'That would have been very wrong.' She grinned. 'But I did say that I'm a detective sergeant, and that while I was outside, queuing, I'd take the opportunity to see if the fire doors came up to the standards laid down in the new regulations.'

'There haven't *been* any new regulations,' Paniatowski said.

'Haven't there?' Meadows asked, guiding her boss towards the door. 'Dear me, what an airhead I am.'

Bill Sikes had decided to film the first night of the play, and had positioned one of his cameras in the left wing, and the other in the right.

It wouldn't produce perfect results.

He knew that.

For a start, the lighting had been set for the play, rather than for the cameras. And then there was the fact that, though the cameras were on tracks, they would have to remain static that night, because, once again, the documentary must play second fiddle to the drama.

None of that mattered, he thought as he headed for the stage to carry out a last-minute check on the cameras, because he was not filming the play itself, but what went into *making* the play, and if some of the shots were grainy and slightly out of focus, then that would only add to the authenticity of his finished product.

And it *would* be authentic, Sikes thought, chuckling to himself. Mark Cotton – who was not only arrogant but also stupid – had tried to manipulate the documentary with his staged pieces, and it had all gone disastrously wrong for him. The conversation with Sarah Audley had been a true television classic, and the way he had handled the Friday morning rehearsal had clearly demonstrated what a nasty little shit he really was.

He climbed the steps to the stage and saw that one of his cameramen seemed to be almost wrestling with his camera.

'Have you got a problem there, George?' he asked.

The cameraman jumped like a scalded cat.

'No, I . . . err . . . was just finding out how easy it would be to film the audience,' he spluttered.

Sikes crouched down beside the camera.

'Filming the audience in the stalls would be a doddle,' he said. 'What you seem to be trying to do is find a way to film one of the boxes. Now why would you want to do that?'

The cameraman said nothing.

'A few years ago, I shot a documentary about the posh people who live in the Cotswolds, and one of the local mini-celebrities was so keen to be in it that he bribed one of my cameramen – let's call him Dirty Dick – to take lots of shots of him,' Sikes said. 'There wouldn't happen to be a local mini-celebrity who's planning to sit in that box tonight, would there, George?'

'Not that I know of,' the cameraman said, unconvincingly.

'Good,' Sikes said. He looked pointedly up at the box. 'I'd have liked to get that Dirty Dick fired, you know, but your union would never have stood for that.'

'No, it wouldn't have,' George agreed, with a slight smile he couldn't quite hide.

'So what I did do was to have a quiet word with all my mates in the business – and you'd be surprised just how many of the other directors *are* my mates. I suggested to them they should think twice before they used Dick again themselves, and they agreed they would.' Sikes paused. 'You get the point, do you, George?'

'Yes,' the cameraman agreed. 'I get the point.'

Getting into the theatre was easy for Paniatowski, Meadows and Louisa. They simply handed over one half of their tickets to the girl on the door, and stepped into the foyer. It was once they were inside that they found their route blocked by two hard men in suits.

'Are you Buds?' one of the hard men asked. 'If you are, I have a personal message for you from Mark Cotton himself. Mr Cotton doesn't think you'll enjoy seeing him in this play. He'd like to give you your ticket money back, and if you leave your names and addresses, he'll see to it that you get a studio pass for the next series of DCI Prince.'

It sounded like a rehearsed speech, and it probably was.

'Why doesn't Markie-Parkie want us in there?' Meadows asked, with that slightly-mischievous, slightly-dangerous tone in her voice that Paniatowski had learned to recognize. 'Is he afraid we'll go completely ape shit when he appears on stage?'

'I couldn't say.'

'But what if we *are* Buds, and we don't want his bribe? What if we really want to see the play?'

'If you're Buds, you're not going in,' the heavy said firmly.

Meadows smiled. 'You actually think that you could stop us, do you?' she asked.

'I *know* I could stop you,' the bouncer said, prodding her shoulder lightly with his index finger.

Meadows had had her fun, but now it was time to step in before the bouncer got hurt, Paniatowski decided.

'We're not Buds,' she said.

'Are you sure?' the bouncer asked suspiciously.

'Yes.'

'I *might* have been a Bud, if I hadn't been so terrified of my mother,' Louisa said sweetly.

EIGHT

Off-stage, he is Mark Cotton, as adored by his fans as he is despised by many of his fellow actors, but he is on stage now, and the body which Mark Cotton once owned is possessed by Hieronimo, the noble Marshal of Spain. He is grieving over his son Horatio's death, and the knowledge that he cannot touch that son's murderers – Prince Balthazar of Portugal and Lorenzo, the son of the Duke of Castile – is almost destroying him.

> With what excuses can you shield yourself,
> Thus to neglect the loss and life of him
> Whom both my letters and your own belief
> Assure you to be cruelly slaughtered?
> Hieronimo! For Shame, Hieronimo.

The speaker looks like Sarah Audley, but at this moment she is Bel-Imperia, sister of Lorenzo and very reluctant bride-to-be of Balthazar. And in words that prick him like heated needles, she is both reaffirming her own love for the dead Horatio and questioning the love his father holds for him.

He has a plan by which they may both get their revenge, Hieronimo tells her. He will propose putting on a play to entertain the wedding guests, and will persuade the two murderers to act in it. And it is in the course of this play that the mourning lover and father will wreak their revenge.

'You see what I mean about him, Mum?' Louisa asked in a whisper. 'He is *so* sexy, isn't he?'

'Shush!' Paniatowski said. 'Remember where you are.'

But she *did* see what her daughter meant. Even with all that make-up on – even playing old – Mark Cotton was undoubtedly sexy.

Undeterred, Louisa turned to Meadows.

'What do you think of him, Kate?' she asked.

'In my opinion, going on a date with him would be like flogging a dead horse,' Meadows told her.

'What do you mean, flogging a dead—'

'Louisa!' Paniatowski hissed, jabbing her daughter with her finger.

Louisa turned to face the stage. Her first inclination was to sulk, but then she conceded that, in all fairness, her mother was right, and that they should appreciate the performance rather than lusting after one of the actors. Still, she couldn't help wishing that she could magically become twenty years older – or that, by the same process, Mark Cotton could become twenty years younger.

The wedding party has assembled to watch the play, and Hieronimo hands them the script to make it easier for them to follow the proceedings. They leaf through it, not realizing that what they are reading is not an improbable fiction, but the clearly set out plan for the murders they are about to witness.

In the play-within-a-play, Pasha stabs Erasto, but in the play that *is* the play, Hieronimo sticks his knife hard into Lorenzo's soft flesh. And scarcely has he had time to die before Bel-Imperia kills Balthazar, and then immediately turns her dagger on herself.

Hieronimo has had his revenge, and considers his own life at an end.

> And, princes, now behold Hieronimo
> Author and actor in this tragedy,
> Bearing his latest fortune in his fist.

A spotlight shines briefly on the balcony above, revealing a noose hanging there.

> And will as resolutely conclude his part
> As any of the actors gone before.
> And, gentles, thus I end my play!
> Urge no more words, I have no more to say.

It is Hieronimo who speaks these words, but it is Mark Cotton, the actor – conscious of how little time he has to take up his position on the balcony – who turns and runs off stage.

And as he runs, a conversation – a time-echo from twenty years earlier – is playing in his head.

'Geoff let us down. We're a bloody company – and now we're all out of work. Who else is to blame?'

'*As Joan said, times are hard . . .*'

'*Then why haven't other companies gone under as well?*'

'*Perhaps because their leads weren't two beats too late on the hanging scene.*'

Well, he'd had to wait twenty years for his revenge, but, in the end, he had got it, and it had given him boundless pleasure to make Jerry Talbot keep on rehearsing the scene until he was almost dead on his feet.

But that does mean that he cannot afford to be late himself – because if he is, Talbot will spread the story far and wide, and he will become a laughing stock. Besides, it is not only Talbot he has to consider. There is also . . .

He is clear of the stage and starting to climb the stairs.

And then he slips.

He bloody slips!

He slides down three steps, banging his shins on each one. He grabs on to the rail and hauls himself up again.

The spotlight will be shining on the balcony soon, and if he is not there when it appears . . .

He reaches the platform and quickly clips on his harness. He grabs the noose, and slips it around his neck.

He could use a second or two to compose himself, but he can manage without them if he has to. And he does *have to* manage without them – because now the spotlight hits him.

He steps off the platform into empty air. He hears the cries of horror from the audience, and anticipates the gasps of relief when, after falling no more than two feet, his harness restrains him.

He feels something snap, and suddenly he is plunging towards the stage, with the noose tightening around his neck.

For a split second, he experiences a terror he never imagined possible – and then there is only blackness.

The rope tightened, and Mark Cotton came to a violent jerking halt. And there he hung, his head twisted at an unnatural angle, his feet swinging gently a mere four feet from the stage.

Some of the company froze. At least two of them screamed. Only Phil McCann had the presence of mind to gesture frantically to the stagehands that they should close the bloody curtains.

The curtains *did* close, leaving the audience on the other side of them somewhat perplexed.

The actors had saved the biggest shock for the end, the audience thought – and it certainly had been shocking enough.

But was it, *in fact*, the end?

It all seemed a little too abrupt.

Yet perhaps that was how it had been written – perhaps that was how plays *did* end in those days.

And if it *was* the end, it seemed only polite to clap – so why wasn't everybody else doing just that?

Eventually, embarrassment – and the fear of being thought rude – led one section of the audience to start applauding, and then the rest joined in.

But it was half-hearted at best, because though the audience knew that they couldn't *really* have just seen a man die – though it had to be a very clever trick – they still felt vaguely uneasy.

'I'll handle this, boss.' Meadows said, standing up. 'You stay here with Louisa.'

She edged to the end of the row, walked down the aisle, climbed the steps, and stepped through the curtain. The scene which greeted her on the stage had not changed much. Most of the actors were still where they had been when the curtain closed. The only one who had moved was the actor playing the King of Spain. He was now standing centre stage, holding Mark Cotton by the legs, and lifting him slightly, so that the rope was not quite so taut.

Not that that would do any good, Meadows thought.

She held up her warrant card, for them all to see.

'Who's in charge here?' she demanded.

The actor who played the Duke of Castile raised his arm and pointed to the hanging man.

'He is,' he said, in a voice as hollow as if he'd spoken the words into a bucket.

'Then who's his assistant?' Meadows said.

A man in cord trousers and a thick woollen cardigan walked unsteadily on to the stage.

'I'm the manager,' he said. 'Or, at least, I used to be.'

He was drunk, Meadows thought, but he still seemed a better option than any of the others.

'Get the ushers to evacuate the theatre,' she said. 'Make sure they tell the audience that there's absolutely no need for panic, but that they must leave as soon as possible. Have you got that?'

'Yes.'

'And somebody get me a knife, so I can cut this poor bastard down!'

By the time Dr Shastri arrived at the theatre, uniformed constables had been posted at each of the exits to ensure that no one entered or left the building. Two more constables stood at either end of the stage, securing the crime scene. And a fifth constable was in the bar, looking on as the Whitebridge Players took advantage – for purely medicinal reasons – of the fact that though the till was closed, the bar was still very much open.

Shastri was wearing her usual colourful sari and heavy sheepskin coat. She discarded the coat, and walked over to the centre of the stage, where the body was lying.

'Who cut him down?' she asked.

'I did,' Meadows said. 'I gave him CPR. I knew it was a waste of breath, but I did it anyway.'

'Would he have died instantly?' Beresford asked.

Shastri looked down at the body. 'It depends on your definition of death,' she said. 'When one or more of his cervical vertebrae were fractured, he would have been instantly paralysed, and maybe even unconscious. After a short time, his brain would have died, but his heart – which is vitally important but still no more than a pump – could have continued to beat faintly for up to half an hour.'

'Jesus!' Beresford said.

Shastri looked at Meadows, and smiled. 'Men are such squeamish creatures, aren't they?' she asked.

'They are indeed,' Meadows agreed.

Shastri looked up at the platform.

'I take it that's where he dropped from.'

'Yes.'

'And how far were his feet from the stage when the rope stopped him falling?'

'About four feet,' Meadows said.

Shastri shrugged. 'Well, it could have been worse.'

'Worse?' Beresford repeated. 'Worse! I very much doubt that he'd have agreed with you.'

'I meant from the perspective of the people observing it,' Shastri said. 'Unless the weight-to-drop ratio is calculated very precisely – and I assume that was not the case here – there is always a fair chance that instead of just being hanged, the victim will be decapitated. And

I'm sure you'll agree, Inspector Beresford, that while seeing someone hanging there can be upsetting, the sight of his head bouncing around on the stage would be even more distressing.'

'Fair point,' Colin Beresford said, feeling – if not actually looking – rather greenish.

Shastri crouched down and moved her fingers expertly over the dead man's neck.

'It was probably the third cervical vertebra which took the strain, though I won't know for certain until I've opened him up,' she said. She ran her eyes up and down his trunk. 'He appears to have been wearing some kind of harness.'

'That's right,' Beresford agreed. 'It was supposed to restrain him before the rope started to bite.'

'A task at which it appears to have been singularly unsuccessful,' Shastri said. She rolled the corpse over. He was a big man, and she was a small woman, but she made it seem easy. 'It looks to me as if the reason the harness failed was because someone – and presumably not the victim – had weakened it by cutting into it,' she said.

NINE

29th March 1977

When Louisa came down to breakfast the next morning she looked rather pale, and for once she did not have her usual appetite for the 'sensible' breakfast which she always insisted on having.

Still, that was hardly surprising, Paniatowski thought – and considering that the girl had seen a man murdered before her very eyes the night before, it could have been much worse.

'What do you want to do today, sweetheart?' she asked softly.

'I'd like to go to school,' Louisa said.

'Are you sure? If you'd rather stay at home with me, then you can. Or we can go out for a drive.'

Louisa gave her a thin smile. 'Haven't you got a murder to investigate?' she asked.

'You must be joking!' Paniatowski said. 'First of all, I'm a witness, which pretty much rules me out as far as leading the investigation goes. And secondly, murder inquiries can last for weeks – or even months – so the chief constable would never dream of putting in charge someone who might be rushed off to the maternity hospital at any time.'

'I still think I'd like to go to school,' Louisa said.

It was possibly for the best, Paniatowski thought. The mundane normality of school was probably just the thing she needed to blank out the horrors of the night before.

'If you're going to school then I'd prefer to drive you, rather than have you take the bus,' she said. 'You've no objection to that, have you?'

'Why would I object to being driven to school by a pregnant lady in a flashy sports car?' Louisa asked, grinning.

She'd have to get a different car when the baby was born, Paniatowski thought. She hadn't considered that before. In fact there were so many changes she would have to make that she hadn't really considered yet.

'If you need me at any time during the day, you must promise to call me,' she said sternly to Louisa.

'Call you where?' her daughter asked. 'Will you be at police headquarters?'

'No, certainly not,' Paniatowski said firmly. 'Call me here. I'm going to take the day off.'

The phone in the corridor rang.

'I'll get it,' Paniatowski said, rising heavily to her feet. 'You try and finish your breakfast.'

When she picked up the phone, the voice on the other end of the line said, 'DCI Paniatowski?'

'Yes. Who am I speaking to?'

'This is the switchboard, ma'am. The chief constable would like to see you in his office as soon as possible.'

Paniatowski felt the bile rising in her throat. There was only one reason anyone was ever called in for an 'as-soon-as-possible' meeting with the chief constable, and that was because they were in trouble – and she had a pretty good idea *why* she was in trouble.

Noting that her hand was trembling slightly, she replaced the phone on its cradle, and returned to the living room.

'So if I need you at any time during the day, I'm to call you at headquarters,' Louisa said mischievously. 'Have I got that right?'

'You cheeky little madam!' Paniatowski said.

She was trying to sound light-hearted, and hoped she had succeeded – because the last thing Louisa needed at that moment was to be worrying about her.

Acting Chief Constable Pickering was not alone, but instead was sharing his desk space with Chief Superintendent Holmes.

'We've had a report that you were in the theatre last night, when Mark Cotton was murdered,' Holmes said.

'I was,' Paniatowski agreed.

'And that instead of taking charge, you went home. Wasn't that a rather irresponsible thing to do?'

It was as she'd suspected when she got the phone call, Paniatowski thought. George Baxter was no longer there, but his lackeys were carrying on the campaign of persecution he had instigated.

'I had my daughter with me at the theatre,' she said. 'She saw the murder. I thought it best to get her home. Besides, there was another officer present – a very competent officer – and I was confident she could deal with it.'

'Ah yes, DS Meadows,' Holmes said. 'Might it not have been wiser to entrust your daughter to her, and conduct the initial investigation yourself?'

'With the greatest respect, sir, she's not Kate's daughter – she's mine,' Paniatowski said.

'But even so . . .'

'I'm perfectly satisfied with DCI Paniatowski's explanation of her conduct,' the acting chief constable said. 'In fact, I'm sure that, in the circumstances, she did exactly the right thing.'

Holmes shot the chief constable a look of surprise, as if he hadn't been expecting that at all.

Pickering had just pulled the classic good-cop bad-cop routine on her, Paniatowski thought, but Holmes, who hadn't been informed of that, had been expecting it to be more like a bad-cop worse-cop scenario.

'I'd like you to take charge of the investigation into Mark Cotton's death, Monika,' Pickering said.

'But I'm a witness,' Paniatowski told him.

'Strictly speaking, I suppose that's true,' Pickering conceded. 'But another way of looking at it is that the act of murder was all in the preparation, and that Cotton was already a dead man once he'd decided to put the noose around his neck. Hence, all you actually saw was a corpse, which makes it no different to any of your other investigations.'

'That's stretching it a bit, isn't it?' Paniatowski asked.

Pickering gave a dry chuckle. 'Not as much as Mark Cotton's neck was stretched.'

'And besides, I'm about to give birth,' Paniatowski said.

'Well, we certainly wouldn't want you to have to conduct your investigation from the maternity ward,' Pickering said, laughing again, to show that he was still joking, 'but once your investigation is rolling, I'm sure Inspector Beresford can take over if necessary.'

'I respectfully request not to be assigned this case, sir,' Paniatowski said in her most formal voice.

'Request denied,' Pickering replied. 'Look at it this way, Monika, the fact that I'm insisting you take charge just shows how much confidence I have in your ability, doesn't it?'

So that was that.

'You set me up there, sir,' Holmes said resentfully, the moment that Paniatowski had gone.

'Did I?' Pickering asked. 'How?'

'When I told you that DCI Paniatowski had left the theatre instead of taking charge – which, as the senior officer present, was her clear duty – you agreed that we'd call her in for a bollocking.'

'No, I didn't,' Pickering contradicted him. 'I said we'd have her in for a talk – which is just what we have done.' He paused. 'It was George Baxter who started this campaign against DCI Paniatowski, and the fact that you're carrying on with it suggests to me that either you think he was right, or that you're hoping to win some brownie points from him when he returns.'

'Sir, that's simply not—'

'I haven't finished speaking,' Pickering interrupted him sharply. 'I, on the other hand, am banking on George Baxter *not* returning to his post, and on me replacing him on a permanent basis. So what you must decide, CS Holmes, is whether to continue backing your old chief constable or whether you transfer your allegiance to the new one.'

'You of course have my unqualified support, sir,' Holmes said, then he added sulkily, 'but you might have told me what you were doing.'

'I needed to soften her up before assigning this case to her, and you contributed to that process admirably,' Pickering said. 'But if I'd told you what I was doing beforehand, you wouldn't have been half as effective.'

'What I don't understand is why you seem so keen to have her conduct this investigation at all, sir,' Holmes said.

'This is not just a high-profile murder, it's the high-profile murder of a man who played a detective on the television – and that's where the distinction between real life and fiction starts to blur,' Pickering said.

'I'm not sure I'm following you, sir,' Holmes admitted.

'How long do you think it will be before some tabloid journalist starts speculating about the length of time it would have taken the great DCI Prince to solve the murder? My guess would be, they've already started.'

'Possibly you're right,' said Holmes, who had never even considered the possibility.

'And once this identification with Prince is established, expectations are raised,' Pickering continued. 'Prince would have solved the murder in an hour (including advertisements) in actual time, and in a day or two in dramatic time. But real investigations aren't like that. There are promising leads which simply don't work out, and blind alleys that you don't even know *are* blind alleys until you reach the end of them.'

'True,' Holmes agreed.

'So whoever conducts this investigation is going to come under constant criticism from the press, and if that officer makes even the tiniest of mistakes, then God help him or her, because the hacks will be on him or her like a pack of rabid dogs. And that will not only be bad for the officer concerned – it will be bad for the whole police force.'

'I still don't see . . .'

'But the press will find it very hard – perhaps even impossible – to savage an officer who's eight months' pregnant.'

Holmes smiled with grudging admiration. 'You're rather good at this job, aren't you, sir?' he said.

'I'm learning,' Pickering replied.

The barriers were still in place across the street, and the crowd standing behind them was even larger than the night before.

Some of the women were sobbing quietly to themselves. Some were holding on to each other for comfort. And others wandered around like zombies – their eyes blank, their mouths hanging open – unable to fully grasp that the unthinkable had actually happened.

There was a long queue of fans carrying flowers, and the inspector on duty was allowing them through the barrier in groups of ten, so that they could make their pilgrimage to the theatre under the escort of two constables and tracked by the cameras of at least three television networks. Once they reached the theatre, they laid their offerings against the wall, said a few words, and backed away. The bank of flowers was already impressive.

'I keep thinking some of them will get fed up and go away, ma'am,' the inspector told Paniatowski. 'But it hasn't happened yet. They don't seem to feel the cold. They don't seem to need to pee. I've never seen anything like it in my time on the force.'

'And these are mainly his northern fans, Joe,' Paniatowski said. 'Just wait till the southerners and Scots get here.'

'Now that is a cheerful thought,' the inspector said – and shuddered.

Paniatowski drove slowly down the single lane the inspector had kept open, and parked in front of the theatre.

As she got out of her MGA, one of the girls laying flowers broke free from the rest and rushed over to her.

'Have you seen him?' she asked. 'Have you touched him?'

She looked about nineteen, Paniatowski thought – only a little older than Louisa.

'No, I haven't seen him,' she said.

'But will you?'

The girl's eyes widened, and she suddenly seemed quite mad.

'Yes, I probably will see him,' Paniatowski admitted.

'Can I come with you?' the girl asked, in what was almost a scream. 'Can I touch him too?'

One of the constables on escort duty strode rapidly across and put his hands on her shoulders.

'Now you know the rules,' he said sternly. 'We only let you through the barrier because you promised to behave yourself. You really shouldn't be bothering the DCI.'

It was doubtful if the girl even heard him, and when he tried to move her, her feet remained anchored to the ground.

'Let me see him,' the girl implored. 'Please – just for a few minutes!'

'It can't be done, and, trust me on this, you wouldn't like to see him as he is now,' Paniatowski said gently.

The girl started crying, and when the constable spun her around and frogmarched her away, she offered no resistance.

A number of uniformed officers were conducting a detailed search of the auditorium, while Meadows and Beresford, sitting in the front stalls, looked on.

'Well, if you're going to park your arses and do bugger all, I suppose you might as well choose the best seats in the house,' Paniatowski said.

'There's nothing for us *to* do, boss,' Beresford said easily. 'We've covered all the preliminaries, haven't we, Sergeant Meadows?'

'We have,' Meadows agreed.

'So now we're just waiting to hand over to the team which will actually be running the case.'

'That team's already here,' Paniatowski said.

'Is it?' Beresford asked. He looked around him, double-checked to make sure, then turned back to Monika. 'You surely don't mean . . .?'

'Yes, I do.'

'But you're . . .'

'I know.'

'Well, bugger me,' Beresford said.

'So what have you done so far?' Paniatowski asked.

'We've arranged for the uniforms to make an initial search, as you can see for yourself.'

'And what have you asked them to look *for*?'

'Nothing very specific. I didn't want to go treading on the investigating team's toes. But now we *are* the investigating team, I suppose I'd better give it some thought.'

'Good idea,' Paniatowski agreed. 'What else have you done?'

'We've sent the cast to their lodgings – which are, conveniently, just down the street. We've told them they can go out for an hour or two, but not more – and that under no circumstances must they talk to reporters. And we've got Geoff Turnbull, who's the stage manager, and Edgar Gough, who was in charge of Cotton's personal security, waiting in the bar.'

'What made you single out those two as the starting point of the investigation?' Paniatowski asked.

'One of them can tell you how it was done, and the other can tell you who couldn't have done it,' Meadows told her.

'Then I'd better go and talk to them, hadn't I?' Paniatowski said.

The bar looked like practically every other small theatre bar in the western world – which was to say it had aimed at being artistic, but only succeeded in being slightly pretentious.

Geoff Turnbull and Edgar Gough were sitting at opposite ends of the room. They could have been talking earlier and just got bored with each other's conversation, but they were such totally different people that Paniatowski didn't really think that was likely.

'I'll find out *how* it was done first,' she said to Meadows.

She walked over to Turnbull, introduced herself, and held out her hand. His grip was weak and slightly clammy, and even at that hour of the morning, she thought she could smell alcohol on his breath.

Paniatowski sat down opposite him and gave him the quick once-over.

Geoff Turnbull was probably no more than fifty-one or fifty-two, but if that *was* the case, he certainly hadn't aged well. He had very bloodshot eyes and bitten-down fingernails, and he seemed to Paniatowski to be carrying a huge weight of defeat on his shoulders.

'My colleagues tell me you can explain how it was done, Mr Turnbull,' Paniatowski said.

'Oh yes, that's easy enough,' Turnbull agreed. 'Both the rope and the harness were attached to a bar up in the fly system and—'

'The fly system? What's that?'

'It's a system of ropes, pulleys and weights high above the stage. It's what we use to raise and lower curtains, move scenery on and off the stage, and allow Peter Pan and his ilk to fly. Some of the lighting is up there, as well.'

'I see. Carry on.'

'It was the harness which took all the weight. The noose looked, from the front of the house, as if it was drawn tightly around the neck, but it wasn't. It was only just starting to close fully when the harness did its work. It was all perfectly safe if it had been left as it was.'

'What do you mean? Left as it was?'

'Well, somebody interfered with the harness, didn't they?'

Paniatowski shot Meadows a look which said, Has anybody been talking out of turn?

And Meadows shook her head to indicate that no one had.

'How do you know someone interfered with the harness, Mr Turnbull?' Paniatowski asked.

'It's obvious. If someone *hadn't* interfered with it, it would never have broken.'

'It may have got worn.'

'It hadn't. I checked it yesterday lunchtime, after we'd done a final run-though, and it was fine. And it wasn't just the harness which was interfered with – it was the rope, as well.'

'Could you explain that?'

'Even with a broken harness, Mark Cotton shouldn't have been in that much trouble, because he'd only have fallen a couple of feet. That's what they call a short-drop hanging. It was how they executed people until about 1850, and it was slow death by strangulation. With the short drop, it took between ten and twenty minutes to die, and Mark would have been pulled back on to the platform after only a few seconds. He'd have had some bruising and a sore throat – he might even have put his back out a little – but that would have been the full extent of it.'

'And that didn't happen because . . .?'

'It didn't happen because somebody must have replaced the rope that was already there with a longer one, so that instead of falling two feet, he fell round about eight.'

'You seem to know a lot about it, Mr Turnbull,' Paniatowski said.

'Are you saying I did it?' Turnbull demanded, with a sudden show of aggression.

'No, I'm not saying that at all – I'm just saying you seem to know a lot about it.'

Turnbull sighed. 'Before we put the play on the first time, back in 1957, I consulted Albert Pierrepoint, who ran a pub over in Much Hoole, near Preston. Have you ever heard of him?'

'He was England's Chief Executioner.'

'That's right. In his time, he hanged four hundred and thirty-five people, including a number of German war criminals, so he probably knew what he was talking about. And when we put the play on this time, I read through the notes I'd made back then, and checked to see if Mark Cotton was still the same weight – which he was. So yes, I do know a lot about it.'

'And you're convinced that the rope was substituted.'

'It had to have been.'

'Do you have any idea at all where the killer might have got the second rope from?'

Turnbull laughed. 'This is a hemp house,' he said.

'What's that?'

'Some theatres use steel cables in the fly systems. They can carry heavier loads, but they're very inflexible, and when you are a repertory theatre, flexibility is what you need, and so you tend to stick to rope – hence, hemp houses. So where could the killer have got the rope from, you ask. From here! We've got bloody miles of the stuff.'

'And is getting up to the fly system difficult?' Paniatowski asked.

'There's a ladder up to it, and once you get there, there's a series of interconnecting walkways around the whole system, so it's only a problem if you have no head for heights,' Turnbull said.

'Great!' Paniatowski said. 'Bloody superb!'

The last time Paniatowski had seen Edgar Gough, it had been when he was briefing the senior officers' meeting about the Bad Buds. He had seemed supremely confident then, but now he looked a little shaken – which, given the circumstances, was perfectly understandable.

'It wasn't my fault,' he told Paniatowski.

'Did I say it was?'

'No, but it's what you're thinking. For a start, you're wondering why I didn't have my people inside the theatre last night, aren't you?'

'And why didn't you have your people inside?'

'Mr Cotton wouldn't allow it. He said he felt safe in the theatre. Besides, he didn't want the other actors thinking he was a wimp.'

'So what did you do?'

'Yesterday morning, I sent a team to check the theatre before Mr Cotton arrived,' Gough said crisply. 'Once he was inside, I posted men in the street, next to the entrances, and they remained there for the rest of the day, because we didn't want any Buds sneaking in while the place was empty.'

'What happened at lunchtime?

'I personally escorted Mr Cotton to his hotel, and then back to the theatre in the late afternoon.'

'And during the performance?'

'I was at the stage door with one of my operatives – that's where the Buds usually try to get in – and I had a couple of my men posted at the main entrance. We were there until your lot took over from us.'

The harness must have been safe enough during the morning run-through, so it had to have been sabotaged some time after that, Paniatowski thought. And if Gough was sure that absolutely no one but the cast and crew had been allowed in the theatre . . .

'Did everyone leave the theatre at lunchtime?' she asked.

Gough took a notebook, and flicked it open.

'Yes.'

'Did they leave as a group – or individually?'

'Individually – apart from the camera crew.'

So the rope and the harness must have been tampered with either just before lunch or during the early evening – and whoever the murderer was, he or she *had to be* either a member of the cast or one of the stagehands.

The two uniformed constables who'd been assigned to search the dressing rooms, toilets and props rooms were called Hollis and Grimshaw. It was not the happiest of pairings, since Hollis, as a keen member of the Whitebridge Gilbert and Sullivan Society, was in seventh heaven at finally getting behind the scenes in a professional theatre, whilst Grimshaw, a hard-headed rugby player, thought that all actors were poofs.

The two officers had already searched the dressing rooms – Hollis fighting the urge to fondle all the props, Grimshaw afraid that if he touched anything he might catch homosexuality – and had finally reached the props room.

It was a big space, large enough to accommodate scenery for everything from a Shakespeare historical play to a Noel Coward drawing room comedy, but since the repertory company was only just starting up again, it was mostly empty, except for shelving and several large wood and canvas flats which had proved to be surplus to requirements.

'Well, here we are, in the hall of the fairy king,' Grimshaw said.

He sniffed loudly, to make his disdain for the place even more evident than it already was, sniffed again, then sniffed for a third time.

'If you ask me, something has definitely gone bad in here,' he said.

'Methinks there is something rotten in the state of Denmark,' Hollis misquoted.

'Yeah, I wouldn't be the least surprised,' agreed Grimshaw, who included foreigners in his long list of dislikes.

He walked around the room, continuing to sniff, and came to a halt in front of one of the larger flats, which was leaning against the wall.

'It's behind here,' he said.

He took one corner of the flat in his massive rugby-player's hands, and tilted it so he could look behind it.

'Oh, Jesus,' he said.

'What's the matter?' Hollis asked alarmed.

'Go and get the DCI,' said Grimshaw, who looked as if he was about to throw up. 'Go and get her right now.'

TEN

Paniatowski glanced briefly behind the large canvas flat, then took a few steps backwards.

'Could you shift that for me, lads,' she said.

The constables took one end of the flat each and lifted it clear to reveal the squalor which lay behind it.

There were empty corned beef cans and crushed crisp packets. There were plastic bottles and half-eaten sandwiches. And there was the woman.

She was lying on the floor with her face towards the wall, and though she was breathing regularly, she had not moved an inch while the flat was being removed. She was wrapped in a black-and-white coat and wearing high-heeled shoes which were much too dainty for her large ungainly feet – and from the smell, it was clear that she'd soiled herself quite spectacularly.

Paniatowski squatted down beside her.

'Can you hear me, love?' she asked gently.

There was no response.

Paniatowski grasped the woman's shoulder, and slowly rolled her over on to her back.

'Can you hear me now?'

The woman's eyes were open, and when Paniatowski waved her hand over them, she blinked. But though the eyes were working on a purely biological level, there was no sign in them of any under-standing of her current situation.

'Call the hospital,' Paniatowski said to PC Hollis. 'I want a stretcher team down here right away.'

Florrie Hodge liked to think of her establishment more as a commu-nity – albeit a temporary one – than a boarding house, and she saw the lounge as being at the very heart of that community. In the fifties, she'd decorated it with signed photographs of her paying guests. Some had gone on to acquire modest fame as minor char-acters in soap operas or loyal assistants in low-budget detective series, though there were others who had long ago given up the struggle and allowed themselves to be sucked deep into the whirlpool of obscurity.

After the theatre had closed, the commercial travellers, who had become her core business, had made unkind comments about the 'nancy boys' on the wall, and to protect the actors' dignity, Florrie had taken the pictures down and replaced them with prints of Highland glens and steam trains, which these philistines who sold dental powder and corn plasters found much more appropriate. But now, her thespians were back, and so were the signed photographs – some of which were of people who, twenty years on, were in the lounge at that moment.

No one had summoned the company to the lounge – no one had even so much as suggested holding a meeting – yet there they all were.

'The police are bound to suspect that it was one of us who killed Mark, don't you think?' Tony Brown asked.

Bradley Quirk laughed. 'Well, of course they are – after all, it *was* one of us who *did* actually kill him.'

'You can't know that for sure,' Phil McCann said.

'Then who else could have done it?' Quirk demanded. 'Are you suggesting that one of the audience managed to sneak out of his seat, make his way up to the fly loft unobserved, and switch the ropes?'

'It could have been one of the crew,' Lucy Cavendish suggested. 'They'd know how to do it.'

'Yes, they would,' Quirk replied, 'but what would be their motive? Did they hate him?'

'They could have.'

'Listen, whilst I've always had the greatest faith in Mark Cotton's ability to piss people off, it's stretching that faith beyond credulity to believe that in one short week he could have pissed off one of our petty bourgeois stagehands – who he'd never met before – to such an extent that they would kill him and damn the consequences. Oh no, my dears, you have to face the facts – this is purely a family affair.'

'We need to have a united front,' Jerry Talbot said.

'And what exactly do you mean by that?' Phil McCann wondered.

'We should all try to remember when we were alone last night, and then ask another of the cast to say that they were with us. If everybody has an alibi for the whole of the evening, we should be safe.'

'I can think of three good reasons why we shouldn't do that,' Phil McCann said. 'The first is that the police would never believe it – because nobody could possibly have an alibi for the whole time. The second, which follows on from the first, is that they'd probably charge us all with obstruction of justice, because what you're proposing *is* illegal, Jerry.'

'And what's the third reason, Phil?'

'The third is, at least from my own viewpoint, probably the most important of all. I didn't like Mark Cotton twenty years ago, and I liked him even less this time around – but I still want to see whoever did it tracked down and punished.'

'Well, of course, we *all* want that,' Jerry Talbot said, somewhat unconvincingly.

'Hello, Mrs H,' Tony Brown said loudly, since he seemed to be the only one who had noticed that the landlady was standing in the doorway.

'Can we help you, Mrs Hodge?' Phil McCann asked.

'I was just wondering if any of you boys and girls fancied a cup of tea,' Florrie Hodge said.

'No, thank you,' Phil McCann replied.

'I'd put out some biscuits, as well.'

'We really don't want anything at all.'

'Oh, all right.' Florrie Hodge turned her attention to Bradley Quirk. 'While I was cleaning your room, I noticed that one of your socks had a hole in it,' she said with a smile, 'and luckily, I had just the right coloured wool in my wool basket, so I darned it for you.'

'You're just like a big sister to me, Mrs H,' Quirk said.

'I don't know about that,' the landlady said, blushing. 'Well, if there's nothing else you want, I'd suppose I'd better get on with my jobs.'

'What a remarkable woman she is,' Bradley Quirk said. 'I swear that if she walked in here and three of us were lying dead on the floor, she'd ask the survivors whether they wanted chocolate biscuits or digestives.'

'Let's get back to the matter in hand,' Phil McCann said. 'Do either of you girls have any thoughts?'

The Audley sisters had been sitting slightly apart from the rest of the group, and so far had kept very quiet, but now Sarah burst into tears.

'I miss him so much already,' she sobbed. 'I know he was a bit of a bastard, but I really do miss him.'

Ruth put her arm around her younger sister's shoulders.

'There, there,' she cooed.

'I think . . . I think that perhaps I was still a little bit in love with him,' Sarah said.

Most of the company looked down at their own knees, and were silent, but Bradley Quirk put his hands together and applauded.

'Bravo,' he said. 'A truly outstanding performance. And now you think you've completely ruled yourself out as a suspect – because how could you have killed him when you were still in love with him? But you see, my dear, we're all actors here – and we can all put on a show when the occasion demands it.'

'You're being horrid,' Ruth Audley said.

'I'm being truthful,' Quirk countered.

'Has it ever occurred to you that people might think that this cynicism of yours is just as much a mask as Sarah's tears?' Phil McCann asked. 'And that they might further conclude that behind the mask, you did actually hate Mark enough to kill him?'

'So you admit Sarah's tears are, in fact, nothing more than a mask?' Quirk said.

'*Has* it occurred to you?' Phil McCann persisted.

'Well, of course it has,' Quirk said. 'I doubt that you've ever had a clever thought that hasn't occurred to me first. But you see, I'm not bothered, because I know I didn't kill Mark Cotton.'

'That could be just another bluff,' Jerry Talbot said.

'Yes,' Quirk agreed, 'it could.'

The woman being carried out of the theatre on a stretcher showed no more awareness of her situation than she had when she'd been discovered, hidden behind the flat, by Constable Grimshaw.

Edgar Gough watched her progress. His face was mostly impassive, though occasionally a look which seemed to combine shame and anger flashed across his features.

When he saw Paniatowski looking at him, he shrugged and said, 'What can I tell you? One of my men screwed up, and when I find which one it was, he'll be looking for a new job – as a eunuch.'

Paniatowski laughed – though she wasn't entirely sure that he was joking.

'She probably hadn't shat herself when your men were searching,' she said charitably. 'That was a great help to us.'

'I know her,' Gough said. 'She's Maggie Maitland, Queen of the Bad Buds.'

'Tell me about her,' Paniatowski suggested.

The first time Mark Cotton comes across Maggie Maitland is in the Grand Hotel in Leeds. He is doing a promotional tour for the second series of DCI Prince. He hates the tour, because it necessitates him being nice to people all the time – and that kind of acting can be very tiring. Still, it will soon be over, he thinks as he waits for room service to bring him his breakfast.

A maid arrives, pushing a trolley, and his first thought on seeing her is that surely an expensive hotel like the Grand could afford to employ somewhat prettier staff.

'Leave the trolley by the table,' he says, and although he normally enjoys being waited on hand and foot, he adds, 'I can serve myself,' because – in all honesty – the woman's face is enough to put him off his breakfast.

The maid parks the trolley, and then stands next to it.

'You can go,' Cotton said.

But she shows no sign of leaving. Instead, she unbuttons her dress, lets it fall to the floor, and stands there naked.

'Look what Santa's brought you,' she says in a grotesque parody of a coquette.

Her breasts are large and floppy, her stomach sags, and her legs are thick and ungainly.

'Well, what are you waiting for?' she asks, with a hint of puzzlement in her voice.

'I shall report you to the management,' he says.

She smiles. 'Oh, I don't work here. I've bribed the real maid to let me take her place.'

'How much did you give her?' he asks, knowing it's a stupid question and wondering what could have induced him to ask it.

'I gave her a hundred pounds,' the woman says.

And now he is getting seriously worried, because, as successful as he is, a hundred pounds is still quite a lot of money to him, and must be a small fortune to the woman.

'You really do have to go,' he says.

She walks over to the door, still naked, and then, having effectively cut off his retreat, she turns round again.

'You know you want to,' she says. 'Any man would.'

He is so horrified that even the little tact that he has in him simply melts away.

'You're disgusting,' he says. 'I'd rather screw a greyhound than have sex with you.'

'You don't mean that,' she says – and she sounds like she really believes that's true.

There is a knock on the door, and then he hears Edgar Gough's voice say, 'We need to leave in ten minutes, Mr Cotton.'

'Get in here now, Gough!' he shouts. 'I'm about to be attacked by a crazy woman.'

The door bursts open, knocking the woman off her feet. Gough quickly assesses the situation, then strides across the room and picks up the dress.

'Tell him to go away, Mark,' the woman says.

Gough pulls the woman to her feet, and wraps the dress around her.

'Tell him to go away, Mark,' she says. 'Tell him to go away.'

She is still saying it as Gough bundles her into the corridor.

'What did you do next?' Paniatowski asked.

'I took her to the room I was sharing with one of my operatives.

We managed to get the dress back on her, then we frogmarched her down to my car, and drove her to the other side of Leeds – where we dumped her.'

'And that was it?'

'That was it.'

'But you saw her again?'

'Oh yes, we most certainly did.'

They are filming the season closer of DCI Prince, a few weeks before Mark Cotton is due to go to Whitebridge. Now that the show is so popular, they have a far bigger budget than they had for the early series, and are doing much more filming on location.

This final episode is set in a seaside village in South Wales. Filming has finished for the day, and Cotton decides he would like to take a walk along the cliff top.

Gough goes with him, but not by his side, because Cotton has made it plain that he has no wish for conversation with the hired help.

They start the walk separated by a distance of five yards, but there is no one else on the path, so Gough drops back further, to give Cotton more space.

There are fifty yards between them when the woman rises up out of the bracken.

'Here I am, my darling,' she says.

It is only the fact that she is so very ugly that makes Cotton recognize her.

'You again!'

She rushes over to him and throws her arms around him, thus effectively pinning his arms to his sides.

He tries to break away.

It should be easy, but it isn't, because the woman has the strength of the insane.

And then she starts to push forward, moving him towards the edge of the cliff.

He is no longer trying to push her away, because there's a chance that even if he succeeds, the force will pitch him backwards and over the edge.

Instead, he tries to manoeuvre them both away from the drop – but it isn't working!

'Please,' he blubbers, 'if you want me to sleep with you, I will. I promise I will.'

And in the time it has taken him to say that, he has lost another few precious inches of firm ground.

Suddenly, the woman's head jerks to the side and her grip slackens. And at almost the same moment he feels a strong pair of hands grab him and pull him away from the edge.

He looks at the woman – felled by a punch in the face – who is lying on the ground and groaning.

He looks at the man who has saved him.

His first feeling is relief, but that quickly turns to anger.

'You took your bloody time getting here,' he says.

'I take it that this time, you reported it to the police,' Paniatowski said.

'No,' Gough replied. 'I didn't.'

'Have I got the wrong end of the stick?' Paniatowski wondered. 'Are you saying she wasn't trying to push him over the cliff after all?'

'No, you've not got it wrong.'

'Then how could you *not* report it?'

'Mr Cotton wouldn't let me. He said he didn't want his fans thinking that there were people out there that hated him.'

'Was that the real reason?'

'It was part of the real reason. The other part was that he didn't want them to know he'd had to be rescued from a mere woman. So what he said was, we'd let her go and I'd better do a more effective job of protecting him in the future, or I'd find myself down at the labour exchange.'

'It sounds like he wasn't a very nice man,' Paniatowski said.

'He wasn't nice – but his money was delightful,' Gough said. He paused. 'Do you know, I'm almost certain that I saved two lives that day.'

'What do you mean by that?'

'Well, I don't think she was just intending to push him off the cliff – I think she was planning to go with him.'

ELEVEN

'We've investigated cases before in which we've started out with eight possible suspects, and in at least half of them the man or woman we ended up arresting wasn't even on the list,' Paniatowski said. 'What makes this case unique is that this time the killer simply *has to be* on it.'

'Does that mean you're ruling out the stagehands?' asked Beresford, lighting up a cigarette.

Paniatowski tried not to hate the fact that he could drink and smoke while she couldn't. In some ways, she thought, it might be nice to be Meadows, who didn't do either, and who, but for her habit of occasionally inviting strangers in leather masks to whip her, could almost have been called a Puritan.

'Give us a quick thumbnail sketch of the stagehands, Kate,' she said to her sergeant.

'They were all born and bred in Whitebridge,' Meadows said. 'One's a shop assistant, one's a fishmonger, and two work in the council offices. They're all married with teenage kids. A couple of them have picked up the odd parking fine, but that's it as far as brushes with the law go.'

'We'll interview them, simply because they might have seen something suspicious backstage, but I'd be amazed if one of them turned out to be the killer,' Paniatowski said.

'Are you also dismissing the idea that the nutter we found in the prop room could have done it?' Beresford asked.

'Yes.'

'Why? According to Gough, she tried to kill him once before.'

'Yes, and look at the *way* she tried to kill him,' Paniatowski said. 'She was attempting to push him over a cliff – which is just about as crude a way of murdering somebody as you could think of. Now, if we'd found Cotton's body with a knife sticking in it, I might have been prepared to consider her as the prime suspect. But what actually happened was much more sophisticated, and the murderer would have needed some knowledge of how the hanging trick worked.'

'Besides, he was killed by someone *from* the theatrical tradition who was operating *within* that tradition,' Crane said.

Beresford looked uncomfortable. He always did when the DC started showing signs of erudition, because while he knew that he himself was a pretty good bobby, he recognized that Crane was good, too – and Crane, in addition, had a first-class honours degree from Oxford University.

'What do you mean, Jack?' Paniatowski asked.

'*The Spanish Tragedy* is a revenge play,' Crane said, 'and the central character, Hieronimo, uses the-play-within-the-play as the vehicle for getting his revenge. And that's just what's happened here. Whoever killed Mark Cotton used the play as his vehicle in much the same way.'

'You're serious about this, aren't you?' Beresford asked.

'Absolutely. Hieronimo could have killed Balthazar and Lorenzo at any time, yet he *chose* to kill them when he had an audience. Now look at our murder from the same perspective – the killer could have run Mark Cotton over, or poisoned him, or got hold of a gun and shot him. But he didn't do any of those things – because he wanted an audience.'

'Jesus, who thinks like that?' Beresford said.

'Actors,' Crane replied.

'Normally, we need as many bobbies as we can drum up to pound the streets and knock on doors,' Paniatowski said. 'But there's no call for that kind of legwork on this investigation, because we know where to find Mark Cotton's killer – he, or she, is either in the boarding house two doors down from the theatre, or at . . . where do the Turnbulls live, Kate?'

'Twenty-seven Ashley Close.'

'Or at twenty-seven Ashley Close. So here's how we'll run the investigation. Inspector Beresford will take an overview of the whole case. He'll contact Scotland Yard to see if any of the suspects has a criminal record, and – if they have – what kind of criminal record. In addition, he'll ring up each suspect's local nick, and use his famously silver tongue to charm the DCI at that nick into assigning some of his lads to a background check. And if any of those background checks throw up anything interesting, he'll pack his little suitcase and follow up that lead himself.'

'Got it,' Beresford said.

'Sergeant Meadows and I will interview suspects,' Paniatowski continued, 'DC Crane will spend a couple of days as a couch potato.'

'Sorry, boss?'

'The BBC has been filming the production for over a week. I want you to go over every foot of film they've got, and then I want you to go over it again – and again – until you find something useful.'

When Geoff Turnbull walked into the living room of twenty-seven Ashley Close at half-past twelve, he was wearing his best suit.

'You look like you're dressed to go somewhere special,' said Joan, who was doing the ironing in front of the television.

'I am,' Geoff agreed. 'I'm going down to the town hall first, and then I'm going to police headquarters.'

'Whatever for?'

'I want to know from both of them when they'll allow us to put the play on again.'

'You want to know *what*?'

'I realize that the police still have things to do in the theatre – looking for fingerprints and suchlike – but I'd imagine they'll be out of there by Wednesday, or Thursday at the latest. So we could open again on Friday night and put on a special matinee on Saturday. With the professional cast reduced by one, I'll have to take over some of the stagehands' jobs, thereby freeing them up to play a few more of the minor parts, but I don't mind that, because—'

'Have you gone mad?' Joan interrupted him. 'Have you completely lost your mind?'

'I don't know what you mean,' Geoff said.

And from the expression on his face, it was clear that he didn't.

'There's been a *murder* in that theatre, for God's sake!'

'True, but they always say, don't they, that whatever happens, the show must go on?'

'Even if the police had no practical objections, the town council would never agree to it.'

'They might.'

'If they gave you the go-ahead, everybody from local church groups to the national press would be down on them like a ton of bricks. What you're suggesting is bad taste, Geoff – and you *know*, deep down inside, that it's bad taste.'

Turnbull's lower lip quivered. 'But I do so want to direct again,' he said. 'I really do.'

'I know you do – and you will,' Joan promised. 'The council won't waste a good theatre now that they've got one, and in a couple of months – when all this has died down – they'll start thinking about setting up a permanent repertory company. And that's when you should approach them.'

'Maybe you're right,' Geoff agreed.

'And you can use the time between now and then to straighten yourself out,' Joan said.

'What are you talking about?'

'I'm talking about your drinking, Geoff.'

'I do like the occasional drink, sweetheart, I'll readily admit to that, but to say that I . . .'

'You've been drinking this morning, haven't you?'

Turnbull suddenly looked very uncomfortable.

'Just the one,' he said.

'It's got as bad as it was in those last few weeks of the old Whitebridge Theatre,' Joan said. 'I understand. I really do. But if you're to have any chance of getting your job back, you're going to have to rein the drinking in again. Will you do that for me?'

'I'll try,' Turnbull promised, 'but it won't be easy.'

'Maybe it won't,' Joan agreed, 'but it should be considerably *easier,* now that the reason for all that heavy drinking is no longer around.'

Based on his appearance the doctor could have been thirty-five or thirty-six, but there were so many framed certificates mounted on his office wall that Paniatowski assumed he had to be older.

'So how's the pregnancy going?' he asked.

'Fine,' Paniatowski said, non-committally.

'How many other children do you have?'

'One. A daughter. But she's adopted.'

'So this is the first time you'll have given birth.'

Paniatowski smiled. 'With deductive powers like yours, you're wasted in medicine,' she said, and then, hoping to change the subject, she added, 'Why don't you jack all this doctoring in and join the force?'

But the doctor was very much in professional mode and was not to be diverted.

'Since you are relatively mature for a first birth, I assume you're having regular check-ups,' he said.

'I'm doing all the things my own doctor told me to do,'

Paniatowski replied. 'I've stopped smoking and drinking, I'm eating properly, I'm getting plenty of rest, and I'm avoiding doing anything that might be physically straining.'

'All that's very good, but since this *is* the first time for you, I really think you should—'

'Good heavens, what a scatterbrain I am,' Paniatowski interrupted. 'I was supposed to be going to the psychiatric unit, and yet somehow I've ended up in obstetrics.'

The doctor smiled. 'You're telling me to shut up about your condition, aren't you?' he asked.

'That's right,' Paniatowski agreed. 'I'm not here to talk about me – I've come to talk about Maggie Maitland.'

'Ah yes, our theatre bag lady.'

'If it's at all possible, I'd like to ask her a few questions.'

'It's perfectly possible. As far as I'm concerned, you can question her until you're blue in the face. But if you're expecting her to answer your questions, you're in for a big disappointment, because she's still traumatized.'

'What caused the condition?'

'There's no physical reason for it, as far as we can tell, so the chances are she was reacting to some kind of shock.'

'Like seeing the man who she loved murdered?'

'That would certainly have done it.'

'Do you think there's any chance she might have killed Mark Cotton herself?' Paniatowski said, because even though she'd pretty much dismissed it as a possibility herself, she had to ask.

'Could you describe to me the way in which the murder was actually carried out?'

Paniatowski sketched out what had happened.

When she'd finished, the doctor said, 'Whoever it was who killed Mark Cotton had to be both cold-blooded and logical. Would you agree?'

'Yes.'

'If Maggie Maitland had had that kind of mind, you wouldn't have found her surrounded by a heap of rubbish.'

'No?'

'Absolutely not. She'd have worked out some way of getting rid of her empty corned beef tins and water bottles, because she simply wouldn't have been able to live with them.'

'What's happening to her now?

'She's currently undergoing treatment.'

'Could you be a little more specific?'

'Would you like the fancy medical name for it, or should I just put it in layman's terms?'

'I'd prefer it in layman's terms.'

'We're pumping her full of all kinds of drugs, and waiting to see how she reacts to them.'

'When can you expect results?'

'It might be half an hour before she's normal again, or it might take much longer. And a word of warning here – when I say normal, what I mean is, as normal as she ever gets.'

'You think she's mentally ill?'

The doctor smiled again.

'Strictly speaking, none of us are completely sane, which means we are *all* mentally ill, Chief Inspector – so what we have to assess is the *degree* of that illness – and anybody who's so obsessed with an actor that she's been hiding in a theatre for perhaps as long as a couple of weeks isn't going to win any sanity Olympics, now is she?'

Jerry Talbot was whistling loudly when he breezed into the boarding house lounge and plopped down in one of the easy chairs.

'Now there's a change,' said Bradley Quirk, who was the only other resident of the lounge at that moment. 'What's put you in such a good mood? Has somebody else who you don't like been murdered? Or have you finally found someone who is stupid enough to give you an alibi?'

'I don't need an alibi,' Talbot said. 'I've been thinking things through, and I've realized that – of the entire company – I'm the only one who can prove he *didn't* kill Mark Cotton.'

'You're not just whistling – and slightly out of tune, if I may say so – you're whistling in the dark.'

'Am I?' Talbot asked complacently.

'Of course you are.'

'Well, if the great Bradley Quirk has made a pronouncement, I suppose there is nothing I can do but to bow to his judgement,' Talbot said.

And then he picked up an old copy of *The Stage* and began flicking idly through it.

Quirk held out for a full five minutes before he finally said, 'All right, how can you *prove* you didn't kill Mark Cotton?'

'You should be able to work that out for yourself.'

'I'm in no mood to play one of your childish games.'

'Then I guess you'll never know.'

Quirk sighed. 'All right, give me a clue.'

'Think back to last night,' Talbot said. 'You and I were sitting side-by-side in the dressing room and—'

'Ah, now I see,' Quirk said.

'And I'm right, aren't I?'

'So it would seem,' Quirk conceded. Then a new thought came into his head, and he smiled. 'But if you *are* right, dear boy, doesn't that mean that your life is in danger?'

'Oh my God,' Talbot gasped, 'I hadn't thought of that!'

'I've called a press conference for you, Monika,' the chief constable said.

'Have you, sir?' Paniatowski replied. 'And why would you have done something like that?'

'So that you can announce at it that you've arrested someone in connection with what the smart-arse broadsheet newspapers are already calling the Revenge Hangman Murder.'

'But I haven't arrested Maggie Maitland, sir. I don't have any evidence to connect her with the murder.'

'Really?' Pickering frowned. 'I've worked with a lot of chief inspectors in my time, and I think that most – if not all – of them would have considered they had ample grounds for charging her.'

Paniatowski said nothing.

'Oh well, if you won't charge her then we'll just have to settle for second best. You can tell the journalists that you're questioning a woman of . . . of whatever age this Maitland woman is.'

'I can't do that, either, because it wouldn't be true. The woman's in a traumatic state. Firing questions at her would be a waste of time. Besides, I don't think she did it.'

'You don't think she did it!'

'That's right, sir.'

'You have a woman who is clearly mentally unstable, who was obsessed with Mark Cotton and who had been hiding in the theatre for over a week, and you don't think she did it?' Pickering asked incredulously. 'So would you like to tell me, Detective Chief Inspector, just how you reached that improbable conclusion?'

Paniatowski outlined the discussion she'd had with her team in the Drum and Monkey, and – for good measure – threw in what the psychiatrist had told her.

'I'm not entirely convinced about any of this,' Pickering said, 'and I find DC Crane's airy-fairy theory *particularly* difficult to take on board.'

'You'll have to trust me on this one, sir,' Paniatowski said firmly.

'All right I'll trust you for the moment – but you'd better not be wrong,' Pickering said. 'And since I am being so accommodating, I'd like you to do me one small favour in return.'

'I'm listening.'

'Half the town council are on the verge of hysterics because we haven't made an arrest yet, and the press are demanding pretty much the same thing, so given that, we're going to have to throw them a bone.'

'What kind of bone?'

'I'd like you to stretch the truth a little, and tell the press conference that we're questioning Maggie Maitland.'

'I can't do that, either, sir.'

'Why the devil not?'

'Because even as we speak, DI Beresford is doing his very best to persuade several police forces spread around the country to cooperate with us on this investigation.'

'And are you saying that if we announce we're already questioning someone, they'll refuse to help?'

'No sir, they'll still help, but they'll assume we've already caught our killer, and they won't exactly bust their guts to get us what we want.'

For a while, Pickering was silent. And then he said, 'I do hope that you and I are going to get along, Detective Chief Inspector Paniatowski.'

'I'm sure we will, sir,' Paniatowski answered. 'How can we fail to, when we've both dedicated our lives to the pursuit of truth and justice?'

'Are you trying to be funny, Chief Inspector?' Pickering demanded.

'No sir.'

Pickering studied her for a second, then nodded his head.

'No, you're not, are you,' he said, in a slightly surprised voice.

TWELVE

The two civilian scene-of-crime officers were known universally as Bill and Eddie. The wages clerk at headquarters probably knew their surnames, too, but no one else in the Mid Lancs police force did.

Bill was tall and thin, and Eddie was small and round. They looked like a sort of Laurel and Hardy in reverse, and while they did clown around, they were quite brilliant at what they did, and, over the years, Paniatowski had grown rather fond of them.

It was Eddie who walked over to greet Paniatowski when she entered the theatre.

'Well, just look at you, Chief Inspector!' he said. 'You're the size of a small family caravan.'

'Thank you, Eddie,' Paniatowski replied. 'I feel much better after your caring comment.'

'I hope you're making sure you go to the doctor regularly,' Eddie said, more seriously. 'When my missus had a bun in the oven—'

'I never knew that you were married,' Paniatowski interrupted.

'Oh yes,' Eddie said. 'I've had five of the happiest years of my life with my wife – which would be great, if we hadn't been married for fourteen.'

'And what about Bill? Is he also a married man?'

'Well, I don't want to go into details, but let's just say that he's known his share of suffering, too.'

Paniatowski grinned. 'Are you done here?'

'Absolutely,' Eddie said. 'You and your team can start rampaging about like a herd of mad rhinos as soon as the mood takes you.'

'Have you found anything I can use?'

'We've found enough fingerprints for you to open a fingerprint emporium, if you were so inclined – and by sometime tomorrow, we should be able to tell you who most of them belong to.'

Which would be of limited value, Paniatowski thought, since the killer – whoever he was – had probably had a perfect right to be wherever the fingerprint was lifted from.

'Anything else?' she asked hopefully.

'Yes, as a matter of fact, there is one thing,' Eddie said. 'Follow me, Your Ladyship.'

He led her through the auditorium, on to the stage, and from there into the right wing.

'See those?' he asked, indicating a set of metal steps running – at a sharp angle – from the backstage floor to the top of some scaffolding.

'Yes.'

'At the top of the steps is the platform which your feller took the big drop from.' Eddie took a powerful torch from his pocket, and shone it on the eighth step. 'What do you see?' he asked.

Paniatowski examined the thick brown substance which looked as if it had been smeared on the step.

'It's some kind of grease,' she said.

'It is. And though we won't know for sure until it's been analysed, I'd put my money on it being actors' make-up.'

'Of which there is a more than plentiful supply in this building,' Paniatowski said.

'The place is swimming in it,' Eddie agreed. 'Now, look at the way that it's spread. It's thinner at the sides than it is in the middle, but in the *very* middle there's a roughly triangular section where there's hardly any grease at all.'

'It's where someone trod.'

'That's what I think. He's coming up the steps in a hurry . . .'

'He has to, because it's only a few seconds before he has to make his appearance on the platform.'

'. . . so he's not putting the whole of his foot on the step, just the toes and the ball of his foot. Then he hits the patch of grease. It's been fairly concentrated up until that point, but now the pressure from his foot makes it squelch to the left and the right. And as for him . . . he loses his footing completely and goes bouncing down four or five steps.'

'How can you be sure of that?'

'We found traces of the grease on the fourth step. Presumably, they came from his shoe. So unless I'm very wrong indeed, you'll find several bruises on the dead man's shins.' Eddie paused. 'He picks himself up and starts climbing the stairs again, and this time – either by luck or because he knows it's there – he avoids the grease and reaches the platform.'

It would have been by luck, Paniatowski thought, because if he'd known it was grease which had made him lose his footing, he would have realized something was seriously wrong – and then he might have thought twice about pulling the stunt with the noose.

'He was probably taking two steps at once, to make up for the time he'd lost, so, on his second attempt, he didn't make any contact with the greased step at all,' she said.

'That's more than likely,' Eddie agreed.

'There's no chance the grease got there accidentally, is there?' Paniatowski asked.

Eddie shrugged. 'Anything's possible in this world, but from the state it's in now, I'd say it had been laid down very precisely.'

Charlie Woodend had always established his centre of operations near to wherever the crime he was currently investigating had been committed – which usually meant the nearest pub.

'You need to be close to the crime scene, Monika,' he'd told Paniatowski at the very start of their partnership. 'You need to able to walk around it – to feel the heart of it beating beneath the soles of your feet.'

By the time they had wrapped up their second investigation together, Paniatowski had been convinced that Woodend was right, which was why, once Eddie had given her the all-clear, she had rung through to police headquarters and set in motion a process that would convert the bar in the Whitebridge Theatre into a place where she could work.

In less than an hour, the transformation had been completed. The mock-Edwardian chairs and low tables had been stacked neatly in the corner, and been replaced by three businesslike desks. Heavy framed portraits of David Garrick, Henry Irving and Ellen Terry had been taken down, and blackboards had been hung in their stead. Police technicians had installed extra phone lines, and grey metal cabinets now stood where only recently there had been a one-armed bandit.

'What I don't understand,' said Meadows, once they had the bar to themselves, 'is why the killer bothered with the grease at all.'

'Go on,' Paniatowski said.

'I can't see why he would do something so petty – something that would only give Cotton a few bruises – when he'd planned it so that the man would hang himself. In fact, by greasing the step, wasn't the killer running the risk that he wouldn't get what he really wanted at all?'

'You mean that Cotton could have hurt himself so badly that he'd never even have reached the platform?'

'Exactly.'

'The picture I've been building up of Mark Cotton is that of a man who was both very fit and very ambitious. Nothing short of a broken leg would have prevented him from picking himself up and making his entrance.'

'It was still a risk.'

'I think the killer may have decided it was a risk worth taking. By slowing him down – by robbing him of vital seconds – he was ensuring that Cotton didn't have time to give the harness even a cursory inspection.'

'But would he have inspected it anyway?' Meadows wondered. 'Time was tight even without the fall, and until the spotlight hit the platform, it was very dark up there.'

There was a knock on the door, and one of the uniformed constables posted at the front entrance came in.

'Sorry to disturb you, ma'am, but there's a man outside who wants to see you urgently. He claims he's one of the actors.'

'What's his name?'

'Jerry Talbot. He says he was the victim's – what's the word? – he was the victim's understudy.'

'And so he was,' Paniatowski said. 'Show him in.'

Jerry Talbot looked bloody awful. His eyes were wild and darting, and when he sat down and put his hands on the desk, it was obvious that he was unable to control his trembling.

'We're not actually ready to begin our round of witness interviews, Mr Talbot,' Paniatowski said, 'but since you seemed to think it was important that you should see me right away—'

'You have to give me police protection,' Talbot interrupted, in what was little more than a croak.

'From whom?'

'From the killer, of course.'

'And why should he be interested in you?'

'I don't know, but I'm sure he is. I've *always* been the one who he was interested in.'

'What leads you to that conclusion?' Meadows asked.

'Look, I was due to play Hieronimo last night. The whole cast knew that. And then, less than an hour before I was due to go on stage, that bastard Mark Cotton marches into the dressing room and says he's going to play the lead instead. Do you see what I'm getting at?'

'You're saying that the faulty harness was intended for you, and not for Mark Cotton,' Meadows said.

'Yes.'

'Is there any chance that the killer could have meddled with the harness and the rope *after* he'd learned that it would be Cotton playing Hieronimo?' Paniatowski wondered.

'No. I mean . . . I don't think so. No, I'm sure there isn't. I went on to the stage immediately after the swine had told me he was replacing me. I stood by those stairs which lead up to the platform. If anybody had been messing with the harness, I would have seen him.'

'What were you doing standing next to the stairs, Mr Talbot?' Paniatowski asked.

'What do you mean?'

'You weren't going to play Hieronimo that night, so you had no real reason to be there, did you?'

'I . . . I . . .'

'Yes?'

'I suppose I just wasn't thinking. All right? I was angry and I simply went where my legs took me. Perhaps there was even some part of me that wanted to revel in my own misery. But that's not the point.'

'Then what is the point?'

'I wasn't the only one around – not by a long chalk. To exchange one rope for another, I would have had to go up to the fly loft, and it would have taken me at least five minutes. Someone would have been bound to notice me, just as they'd have noticed anybody else. So it must all have been set up beforehand – when everybody thought *I* was playing Hieronimo.'

'Can you think of anyone in the company who might have wanted to harm you?'

'I couldn't stand that bastard Mark Cotton, and he couldn't stand me,' Talbot said. 'I nearly didn't come here at all because of him, but then I let Phil McCann talk me into it. He said Cotton would have changed – but he couldn't have been more wrong about that. He was worse than ever – cocky, bullying, vindictive – and I hated him even more than I did in the old days.'

'When did you have this conversation with Phil McCann?' Paniatowski asked.

'Why does that matter, when my life's in danger?'

'Because you want us to catch the killer, and that's what we want, too. And the *way* we'll catch him is by collecting as much information as we can, even information that probably seems irrelevant to you – and may turn out to be just that. So I'll ask you again, Mr Talbot – when did you have this conversation with Mr McCann?'

'It was the week before last. We met in a pub in London.'

'So if you'd suspected anybody of wanting to hurt you, it would have been Mark Cotton,' Meadows said. 'The only problem is that if it had been Cotton who set up that death trap for you, he was hardly likely to walk into it himself.' She paused. 'You do realize you've just established that you had reasons for wanting him dead, don't you?'

Talbot groaned. 'I just don't believe this,' he said. 'I was supposed to be playing Hieronimo. Can't you get that into your thick head? *I was supposed to be playing him.*'

'Maybe, after setting up the death trap, you suggested to him that he might want to play the role on Monday night,' Meadows said.

'I desperately wanted to play it. I thought I *was* playing it. It came as a big shock when Mark Cotton told me I wasn't – and if you don't believe me, ask Bradley Quirk.'

Bradley Quirk was a good-looking man – possibly better looking than Mark Cotton had been – yet Paniatowski could not picture him in her bed, nor could Meadows imagine tying him up.

He walked into the room with breezy confidence, and sat down opposite the two officers without waiting for an invitation.

'You summoned me, and like the good and faithful knight that I am, I have been fleet of foot in answering that summons,' he said.

'He means he got here about as quickly as a middle-aged man like him could have got here,' Meadows translated.

'Cruel – but fair,' Quirk agreed, taking the remark in his stride.

'We've just been talking to Jerry Talbot, and we'd be grateful if you'd either confirm or deny what he told us,' Paniatowski said.

She repeated what Talbot had said about the conversation in the dressing room.

'Yes, things happened pretty much as Talbot described them to you,' Quirk said, when she'd finished, 'although dear old Jerry seems to have edited out the more humiliating bits.'

'So put them back in,' Paniatowski suggested.

'Cotton came into the dressing room, already half made up, and told Talbot he wouldn't be going on that night. At first, Talbot pleaded with him. Then – when it became plain Cotton wasn't going to change his mind – he got angry. At least, that's what appeared to be happening.'

'What do you mean by that?'

'Talbot's an actor, and though I hate to admit it, a rather good one. So what I saw could have been real, or it could merely have been a performance.'

'Have you any reason to assume it *was* a performance, Mr Quirk?' Paniatowski asked.

'No,' Quirk said, perhaps a little too quickly.

'You won't believe how nasty we can get when we think we're being lied to,' Meadows growled.

Quirk laughed uneasily. 'She's a bit of a Rottweiler, this sergeant of yours, isn't she, Chief Inspector?' he said.

'I'm waiting,' Meadows said, with added menace.

Quirk's bravado crumbled. 'Look,' he said, 'what I have to tell you is tenuous – at best.'

'Tell us anyway,' Paniatowski said.

'A few years ago, Talbot and I were working together in rep somewhere in the dark north, and one of the plays we put on was called *The Real Target*. It was a very bad play – I think it was written by the idiot daughter of the man who owned the theatre – and though we put it on because we were ordered to, no other theatres followed our example, and it sank without trace. But I think you'll find the plot interesting.'

Now that he was holding the centre stage, he was getting his confidence back, Meadows thought – and they couldn't have that.

'Get on with it,' she said.

'I can't remember what the central character's name was – bad playwrights rarely manage to create characters with memorable names, in much the same way as they never—'

'You are really starting to get right up my nose now, Brad,' Kate Meadows snarled.

'Let's call him Fred Bloggs,' Quirk said hurriedly. 'Anyway, at the start of the first act, he's walking through the park and someone hidden in the bushes takes a pot shot at him. He reports it to the police, and they decide that the shooter was a lunatic, and the only reason he was a target was because he was in the wrong place at the wrong time. Act two opens with Bloggs and his business partner – we'll call him Joe Soap – coming out of a restaurant. There's the sound of a shot, and Soap falls dead. Now the police realize they've been thinking along the wrong lines and Bloggs has been the real target all along, which means, of course, that Soap was killed by mistake. Except . . .'

'Except he wasn't,' Paniatowski supplied. 'It was Bloggs who hired the gunman in the first place, because he'd worked out that if the police thought he was the real target, they'd never suspect him of plotting to kill his partner.'

'Quite right, Chief Inspector,' Quirk said. 'You should be a detective.' He glanced quickly at Meadows to see if he'd gone too far, and decided he was safe for the moment. 'You get the point, don't you? Talbot claims he can't be the murderer because someone had been trying to kill *him*. But maybe nobody was – maybe he got the whole idea from *The Real Target*.'

'But how could he be so sure that Cotton would insist on taking the role off him at the last moment?' Paniatowski asked.

'I don't know,' Quirk admitted. 'Perhaps he was just banking on Cotton acting like the greedy egomaniac we all know him to be.'

'You do appreciate, don't you, that since you were in the same play, what could have been a blueprint for Talbot's murder plan could also have been a blueprint for yours?' Meadows asked.

'Mine!' Quirk exclaimed.

He sounded genuinely surprised – but then he was an actor.

'Yours,' Meadows repeated.

'But why should I want to kill Mark Cotton?'

'You didn't like him – that much is obvious.'

'True, but if I murdered everyone who I didn't like, there'd be many fewer people walking around. In fact, I'd probably be the only surviving member of the Whitebridge Players.'

'And you were jealous of him, weren't you?'

'Well, of course I was jealous of him – but not in the same way that Jerry Talbot was.'

'How are you different?'

'Jerry thinks that he could have *been* Mark Cotton – that he *should* have been Mark Cotton. And he's got a point. He's at least as good an actor as Cotton, yet Cotton is a towering presence and he's nothing but a small dog yapping from within the great man's shadow.'

'And you don't think *you're* as good as Mark Cotton?'

'I know I'm not,' Quirk said, and his eyes were starting to water. 'I'm very good at acting the part of an actor when I'm off the stage, but once I'm on it, I'm only a little better than adequate. I've always known that – deep down – and in the last few years I've even come to accept it.'

But it still hurts, Paniatowski thought – it still hurts a lot.

'If you really believe that you're not that good, why do you carry on acting?' Meadows asked.

Quirk shrugged. 'What else could I do? What else am I *qualified* for? Besides, it's not a bad life. It supplies me with a constant stream of new people to dislike, and at least the sex is varied and plentiful.'

'But even there, you've had to settle for Mark Cotton's rejects,' Meadows guessed.

Quirk seemed genuinely amused by the suggestion – but then how *could* you tell with actors, even those who claimed to be bad at it.

'You've got me all wrong,' he said. 'I didn't have to compete with Mark Cotton in that particular sphere at all.'

'Why not?'

'Because I'm as bent as Dickie's hatband.'

'You're what?'

'I'm an old stage queen – just like my heroes, Noel Coward and Oscar Wilde.'

THIRTEEN

Crane sat in what had been the cast dressing room, facing two monitors and video playback machines, and surrounded by a mountain of tapes.

'I like to combine the conventional documentary style with fly-on-the-wall filming,' Bill Sikes said. 'What that means, in effect, is that sometimes the subjects are very conscious that they're being filmed, and sometimes they're not.'

'Are you saying they actually forget the cameras are there?' Crane asked sceptically.

'No, they know the cameras are there, but they've forgotten what they're there *for*,' Sikes said. 'I'll show you what I mean.'

He leant forward, and clicked two switches.

Both monitors came to life. On the first, the dead man was talking into the camera.

'Thomas Kyd was born in 1558, which made him six years older than William Shakespeare . . .'

On the second, Bradley Quirk and Jerry Talbot stood watching the interview from the back of the stage. Their mouths were opening and closing, but no sound was coming out of them.

'See what I'm saying?' Sikes asked. 'That pair are paying no more attention to the camera than they would to an armchair.'

'Why can't I hear what they're saying,' Crane wondered.

Sikes grinned. 'You're a bright lad – can't you work that out for yourself?'

'Because there are no microphones close to them?'

'That's right. I've learned from experience that it takes people a lot longer to forget about a mike than it takes to forget about a camera, and when they see a mike, they automatically switch to their best-behaviour mode. They're worried that their words will betray them, but they never think their bodies will. And that's true of everybody – even actors, who should know better.'

'But surely, without sound the tapes are of no use,' Crane said.

Sikes chuckled. 'You couldn't be more wrong. What this silent film is providing me with is excellent material to go with the commentary.'

He reached out and turned down the volume, so that Mark Cotton fell silent.

'Watch Quirk and Talbot, and listen to me,' he said.

Quirk made a savage waving gesture with his hand, and Talbot nodded. Neither of them looked happy.

'There is obvious discontent amongst some of the cast members even at this early stage of the production,' the director said in his authoritative commentary voice. 'This may well be because they feel that Mark Cotton is grabbing too much of the limelight for himself, but only time will tell whether this leads to further problems.'

He paused for a moment. 'Get the idea?' he asked in his normal voice.

'You're doing a hatchet job on him,' Crane said.

'No, I'm making a documentary,' the director countered, sounding slightly offended. 'My original intention was to give it a strong artistic bias, like the one I did on John Gielgud's one-man show.'

'That was you, was it?' asked Crane, impressed. 'It was very good.'

'Thank you,' Sikes replied. 'But I'd only been here for five minutes when I realized this whole production wasn't about art at all – it was about Mark Cotton. So I needed another focus for the documentary, and the only one open to me was an examination of what happens when a complete arsehole tries to run a theatre company solely for his own ends.'

'You would have ruined him if you'd produced a documentary like that,' Crane said.

'If he had been ruined, then he would have ruined himself, and I would merely have recorded it. But I don't think he would have been ruined. He wouldn't have been able to play characters like the noble DCI Vic Prince again, but he'd have become an anti-hero – the man the public loves to hate – and anti-heroes are *never* short of work.'

On the monitor, Quirk mimed opening a book, and then peered into the imaginary book as if he were having trouble reading it.

Talbot shook his head in what may have been disbelief.

Quirk mimed closing the book, and then pretended to throw it over his shoulder.

'Actors, eh?' the director said. 'They can't stop showing off, even if they've only got an audience of one – and that audience also happens to be an actor, so is very unlikely to be impressed.'

Bradley Quirk held up six fingers, and, a moment later, Jerry Talbot held up two.

'I don't know whether Talbot's answering the question, or just telling Quirk to sod off,' the director said.

'Six could be the number of nights the play was meant to run,' Crane suggested, 'and two could indicate the number of nights on which something was supposed to happen.'

'The number of nights that Talbot would be allowed to play Hieronimo,' Sikes said. 'I'd stake my granny's old age pension on that.'

On screen, Bradley Quirk drew a finger across his throat.

The director stood up.

'Well, happy viewing,' he said. 'By the way, I will get all this video tape back, won't I?'

'I imagine so, unless we need it as evidence,' Crane replied. 'But why would you want it? You can't possibly show your "Mark Cotton is an arsehole" documentary now.'

'That's where you're wrong,' the director said. 'It'll need a bit of rejigging and some additional material, but once it's retitled as "Who killed Mark Cotton?" it'll be a real winner.'

Ruth Audley was the older of the sisters but she had none of Sarah's confidence or glamour. It would have been totally unfair to describe her as dowdy, but it would certainly have been easier to imagine her running a quiet village post office than it was to picture her dominating a stage.

'We like to start by asking you to give me an account of your movements yesterday,' Paniatowski said.

'We had the full rehearsal in the morning.'

'A dress rehearsal?'

'No, we did that on Friday. Most of the cast didn't think the Monday rehearsal was necessary at all. Some even worried it would take the edge off their performance. But Mark wanted it – and it was Mark who was calling the shots.'

'What happened after the rehearsal?'

'I had lunch and went back to the boarding house for a rest. I took a half an hour walk before the performance – it's something I always did in the old days – and arrived back at the theatre in time to dress and apply my make-up.'

'Did you go up to the fly loft between the dress rehearsal and the performance?'

'No.'

'Did you see anyone else go up to the fly loft?'

Ruth Audley smiled. 'If I had, do you think I'd have waited to be asked before mentioning it?'

'No, I suppose not.'

Ruth Audley took a deep breath.

'What I think I *should* tell you now is that I had an affair with Mark Cotton back in 1957,' she said.

'You think that's important?'

'No, not to me.'

'Then why are you telling us?'

'I'm telling you because it will save you some time when you start taking a closer look at the company as it was in 1957.'

'And you think we'll do that?'

'Yes.'

'Why?'

'Because you'll reach the conclusion that however obnoxious Mark has been over the last week, it probably wasn't enough – on its own – to drive someone to kill him, so the roots for the hatred must lie back in the fifties.'

'Hasn't it occurred to you that the real intended victim might have been Jerry Talbot?' Meadows asked.

'Good God, no!'

'Why not?'

'Jerry isn't the sort of person you would *want* to kill.'

'No?'

'No. I mean, I don't think he'd be anybody's choice as the ideal companion on a desert island, but neither can I see anyone lying awake at night planning ways to kill him.'

'But you can see people lying awake and having those thoughts about Mark Cotton?' Meadows asked.

'I couldn't see *myself* doing it, nor, really, any of the others. But if one of them *was* plotting a murder, it would be Mark's, not Jerry's.'

'How did your affair with Mark Cotton end?' Paniatowski asked.

'I broke it off.'

'Why?'

'If you'd known him yourself back then, you wouldn't need to even ask that question.'

They are putting on George Bernard Shaw's Arms and the Man *the following week, and have just finished their last rehearsal. Ruth is playing Raina, the beautiful-if-deluded aristocratic heroine, and Cotton has the role of Sergius, the dashing-but-pompous hero.*

As they walk off the stage and back towards the dressing rooms, Cotton says, 'So what's it to be? Shall we go out and have a meal, or should we go straight back to the lodgings and jump into bed?'

'Neither,' Ruth says.

'Then what will we do?'

'We won't be doing anything. I'm breaking up with you.'

'You can't do that,' Cotton says incredulously. *'Women never break up with me.'*

'I just have.'

'Tell me why?'

'Because all we have in common is sex – and even that isn't as much fun as it used to be.'

'How did he take it?' Paniatowski asked.

'At first, he took it very badly. Not because he had any real affection for me, you understand, but because, as he'd said, he just wasn't used to being jilted. But then, Mark being Mark, he moved on – and unfortunately, his next conquest was my sister, who was only seventeen and had just joined the company.'

'Only seventeen,' Meadows repeated musingly. 'She didn't go to drama school, then?

'No, she didn't.'

'I thought that going to drama school was pretty much a requirement for the job.'

'It is the commonest route into the theatre, but it's by no means the only one. Michael Caine, who's one of the most successful actors this country's ever produced, never went to drama school, for example.'

'Did you use your influence to get your sister Sarah into the Whitebridge Players?

Ruth smiled again. 'I suppose so, though I never thought of it like that. Sarah needed to get away from home . . .'

'Needed to?'

'Felt the need to. She was young and restless. My mother asked me if I could get Sarah a job in the company, and –' another smile – 'my mother was not someone you said no to. So I asked Geoff if he'd take her in, and he said he would. That's how it worked in those days. It was a really nice company – which is probably why it went broke.'

'Given your opinion of Mark Cotton, did you try to talk Sarah out of having an affair with him?' Paniatowski asked.

'Of course I did, but it had no effect – when you're seventeen, nobody can tell you anything.'

'And how did their affair end?'

'I think it would be better if you asked Sarah about that,' Ruth said, suddenly cagey.

'Apart from your sister, have you seen any members of the cast since the theatre closed?' Paniatowski asked.

'For the first few years, I would occasionally run into one or other of them at auditions, but then my mother became seriously ill, and I gave up the theatre to nurse her.'

'That was a big sacrifice, wasn't it?' Meadows asked.

'Not really,' Ruth said. 'I'm sure if either of you ever found yourselves in my situation, you'd gladly have done the same.'

Paniatowski found herself thinking of her own mother, who must have known that she was being abused by her stepfather, but who had said nothing. But she couldn't really blame the woman for that, she supposed – her mother had had a very difficult life, and simply hadn't been able to summon up the strength to abandon the security and comfort that Arthur Jones could offer her.

She turned to look at Meadows, and saw that her sergeant was similarly deep in thought.

'My career wasn't exactly soaring towards stellar heights at that point, and, to be honest, I was growing a little tired of the life.' Ruth said. 'Besides, I really *did* want to look after Mother.'

'Did your sister help?'

'I'm sure she would have if I'd asked, but I didn't. The truth is – and I'm a little ashamed of this – I was being a bit greedy. I'd been away from home for several years by then, and I wanted Mother all to myself, if only for a short time.'

'How long did it turn out to be?'

'Ten years. She died quite recently.'

'So, for the last ten years you've been looking after your mother full-time,' Paniatowski said.

'Not full-time. At least, not full-time *all* the time. She had her good periods and her bad periods, and when she was having one of the good ones I'd get a job as an office temp. I enjoyed it. There's something relaxing about typing. You don't really have to think, and yet, at the end of the day, you've produced something which will be useful. There's a lot to be said for that.'

'What made you come back for this reunion?'

'I promised I would, twenty years ago. In fact, the whole thing was my idea. And Sarah was most insistent that I come. She said it would help to relaunch my career. She seemed to assume that was what I wanted.'

'And don't you?'

'I don't think so.'

'So what will you do now?'

'Go back into secretarial work. It's still not too late for me to build up a career.' Ruth sighed. 'It's the others I feel sorry for. They have nothing to fall back on, you see.'

'Won't they want to continue in the acting profession?'

'They may want to, but it will be harder for them now – perhaps even impossible. Actors are very superstitious. Did you know they won't even say *Macbeth* because it's considered bad luck?' They have to say "the Scottish Play" instead.'

'I don't quite see . . .'

'This has been a very unlucky production, and as far as most of the theatre world is concerned, they'll all carry that bad luck with them forever.'

'Do they know that?'

'They *should* know that, but you know what actors are like. They're very self-confident – perhaps even arrogant. They have to be, in order to survive, so some of them will automatically assume that, with a massive talent like theirs, they'll be able to overcome any obstacle.'

'Were you surprised when Mark Cotton took over the role of Hieronimo at the last minute?' Paniatowski asked.

'Not really. Mark had made it very plain over the last week that he considers us little more than serfs whose duty it is to serve him.'

'Do you think any other members of the cast were surprised?'

'No.'

'Not even Jerry Talbot?'

'Ah,' Ruth said, 'that's a different matter. He was so desperate to play Hieronimo that he may have talked himself into believing that it was really going to happen. I saw him after he'd got news that Mark had snatched the role from him. He was standing by the steps to the platform and breaking his heart. Then he noticed me and walked away. But two minutes later, he was back.'

'Is there anything else you'd like to tell us before you go, Miss Audley?' Paniatowski asked.

Ruth Audley hesitated. 'I know you have your job to do, but I'd appreciate it if you weren't too hard on my little sister,' she said finally. 'This has all been a great shock to her, and she's much more vulnerable than she seems.'

'We have to start making some assumptions,' Paniatowski said, when Ruth Audley had left the bar, 'and my first assumption is that it probably *was* Mark Cotton who was the intended target.'

'I agree,' Meadows replied.

'And my second assumption is Jerry Talbot probably wasn't the killer.'

'Agreed again,' Meadows said. 'Ruth Audley says he desperately wanted to play Hieronimo – and he must have known that with Mark Cotton dead, there was no chance of that. Besides, a potential murderer – even a particularly stupid one – wouldn't have stood there looking wistfully up at the platform.'

'I don't think he was *just* standing there and looking wistful,' Paniatowski mused.

'What do you mean, boss?' Meadows asked.

'I'm not sure,' Paniatowski admitted. 'I've got an idea, but I need time to think it through.'

She opened her handbag, reached for her cigarettes and then realized they weren't there because she wasn't allowed to smoke.

'Moving on, then,' she continued. 'Do you think Ruth Audley killed Mark Cotton?'

'My gut feeling is that she didn't,' Meadows said, 'but then, my gut's let me down before.'

'Assuming that she didn't do it, do you think she knows who did?'

'Again, my gut says no.'

'Then let me throw a really tricky one at you,' Paniatowski said. 'If she *did* know, do you think she'd tell us?'

'No, I'm pretty sure she wouldn't.'

'And what *makes* you pretty sure?'

'She has so much obvious contempt for Mark Cotton that she probably thinks killing him was no more than a waste of good rope. On the other hand, she's more than willing to respect the opinion of anyone else who thinks he *was* worth killing.'

Paniatowski nodded.

'I couldn't have put it better myself,' she said.

FOURTEEN

Beresford sat at his desk in Whitebridge police headquarters, a list of phone numbers in front of him and the prospect of several – possibly fruitless – hours on the phone ahead of him.

He knew, from his previous experience of making contact with other police authorities, that the chances were he'd either end up speaking to the type of officer he privately thought of as a Glum, or the kind he had classified as a Gabbler.

The Glums were precise and unemotional, and though they were police officers, they could just have easily been undertakers or tax inspectors. They were usually perfectly willing to help, but only if it could be done strictly by the book, and to expect from a Glum one of those imaginative leaps which are often so necessary in police work would have been like expecting Vlad the Impaler to agree to become the honorary president of his local ladies' knitting circle.

The Gabblers were quite the reverse. They talked to you as if you were sitting side by side in a pub, with several pints of best bitter already swilling around in your belly. In a way, the Gabblers were harder work than the Glums, because they gave you so *much* unfiltered information that vital details could quite easily slip through the cracks.

The first name on Beresford's list, a chief inspector in Hereford, was a Gabbler.

'As a matter of fact, I think I can save you a little time here, because I know Phil McCann personally,' he said. 'He's my bank manager. And he plays an active role in the local community. For instance, he runs an amateur theatre group in which his elder daughter is one of the stars. I know what you're thinking – a whiff of nepotism there.'

'I wasn't thinking that at all,' Beresford said.

'But, in fact, it's not nepotism at all. She's a wonderful little actress. He's also a big wheel in the Rotary Club – no pun intended, and—'

'I'm more interested in things that might relate to the murder

I'm investigating,' Beresford interrupted. 'Has he been involved in any local scandals, for instance?'

'Scandals? What precisely do you mean by that?'

'I don't mean anything *precisely*,' Beresford said. 'I'd just be interested in anything he's been connected with which might have brought him to the attention of the police.'

'Good God, there's been nothing like that. I told you, the man's a pillar of the community.'

'Does he have any kind of criminal record?'

'I shouldn't think so. He might have a couple of speeding fines – but nothing more than that.'

'Could you get someone to check for me?' Beresford asked wearily.

'Scotland Yard holds every criminal record in the country. Why don't you check with them?'

'I am checking with them, but they can't get the records to me until tomorrow morning. And anyway, local stations don't always bother to inform Scotland Yard if it's only a minor infringement . . .'

'They should! It's right there in the protocols.'

Idiot! Beresford thought.

'. . . so the Yard's records are sometimes incomplete,' he continued. 'That's why I need both sets of records.'

'You've lost me,' the chief inspector admitted.

'I need both sets so I can cross-reference them.'

'All this paperwork, hey?' the chief inspector said sympathetically – and completely missing the point again. 'In my opinion, it's paperwork that's killing this job. Oh, for the good old days, when it was all constables on bicycles, and most offenders were given a clip round the ear and warned not to do it again.'

The good old days, when everybody was happy, and kids didn't mind being hungry and suffering from rickets, and being out of work for years was a real laugh, Beresford thought.

'Could you do that, sir?' he asked. 'Could you get someone to check your records?'

'Oh, I suppose so,' said the chief inspector, slightly huffily. 'I'll get back to you sometime tomorrow.'

And it was even possible that he might, Beresford told himself, as he replaced the phone.

*   *   *

'You were here in the theatre last night, weren't you?' Paniatowski asked Joan Turnbull.

'Yes, I was.'

'And were you also here for the morning run-through?'

'I was here most of the day.'

'Was there any particular reason for that?' Meadows asked. 'You had no official standing, did you?'

'I've never had any official standing, but I've always been there. Back in the good old days, I was a sort of mother hen to the company.'

'Weren't you rather young to be a mother hen, Mrs Turnbull?' Paniatowski asked.

Joan Turnbull laughed. 'I was about ten years older than most of them – but when you're in your twenties, as they were, someone in their mid-thirties seems almost ancient.'

'I still don't see why you were there last night,' Meadows persisted. 'The cast are a little too old for mothering now.'

'I was there to assist my husband.'

'But from what we can tell, your husband didn't have much to do,' Meadows prodded.

'My husband built this company,' Joan said angrily. 'The Whitebridge Players were a pathetic shambles when he took over. Geoff taught those young men and women their stagecraft. He moulded each and every one of them into the actors that they've become today.'

'Yes, but the fact remains that it was Mark Cotton – not your husband – who was directing this production,' Meadows said, 'so I really don't see why either of you needed to be there.'

'Mark knew nothing about theatre direction,' Joan said, still furious. 'He hadn't even been on stage himself for years and years. So something was bound to go wrong – and when it did, my Geoff would be there to put it right. But before there was *time* for anything to go wrong, Mark was murdered.'

'Some people might say the murder would fit into the category of things going wrong,' Paniatowski pointed out.

She had spoken mildly enough, but her words had the effect of a bucket of cold water on Joan Turnbull.

'Yes, of course . . . I didn't mean that,' she said. 'I was talking about things going wrong in theatrical terms, and I got a little carried away.'

'Did you go up to the fly loft at any time yesterday, Mrs Turnbull?'
Meadows asked.

'No. I don't think I've ever been up to the fly loft in my life.
I'm not interested in the technical aspects of the stage – only the
people.'

'But you know where the fly loft is?'

'Of course.'

'And you didn't see anyone up there on Monday?'

'I did not.'

'One last question,' Paniatowski said. 'Have you seen any of the
actors between the time the company disbanded and it being reunited
last week?'

'I have not,' Joan said. 'I would have thought one or two of them
would have visited us – if only to thank my Geoff for what he'd
done for them – but none of them did.'

Crane was watching a tape of the Friday rehearsal. He had done a
little treading the boards himself, while he'd been up at Oxford,
and though he didn't consider himself an expert on theatre, it was
perfectly clear to him that the rehearsal was not going well, and
that most of the responsibility for that lay with the director.

A few minutes earlier, he had seen how Mark Cotton had left
Jerry Talbot hanging in the harness, while he harangued him for
missing his cue. Since then, he had seen Talbot repeat the scene
three times, and even that had failed to satisfy Cotton. Finally,
when Geoff Talbot had complained that he was being unreasonable, Cotton had exploded and forced him into a humiliating climb
down.

Crane ran the tape again, and this time he concentrated his attention on the other actors. He couldn't always see their faces clearly,
but from what he read of their body language he was convinced
that Mark Cotton didn't have a friend in the entire theatre.

Joan Turnbull had made what she considered quite a calm exit from
the bar, but once she was out on the street, she felt herself fighting
for breath, and had to clutch the doorpost for support.

She had told the two female detectives too much, she thought
– far too much – but at least, thank God, she hadn't told them about
what happened between her and Mark Cotton.

* * *

*She is lying in bed with Mark, wrapped up in a blanket of content-
ment and slowly fading sensual pleasure, when Mark goes and spoils
it all.*

'Geoff's been talking about putting on The Spanish Tragedy *next
year,' he says.*

*'I know,' Joan says, hoping she's wrong about what she thinks
he will say next, but almost sure that she isn't.*

*'And do you also happen to know who he's got in mind to play
Hieronimo?' Mark asks.*

She rolls over so that she can look him straight in the eye.

'So that's what all this is about, is it?' she asks.

He doesn't flinch – but then, he is an actor

'I've not got a clue what you're talking about,' he says.

*'Is the only reason you've taken an old bag like me into your
bed because you want the best role in* The Spanish Tragedy*?'*

He laughs, reaches across, and strokes her cheek.

*'Of course not,' he says. 'First of all, you're not an old bag at all –
you're a beautiful woman in her prime. And secondly, you can't expect
actors not to think about acting, even in bed – it's what they live for.'*

'Would you like me to speak to Geoff about it?' she asks.

He plays it very cannily.

*'No, I wouldn't want to force you into doing something you didn't
believe in. But you've been around the theatre a long time, and if
you happen to think that I'd be the best person to play the role . . .'*

*'I'll do it,' she says – because she senses that this is the price he is
demanding for their afternoons of passion.*

*She tries to make the suggestion sound casual – off the cuff – but she
is no actress, and Geoff senses that something is wrong.*

'Are you having an affair with Mark Cotton?' he asks.

*She wants to say no, but she realizes she can never deliver even
that single word convincingly.*

*She gazes down at her feet, which were once young and elegant,
but are now starting to look tired and middle aged.*

'Yes, I've been having an affair with him,' she says.

'But why?' he asks pleadingly.

*Because although she loves Geoff with all her heart, he cannot
excite her in bed however hard he works – somehow cannot bring
her to those levels of ecstasy which handsome young Mark does
almost effortlessly.*

'Why?' Geoff repeats.

'I don't know,' she says.

'I want you to end the affair,' Geoff tells her.

'I will,' she promises.

And she will keep that promise. It will be easy. She has seen a look of anguish on her husband's face which has seared itself on to her very soul, and she can never go to bed with Mark again without that look coming between them.

'If Mark Cotton really wants to play Hieronimo, then the part is his,' Geoff says.

'You don't have to do that,' Joan protests.

'It's the right thing for the company,' Geoff says. 'He'll play the part superbly, but . . .' He pauses. '. . . but if word ever gets out that you've been having an affair with him, he's gone.'

'Word won't get out,' she says.

Mark Cotton will know it's a bribe, but it's a big enough bribe to make him do what Geoff wants.

Mark had pretended to be hurt when she'd told him they wouldn't be seeing each other again, but the truth was, he hadn't really cared, and just a few days later he'd managed to talk Ruth Audley into his bed.

But though Geoff had never mentioned the matter again, she knew he had not forgotten. A small – vital – part of him had died that day, and it showed in his work. In fact, it would be no exaggeration to say that the company had started to decline the moment she had told Geoff about the affair.

She had killed the company and maimed her husband, and though she had spent the next twenty years trying to compensate for that one moment, it had all been a waste of effort.

Until now!

Now, if they could just ride out the storm, she and Geoff might just find they had the foundations on which to start to build a new life.

Sarah Audley's hair was the same shade as her sister's – a deep auburn – and, like Ruth, she wore it long, but while Ruth's hair seemed tired, Sarah's had a bounce in it which proclaimed that it was ready to take on the world. There were other differences, too. Though the two sisters did look alike, Sarah's face was both lively and challenging, while Ruth's always appeared mildly apologetic.

So all-in-all, Paniatowski thought, as Sarah Audley sat down opposite her, the younger sister seemed far less vulnerable than the older sister had led her to expect.

'It's really a waste of time my being here,' Sarah said. 'I didn't see anything yesterday, and since I can't possibly be a suspect . . .'

'Hold on a minute, what makes you think you can be ruled out?' Paniatowski asked.

'Because of all the people who were on the stage last night, I'm the only one who really loses out by Mark's death. The others might have got a small boost to their careers from the documentary – which they've now lost – but I didn't need a boost, because I'd already signed to co-star in DCI Prince – and there can be no DCI Prince without Mark Cotton.'

'How did Cotton feel about you co-starring with him?

'I think he was surprised at first – possibly even a little shocked. But pretty soon he came to realize that since there's such chemistry between us, it could only strengthen the series.'

'You went out with him once, didn't you?' Meadows asked.

'I was talking about chemistry on stage,' Sarah Audley replied, slightly haughtily.

'But you *did* go out with him,' Meadows persisted.

'Yes, for a while.'

'And you were devastated when he jilted you?'

'Who told you he jilted me?' Sarah asked angrily. 'Was it my sister?'

'It doesn't matter who told us,' Meadows said. 'It's true, isn't it?'

'Because, let me tell you, her breaking up with Mark hurt her a lot more than my breaking up with Mark hurt me.'

'You still haven't answered the question,' Meadows reminded her – and she could see, from the look in other woman's eyes, that Sarah was playing out scenes from that relationship in her head.

Mark has just told her that he thinks they should stop seeing each other, and her first thought is that that is a ridiculous way to express it, because whatever else happens, they will *be seeing each other every single day. And then the implications – rather than just the words – begin to sink in.*

'How can you treat me like this?' she asks.

'Treat you like what?' Mark replies. 'It's not as if I've made any promises, is it?'

'You let me tell you I loved you.'

'I couldn't stop you saying it, could I? And, to be fair, I never told you that I loved you in return.'

So that's all right then – that leaves him in the clear.

Like hell it does!

'Are you sleeping with Lucy Cavendish?' she demands.

'That's my affair.'

The word affair enrages her.

'You're a piece of shit,' she screams. 'You're nothing but a filthy piece of shit.'

'I think you should calm down,' he tells her.

She needs to hurt him, but she's not sure how to go about it. And then – suddenly – she is.

'You only get the starring roles because of your looks,' she says. 'But just wait until you try to move on to something bigger than provincial theatre. Then you'll come against other good-looking men, men who have real talent – and you won't stand a chance.'

She can see the barb has hit home.

'You little bitch!' he says.

'The truth hurts, doesn't it?' she taunts him.

'You want the truth?' he asks, really angry now. 'All right, here's the truth. I never really fancied you at all.'

'You're a liar!'

'It's the truth. I only screwed you to get back at your sister.'

'You don't mean that,' she sobs.

But she knows he does. And it really hurts that, for the first time in her life, her older sister has got one over on her – even though that was clearly not Ruth's intention.

'Are you all right, Miss Audley?' Paniatowski asked.

'I lied to you earlier,' Sarah said.

'About what?'

'It did hurt me when Mark chucked me for Lucy Cavendish. I was so upset that I almost left the company, but then Ruth said that throwing away my career because of a rat like Mark Cotton would be a real waste.'

'So you stayed.'

'Yes, it was hard, because every time I saw Mark I thought my heart would break again – but I stayed.'

'What made you agree to come back for this reunion, Sarah?' Paniatowski asked.

'I'm not sure I know what you mean.'

'Well, most of the others came back because they thought it would boost their careers, but – as you've pointed out – your career didn't need a boost. And given your painful history with Mark Cotton, I'd have thought you'd have wanted to stay well clear.'

'I knew that I'd have to come face-to-face with him sooner or later, and I wanted to see if I still had any feelings for him before we started filming the next series of DCI Prince.'

'And did you?'

'Honestly, no – not at all. It was almost as if it had never happened to me – as if it was just something I'd read about. What I was much more concerned about was helping Ruth adjust to being back in the theatre because – now Mother's dead – she really needs to find something to do with her time.'

'You're very close, are you?' Meadows asked.

'Very close.'

'Yet you seemed quite happy to have Ruth shoulder the burden of caring for your mother.'

'Ruth wanted to do it. I'd have been an awful carer, because I don't have the patience for it – and anyway, Mother and I didn't really get on.'

'Who do you think killed Mark Cotton?' Meadows asked.

'Have you asked all the other members of the company the same question?' Sarah Audley replied.

'Yes,' Meadows lied.

'And have they given you a name?'

'Some of them.'

'Have any of them given you *my* name?'

'I'm afraid I can't tell you that.'

'That means yes,' Sarah said. 'But I don't care if someone has pointed the finger at me. I'm not pointing it back, because I have no idea who would have killed Mark, or why they would have wanted to kill him.'

It was the fifth phone call he had made to a local police authority – this time it was to West Sussex, where the Audley sisters came from – and Beresford was starting to work on automatic pilot.

'This is DI Beresford of the Mid Lancs Constabulary,' he told the switchboard in a robotic voice. 'I'm currently part of a murder inquiry in Whitebridge, Lancashire, and I'd like to be connected to –' he glanced down at his list – 'to Detective Chief Inspector Williams.'

'I was told that if you rang up, I was to put you through to Sergeant Lloyd,' the girl on the switchboard said, in a voice which would have been perfect for the sloth in a Disney cartoon.

'You were told *what*?'

'I was told that if you rang up, I was to put you through to Sergeant Lloyd,' the girl repeated.

'Let me get this straight – are you saying that someone there expected me to call?' Beresford asked.

'If you rang, I was told to put you through to Sergeant Lloyd,' the operator said, as if she thought that by turning the sentence around, she might finally make him understand.

'Then will you please do that?' Beresford asked.

'Do what?'

'Put me through to Sergeant Lloyd.'

Sergeant Lloyd, as it turned out, was neither a Glum nor a Gabbler.

'I can have you transferred to DCI Williams and his band of merry men on the top floor, if that's what you want,' he said, 'but in my opinion, you'd be much better talking to Jim Parry.'

'Who's Jim Parry?' Beresford wondered.

'He used to be a sergeant here. As a matter of fact, he was the one who trained me up, and a bloody good job he made of it. Anyway, he's retired now, but he came in to see me this morning, and he showed me the front page of a newspaper, which had that murder on your patch splashed right across it. "If they know their arses from their elbows up in Whitebridge, they'll be ringing you about this very soon," he said. "And if they do ring you, put them on to me, because I'm the one who can give them what they need".'

'What did he mean by that?' Beresford asked.

'I've absolutely no idea, sir. But I'll tell you this for nothing – Jim Parry was one of the finest police officers ever to wear the uniform, and it's a disgrace that he never rose any higher in the force. So if he says he's got something for you, you'd be a bloody fool not to listen.'

'You'd better give me his number, then,' Beresford said.

The sergeant dictated the number. 'But there'd be no point in calling him now.'

'Why not?'

'He'll still be out on the golf links. It'd be best to leave it until seven or eight o'clock.'

FIFTEEN

Tony Brown was wearing a brown cord jacket with leather elbow patches, cavalry twill trousers and stout brogues. He had dark brown curly hair, which made him seem younger than he actually was. He looked every inch a teacher, and the expression on his face at that moment was one of a teacher who was confronting a class with a fearsome reputation for the first time, and was wondering what the best way to deal with them would be.

He answered the standard questions which Paniatowski and Meadows put to him in the same way that everyone else in the company had answered them.

No, he had not been up to the fly loft any time on Monday.

No, he had not noticed anyone else going up there.

'You've left the stage, haven't you, Mr Brown?' Paniatowski asked.

'That's right.'

'What do you do now?'

'I'm a teacher at a place called Walford Hall. It's a small independent boarding school.'

'What do you teach, Mr Brown?'

'English and Drama.'

'Are you happy in your work?'

'More or less.'

'Have you ever thought of returning to the stage, Mr Brown?' Paniatowski asked.

'Definitely not. I'm glad I did it for a time, but that part of my life is behind me now.'

'So why exactly are you here?' Meadows asked.

'It's a reunion,' Brown said, as if that was all the explanation necessary. 'We're all here.'

'Ah yes, but the others' motives are much clearer than yours.'

'What do you mean?'

'With the exception of Phil McCann, they're all actors, and they hoped that this would help them in their careers. Anyway, since they *are* actors, they were probably "resting", so they had nothing to lose,' Meadows said. 'You, on the other hand, you have a real job.'

'I'm still not following you.'

'Did you have to ask your employer for permission to take two weeks off and come here?'

'Well, yes.' Brown grinned. 'You surely don't think I'm playing truant, do you?'

'Is your school paying your salary, or is it *unpaid* leave?'

'It's unpaid leave,' Brown said, sounding slightly defensive now, 'but we are getting paid for performing.'

'But, as I understand it, you're only earning what you would have earned in Whitebridge Rep in 1957.'

'Yes, it's all part of the spirit of the thing. We stay in the same boarding house, we're paid the same . . .'

'How did your wife feel about you losing what – to all intents and purposes – is two weeks' pay?'

'I'm not married.'

'Your girlfriend, then?'

'I don't have one at the moment.'

'I still don't get why you're here,' Meadows confessed.

'I thought it would be fun.'

'Is that what you thought?' Meadows asked sceptically.

'Yes.'

'This is an official police investigation into a murder,' Meadows said, 'so I'd like you to think carefully before you answer what I'm about to ask you. Tell me, Mr Brown, did you *really* expect it to be fun?'

Tony Brown hesitated for a second, then he said, 'No.'

'So what did you expect?'

'I expected it to be just what it was – a showcase for Mark Cotton, an opportunity for the big star to laud it over the rest of us.'

'So why *did* you come?'

'I suppose it was because there were people I wanted to see.'

'Who?'

'Ruth Audley, for one. I've always had a soft spot for her. And

Jerry Talbot – he can be a bit of a prick at times, but we've had some laughs together.' Brown paused for a moment. 'But what I've just realized is that that wouldn't have been enough on its own. What really tipped the balance was that Phil McCann paid me a visit, and pretty much talked me into it.'

As Colin Beresford stood facing the heavy black door, a tired old police joke came into his head.

Q: Why is a chief constable like a sewerage system?

A: Because most of the time you can ignore the fact that he's there, but if you ever have to go and see him, you're probably in the shit.

It wasn't a particularly funny joke, he thought, but what it lacked in humour, it made up for in accuracy.

This wouldn't be the first time he'd spoken to the chief constable, he reminded himself. But 'Yes, sir,' 'No, sir,' and 'Thank you, sir,' couldn't really be called conversations, and when you were personally summoned to the big chief's office, a conversation – or, far more likely, a lecture or interrogation – was what you were about to be on the unpleasant end of.

The green light came on and Beresford knocked on the door, opened it, and stepped into the inner sanctum.

Pickering was at his desk.

'Inspector Beresford,' he said. 'Colin, isn't it?'

'Yes, sir.'

'Take a seat, Colin.'

Beresford sat.

'You've worked with DCI Monika Paniatowski for a long time, haven't you, Colin?' Pickering said.

'I have, sir.'

'And am I right in assuming that she's more than just a colleague – that she is, in fact, a close personal friend?'

'Yes, sir, she is a close friend – but only when we're off duty,' Beresford said cautiously.

'Quite right and proper,' Pickering agreed. 'There are some chief constables, you know, who just fire off arbitrary orders at random, and expect everyone else to jump to it unquestioningly, but that's not my way.'

On the surface, it sounded as if he was changing the subject – but Beresford was bloody sure he wasn't.

'Mine is a more personal style of management,' the chief constable continued. 'I don't like ordering my officers to take certain actions – although I will, of course, if I consider it absolutely necessary. I prefer to let them act on their own initiative, and if I think they're making a mistake, my first step is to try and talk them round to my point of view.'

Here it comes, Beresford thought.

'Both the press and the police authority have contacted me several times during the course of the day, and what they all seem to wondering is why DCI Paniatowski hasn't questioned Maggie Maitland, who is an obvious prime suspect in the murder of Mark Cotton.'

'DCI Paniatowski doesn't think Maggie Maitland *is* the prime suspect,' Beresford said. 'And besides, she's been traumatized.'

'But she's come out of it now, hasn't she?'

'Yes sir, but the doctors think she's still too fragile for them to allow us to talk to her.'

'I think I might be able to help you there,' Pickering said. 'Some of the members of the hospital board are golfing acquaintances of mine, and I know others through various social organizations.'

The bloody Freemasons, Beresford thought – but he was wise enough to say nothing.

'I believe that in the interest of the greater good, those board members could persuade the doctors in the psychiatric unit to change their minds,' Pickering continued. 'But that won't be of any use at all if DCI Paniatowski still refuses to make questioning Maggie Maitland a priority. And that's where you come in. I'm not *ordering* you to try and change your DCI's mind, but I would certainly appreciate it if you would.'

The safest course would be to agree with the chief constable, and then do nothing, Beresford decided.

But he had been knocking around with Charlie Woodend and Monika Paniatowski for so long that part of their general approach to life seemed to have rubbed off on him.

'You're the big boss, sir,' he said.

'Yes, I am,' Pickering agreed.

'But DCI Paniatowski is my *immediate* boss, and whatever course of action she decides on has my complete backing.'

'Then here's something else to consider,' Pickering said, doing his best to hide his irritation. 'A lot of women plan to go back to work after their babies are born, but once it's actually happened, they decide they wouldn't be able to cope with both an infant and a job. And if that happens in DCI Paniatowski's case, then there'll be a vacancy at the DCI level, and that vacancy is likely to filled by someone I think I can rely on.'

Beresford laughed. He didn't mean to, because laughing is not something you do, uninvited, in the presence of the chief constable – but he couldn't help himself.

'If you think there's a possibility she might not be coming back to work, sir, then you don't really know Monika,' he said.

Given that she'd been a member of the Whitebridge Players in 1957, Lucy Cavendish must have been around forty, but she did not look it. She had long hair which was almost platinum blonde, and a face that reminded Paniatowski of an exquisitely delicate china doll.

There was nothing delicate or exquisite about the man she had brought with her.

'This is Mr Graves,' Lucy Cavendish told Paniatowski and Meadows. 'He's my solicitor.'

He might well be, Paniatowski thought, but he was scarcely in the tradition of the friendly *family* solicitors – heavy tweed suits and an avuncular air. No, this man had sharp features and shifty darting eyes, and while he possibly *did* know a little about trust funds and entailments, it was unlikely that they had featured much in his professional life.

'Strictly speaking, you're only being questioned as a witness, Miss Cavendish,' Paniatowski said. 'Our conversation is not being recorded, and in these circumstances most people don't consider it necessary to have their solicitors present.'

'Is my client a suspect in the murder of Mark Cotton?' Graves asked, in a harsh North London accent.

'At this stage of the investigation, everyone in the Whitebridge area – and beyond – is, to a greater or lesser extent, a suspect,' Paniatowski said.

'Everyone in the Whitebridge area and beyond wasn't backstage when Mark Cotton did his neck stretching exercise,' Graves countered, sitting down and indicating to Lucy Cavendish that she should do the same.

'Did you go up to the fly loft at any time yesterday, Miss Cavendish?' Paniatowski asked.

'No.'

'Did you see anyone else up there?'

Lucy Cavendish glanced across at her solicitor, who nodded.

'Yes,' she said.

'Tell me about it.'

'It was just after we'd finished the final rehearsal. Most of the cast and all the stagehands had already gone away, but I was waiting on the stage for Mark, who was still in the dressing room.'

'Why were you waiting for him?'

'He was the director of the play, and my client wished to discuss one of the nuances of her role in it with him,' Graves said, before Lucy Cavendish had time to answer.

'So it wasn't that you were hoping, even at that late hour, to persuade Mark Cotton to take the role of Bel-Imperia off Sarah Audley and give it to you?' Meadows asked innocently.

'No comment,' Graves said.

'What made you look up at the fly loft?' Paniatowski asked Lucy.

'I was practising dying,' the other woman replied.

'Sorry?'

'In the play, I stab myself and then fall to the ground. I was making sure I'd got it right.'

'So you weren't so much looking up at the fly loft as having your eyes directed there by your position on the stage. Is that what you're saying?'

Lucy looked at her solicitor again.

'Yes, that's what she's saying,' he confirmed.

'What can you tell me about the person you saw, Miss Cavendish?'

'It was very dark up there, and I only got a second's glance, but I think it was a woman.'

'She was wearing a skirt?'

'No, she was wearing trousers – or maybe even a tracksuit. But then, so do all the women – myself included.'

'How did you get on with Mark Cotton?' Paniatowski asked.

'I got on with him as well as everybody else did.'

'Which, from what we've gathered in the investigation so far, wasn't terribly well at all.'

'All right,' said Lucy Cavendish, 'I got on much *better* with him than everybody else did.'

'You had an affair with Mark Cotton back in 1957, didn't you?' Meadows asked.

'Who told you that?'

'It began right after Cotton ditched Sarah Audley, didn't it? Or perhaps it began even *before* that.'

'I had a romantic relationship with him, yes, but I will neither confirm nor deny that sex was involved.'

'And have you renewed that "romantic relationship" with him while you've been in Whitebridge?'

'No. Definitely not.'

'Are you still a member of the acting profession, Miss Cavendish?'

'I play the occasional role on television, and I've done some modelling for mail order catalogues. I also own a property and rent out rooms to actors who are on tour.'

'So you're a theatrical landlady?'

Lucy Cavendish wrinkled her nose. 'I don't care for that particular term,' she said. 'It sounds so dowdy.'

'How did you feel when you were asked to come back to Whitebridge after all these years?'

'How do you think I felt? I was over the moon. I was getting a second chance to make it big.'

'Is that right?' Meadows asked.

'Yes, it is! Oh, I know what you're thinking – she looks at least thirty-three, and that's too old to be a star. But that's where you're wrong – there's been a big shift in the last few years, and older women are considered very sexy now. Just look at Sophia Loren.'

'True, but then you're no Loren,' Meadows said, under her breath.

'You didn't need any persuading to come back?' Paniatowski asked.

'None at all.'

'So Phil McCann needn't have bothered coming to see you.'

'How did you know Phil came to see me?' Lucy Cavendish asked. 'Silly me – he probably told you himself!'

'One more question,' Paniatowski said. 'None of the other people we've questioned felt it necessary to have their solicitors present, so why did you?'

And this time, Lucy Cavendish didn't even need to look at Graves before answering, 'No comment.'

'So what did you make of that?' Paniatowski asked.

Meadows grinned. 'I think Lucy Cavendish is either lying or telling the truth,' she said. 'Perhaps she really did see someone up there in the fly loft. Then again, she could have been trying to create some sort of tenuous alibi for herself – because if she saw someone up in the fly loft, she couldn't have been there herself.'

'If she was telling the truth, then she's not really been much help at all, because we know that someone *had to be* up in the fly loft, and she can't even tell us anything about that person.'

'She thinks it was probably a woman.'

'But she can't be sure. That's if she's telling the truth. If she's lying, she's either trying to cover for herself or someone else. Do you think she was being honest when she said she hadn't embarked on another affair with Mark Cotton?'

'No,' Meadows said.

'Neither do I,' Paniatowski agreed. 'So I think I might send young Jack Crane round to the Royal Victoria to make a few inquiries.'

She reached into her handbag for her cigarettes. She wished she could stop doing that.

'Why do you think Lucy Cavendish brought her solicitor with her?' she asked Meadows.

'Because she doesn't trust the police.'

'And *why* doesn't she trust the police?'

'Because she's obviously been in trouble with us before.'

Paniatowski nodded. 'Yes, she has, hasn't she?' she agreed.

SIXTEEN

'*Y*our mind seems to be somewhere else, this afternoon,' Mark Cotton said.

Sarah Audley sighed, wistfully. '*I suppose I was thinking back to the time when we first did this play – twenty years ago. I had quite a crush on you back then, you know.*'

'*Did you? I had no idea. But I'm assuming you've got over it by now.*'

'*Oh yes, I've quite got over it. But I still enjoy working with you. In fact, I adore it.*'

Crane groaned. They were working, he assumed, to a script that Cotton had written – and a bloody awful script it was!

He looked up and saw Meadows standing in the doorway.

'How's it going?' she asked.

'If this were played upon a stage, I could condemn it as an improbable fiction,' Crane replied.

Meadows grinned. 'As your sergeant, I'm really going to have to start rationing your use of Shakespearean quotes,' she said. 'It's the least I can do for the rest of the team.'

'Inspector Beresford wouldn't recognize a Shakespearean quote if you stuffed it up his nose,' Crane said.

'And probably neither would the boss,' Meadows conceded. 'Speaking of whom, she wants you to get off your arse and do some real detective work for a change.'

Crane stood up.

'Thank God for that,' he said.

Paniatowski was looking straight into the camera.

'*A forty-two-year-old man has been taken into custody and is helping us with our inquiries,*' she said.

'*Will you be arresting him?*' asked the person attached to the hand which was holding the microphone.

'*I have no further comment to make at this time.*'

The phone rang in the hallway, and Louisa went to pick it up.

'You're on the telly, Mum,' she said.

'What!' Paniatowski asked, alarmed.

Louisa laughed. 'Don't worry, you've not been caught by *Candid Camera*. They haven't got anything new from you, so they're using old footage – a sort of Monika Paniatowski's Greatest Hits.'

'How were things at school?' Paniatowski asked.

'Awful.'

'I'm so sorry. I should never have—'

'They weren't awful because of what happened last night. And anyway, I'm going to have to get used to seeing stiffs if I'm ever to be the first female chief constable of Mid Lancs.'

'Then what was the problem?'

'My so-called *mature* contemporaries.'

'Come again?'

'The rest of the girls in the Sixth Form. They've been a real pain. "Do you know who did it, Louisa?" "Has your mum told you who killed gorgeous Mark Cotton?" They never bloody stopped.'

'You shouldn't swear, Louisa,' Paniatowski admonished.

'Well, honestly, it was enough to make a saint swear,' Louisa

countered. 'Why couldn't you have been a rock star or something
– that would have caused me *far* less trouble.'

Paniatowski laughed. 'I'll be home as soon as I can,' she
promised.

'I won't hold my breath waiting,' her daughter said.

Tony Brown sat in a lonely corner of the Bull and Bush. He was
holding a gin and tonic in his hand – his third in less than half an
hour – and he was going over, in the minutest possible detail, his
interview with the two policewomen.

He should have done better, he told himself. He was an actor –
albeit a rather rusty one – and he should have been able to project
a much more appealing image than the one he had projected.

He took another slug of his drink.

But it could have been worse, he thought. Meadows and
Paniatowski didn't like him, and they didn't trust him – but at least
they hadn't come anywhere near guessing the truth.

He pushed the interview to the back of his mind, and unwittingly
allowed another interview – a less official but much more unpleasant
one – to slide into the space the first had vacated.

*It is Thursday, which means they have had a full three and a half
days of rehearsals, and it is already plain to the entire cast that
although Geoff Turnbull may be out of touch with contemporary
theatre techniques and, in addition, is rarely sober, he would still
make a much better job of directing* The Spanish Tragedy *than Mark
Cotton is doing.*

*And Cotton knows the tide is moving against him, which is why
he corners Tony when no one else is around.*

*'I need your help,' he says. 'I want you to tell the rest of the cast
that they've got the wrong attitude to these rehearsals, and that they
need to do something about it.'*

'Why would they listen to me?' Brown asks.

*'Why? Because they all like you! Because they all think you're a
nice guy.'*

*That's true. Phil McCann has always been regarded as the
diplomat of the company, but he himself is unquestionably the nice
one.*

*'One of the reasons they like me is because they know I'm
honest,' Tony Brown says. 'If I told them they had the wrong*

attitude, they'd know I was lying, and my credibility would just melt away.'

'Are you saying it's my *attitude that's wrong?' Cotton demands.*

'Yes, isn't that obvious – even to you.'

'If you were still a full-time actor, I'd have no power over you,' Cotton says. 'But you're not an actor any more, are you? You're a schoolteacher – and, because of that, all I need to do to destroy you is to pick up the phone.'

'You won't do that,' Brown says, but there is a fearful note in his voice which says that he thinks Cotton just might.

'I don't know why I ever agreed to do this show,' Cotton whines, suddenly completely engulfed in self-pity. 'I was a huge success on television. I was making a lot of money and my fans adored me. But I wanted more, didn't I? Stupid, stupid, stupid!'

'Mark . . .' Tony Brown says softly.

'I've got a sort of magic about me, and if this play fails, the magic will be gone. If it fails, I go down.'

'It doesn't have to fail,' Tony tells him. 'All you need to do is change your attitude a little – and I can help you with that.'

But Cotton has not been listening.

'And if I go down, I'll make bloody sure that I drag you down with me,' he says.

The gin and tonic was gone. Tony Brown rose to his feet and walked unsteadily across to the bar to order another one. He had tried to do what Cotton had asked, it had cost him his integrity, but it still hadn't worked, and by Friday, he had accepted that he was doomed.

But that wasn't the case any more. If he could just keep his head – if he could avoid the strong urge to confess – then there still might be a light at the end of the tunnel.

'You were around the stage for most of Monday, weren't you, Mr Turnbull?' Paniatowski asked.

Geoff Turnbull stared at the wall, and said nothing. It was hard to work out whether his lack of focus was due to nerves, or to drink, though she suspected it was a little of both.

Paniatowski repeated the question.

'Yes, I was,' Turnbull agreed.

'And you were watching everything that was going on?'

'That was part of my job.'

'So did you notice anybody going up to the fly loft?'

Once more, the witness was silent.

'Mr Turnbull!' Paniatowski said forcefully.

'Do you know how the town council feel about all this?' Geoff Turnbull asked.

'What do you mean?'

'They can't blame me, can they? I wasn't in charge. I should have been – it was only right and proper for me to be in charge – but I wasn't.'

'Did you go up to the fly loft?' Paniatowski asked.

'No, I . . .'

'Did you see anyone else go up?'

'No.'

He was either a brilliant actor or he was coming apart at the seams, Paniatowski thought.

'Thank you, Mr Turnbull, that will be all for the present,' she said.

'If you see someone from the council, will you make it clear to them that Mark Cotton was in charge, and if anyone's to blame for what happened, it's him,' Turnbull said.

The woman behind the reception desk in the Royal Victoria had a name badge that identified her as Elaine Rodgers. She was in her early forties and seemed both smart and competent.

'I'd like to ask you some questions about Mark Cotton,' Crane said, when he'd shown his warrant card.

The receptionist smiled. 'Mark Cotton,' she said, 'born eighth of April 1934 in York, to Arthur Cotton and Doris Cotton née Hoskins. Studied at the Halifax School of Dramatic Art. First major role – Aladdin, in the Kingston-upon-Hull Christmas pantomime.'

'You're a fan of his,' Crane said.

'I *used* to be a fan of his – a very big fan,' Elaine Rodgers said, with some emphasis.

'And why aren't you a fan of his any more, Elaine? It's not because he's dead, is it?'

'No, life or death has got nothing to do with it. James Dean has been dead for over twenty years, you know, and when I see one of his old films I still go weak at the knees.'

'So what did Mark Cotton do to offend you?'

'He didn't so much offend me as shatter all my illusions,' Elaine Rodgers said.

'Tell me about it,' Crane invited.

'Well, I thought all my birthdays had come at once when the manager told us that he would be staying here,' Elaine said. 'Of course, we were instructed not to bother him – we were told that we couldn't even mention the fact that he was staying here to anyone from outside the hotel – but the possibility of just seeing him every day was enough to make me positively giddy.'

'And *did* you see him every day?'

'No, for the first four days, I didn't see him at all, but he was there, all right – room service told me that – so he must have been slipping in through the staff entrance.'

Thus both evading his fans and maintaining his image as a humble actor who was trying to go back to his roots, Crane thought.

'I take it that you did get to see Cotton eventually,' he said.

'That's right. It was Friday lunchtime. He was wearing a hat and a muffler, and if I hadn't known he was staying in the hotel and been on the lookout for him, I probably wouldn't have spotted him at all.'

'You're sure it was him.'

'I'm positive.'

'So what happened next?'

'He stood there, watching the lifts. When one of the lifts arrived, this blonde woman, who'd been hanging about for quite some time, stepped into it. But Mark Cotton didn't follow immediately. He waited until the doors had started closing before he got it. And that's what burst my bubble.'

'I think you'll have to explain that,' Crane admitted.

'Typical man,' Elaine said. 'I've given you all the facts, but you still can't see it from a woman's point of view, can you?'

And then she smiled – to show he should not take the criticism too much to heart.

Crane smiled back.

'So what should I have seen?' he asked.

'This is the 1970s, and I've nothing against people having affairs, as long as neither of them is married,' Elaine explained, 'but the men should show some respect for the women they're having the affair with. And that wasn't respect – it was almost as if he was ashamed to be seen with her, which, as far as I'm concerned, means he was treating her little better than he'd have treated a prostitute. Well, you can't have under-the-blanket fantasies about an insensitive brute like that, can you? And that's why I'm now an ex-fan.'

Crane took a photograph out of his pocket, and slid it across the desk to Elaine.

'Is that the woman who was waiting by the lift shaft?' he asked.

'Yes, that's her,' Elaine confirmed.

So the boss had been right in her suspicions, and Mark Cotton and Lucy Cavendish *had* reignited their affair.

'I don't know if it's important, but there was another woman, as well,' Elaine said.

Crane felt the hairs on his neck tingle.

'Who was she?' he asked.

'I don't know. I'd never seen her before. I don't even know exactly when she came into the lobby, except that it must have been after he did. All I can say with any certainty was that I first noticed her when the lift doors closed.'

'And what was she doing?'

'She was standing there, absolutely rigid, and staring at the lift. She looked so angry that I was half-surprised her gaze didn't melt it.'

Crane took two more photographs out of his pocket, and passed them to Elaine.

'It wasn't, by any chance, either of these women that you saw, was it?' he asked.

Elaine studied the photographs for no more than a couple of seconds. Then she said, 'It was her.'

'Are you sure?' Crane asked. 'They are quite alike, because they happen to be sisters.'

'It was her,' Elaine said, even more definitely.

Well, well, well, Crane thought, and wondered if Mark Cotton had known he was being followed by Sarah Audley.

He rather suspected that Cotton hadn't.

'If you don't mind, I'd like to ask you the same question as I've asked all the others,' Paniatowski said, when the usual opening inquiries had drawn what had become the usual negative responses. 'Why did you decide to come back to Whitebridge, Mr McCann?'

'Nostalgia,' Phil McCann replied.

'But you're a bank manager.'

'An *assistant* bank manager – but hopefully, only for the moment,'

McCann said, with a smile. 'And surely, even assistant bank managers are allowed to revel in their pasts now and again.'

'The thing is, you seem to have gone to a great deal of trouble over the whole deal,' Paniatowski said.

'You're quite wrong about that. In fact, it was very little trouble at all. My manager was more than happy to give me two weeks' leave, my wife and children assured me they could manage perfectly well without me for a fortnight – all I had to do was buy the ticket and get on the train.'

'No, I'm talking about the time *before* that.'

'I beg your pardon?'

'How often have you seen the rest of the Whitebridge Theatre Company over the last twenty years?'

'I haven't seen them all. After I left here in 'fifty-seven, the first thing I did was to enrol in a technical college so I'd have a few more qualifications behind me. And after I'd got those qualifications, I joined the bank.'

'So you haven't seen any of them between the time you left Whitebridge and the time you came back?'

It was a trap, but Phil McCann was too wily to fall into it.

'As it happens, I have seen several of the company within the last month or so,' he said.

'In fact, you've seen *all* of them, with the exception of Mark Cotton and Ruth Audley,' Meadows said.

'Yes, that's right.'

'And you saw them on their territory, rather than your own.'

'I've never thought of it that way, but I suppose you're right about that, too.'

'Specifically, from your base in Hereford, you travelled down to London to see Jerry Talbot, across to Lincolnshire to talk to Tony Brown, down to London a second time to see Lucy Cavendish . . .'

'Yes, yes, I agree that I went to see them, rather than them coming to see me,' McCann conceded.

'The reason for your visits was to try and persuade the rest of the original cast to come to Whitebridge, and some of them – like Jerry Talbot and Tony Brown – needed quite a lot of persuading. So what was that all about?'

'What are you suggesting?' McCann demanded.

'I could be suggesting all kinds of things,' Paniatowski said. 'I could be suggesting that you'd decided to kill Mark Cotton, and, for some reason of your own, you wanted all the cast there to see it. I could be suggesting that you had something else – something entirely different – planned, but Cotton's death got in the way of it. But, in fact, I'm not suggesting *anything*, because I'm hoping that you'll explain to me what was motivating you.'

McCann folded his arms. 'I enjoy setting things up and negotiating deals – that's why I'm so good at my job,' he said. 'You probably wouldn't understand this, but I got almost as much pleasure from persuading people to come as I did from seeing them here.'

It all sounded very plausible, Paniatowski thought, but she was convinced he was lying through his teeth.

'Did you get on with Mark Cotton?' she asked.

'I get on with everybody,' McCann replied. 'And if you don't believe me, just ask the rest of the cast.'

'Sergeant Parry?' Beresford asked.

'I used to be,' the man on the end of the line said, his voice heavy with regret. 'Now I'm just plain Jim.'

'I'm DI Beresford, from the Mid Lancs Police. I've been told by a Sergeant Lloyd that you might have some information relevant to the murder we're currently investigating.'

'I have,' Parry confirmed. 'I most definitely have. But if you want it, you'll have to come here, and meet me face-to-face.'

'That would take a great deal of time, and when you're conducting a murder inquiry—' Beresford began.

'Don't try to tell me what a murder inquiry is like, lad, because I've been part of more murder inquiries than you've had hot dinners,' Parry interrupted him. 'Look, I can see it's a problem for you, Inspector,' he continued in a much softer voice. 'I really can. But I've had my fingers badly burned once before – and I'm not going to let it happen again.'

'What do you mean when you say you've had your fingers badly burned?' Beresford asked.

'And to be quite frank with you, lad,' Parry continued, ignoring the question, 'if I told you what I know over the phone, you'd probably end up thinking I was a bit of a nutter. That's why you need to be down here – looking into my eyes – when I tell you.'

'If you could give me some idea of what kind of information you have . . .' Beresford cajoled.

'Sorry, son, that's as far as I'm prepared to go for now,' Parry said. 'My address is thirteen Elm Drive, Hinton. I'll give up the idea of golf tomorrow, and wait in for you. If you come, I'll tell you what I know. If you don't come – well, it will be you that's missing out, not me.'

SEVENTEEN

T here were things which would have amazed the regular drinkers in the public bar of the Drum and Monkey more – Noah's Ark, floating sedately down the Whitebridge canal, while a dozen trombone-playing chimpanzees stood on the deck giving their rendition of the show-stoppers of the 1940s, would be just one example – but the emptiness of the corner table was certainly well worth raising a quizzical eyebrow over.

There'd been a murder – right? they asked each other, as they took thoughtful sips from their pints of best bitter.

Right.

And DCI Paniatowski was heading the inquiry – right?

Right.

So where was her team?

And what was Terry the waiter supposed to do with the time that was normally employed in ferrying two pints of best bitter, a glass of vodka, and a bottle of tonic water over to the corner table at regular intervals?

Then, looking around them, the locals began to notice several strangers who were wearing expensive suits and seemed very uncomfortable in the spit-and-sawdust atmosphere of the public bar – and they understood.

The big clock on the wall clicked off the minutes, the men in the smart suits grew more and more restless, and eventually one of them crossed the room and sat down at a table occupied by two men from the carpet warehouse.

'I hope you don't mind the intrusion, but I'd like to buy you both a drink,' he said.

The two warehousemen looked at each other, and nodded.

'Fair enough,' the older one said. 'We're on pints of best bitter and Irish whiskey chasers.'

The journalist could find no evidence of whiskey chasers on the table, but thought it best not to argue, and signalled to the waiter.

'I was told DCI Paniatowski always puts in an appearance in this bar when she's working on a case,' he said, once the drinks had arrived.

'She *usually* puts in an appearance,' the older warehouseman agreed, 'but then once in a while – for the sake of a bit of variety like – she takes her team out of town.'

'Do you know where they go, when they do that?'

'They go to the Flying Fox in Accrington, don't they, Sid?' the older warehouseman asked his companion.

'That's right, Albert, they do,' the other man agreed.

The journalist stood up.

'Thanks for the information,' he said, and moved hurriedly to the door.

His place at the table was soon taken by a second journalist.

'Do you want to know where to find DCI Paniatowski?' Albert asked, 'because if you do, it'll cost you the same as it cost your mate.'

The drinks were duly ordered.

'Tell him, Sid,' Albert said.

'They'll be at the Bull's Head in Preston,' Sid said.

It took ten minutes to clear the bar of reporters, and as the last one left, the warehousemen looked down at the table weighed down by pints and chasers. It was going to be heavy work clearing that lot, they thought, but they were confident they were up to the job.

There was no draft beer pump in the theatre, so Beresford and Crane were forced to lower their standards by not only settling for bottled beer, but also – to their great discomfort – drinking it out of *half pint* glasses.

'And ale – any ale – just doesn't taste *right* out of a half pint glass,' Beresford complained.

'Count yourself lucky that you can drink at all,' Paniatowski said waspishly, gently rubbing her stomach. 'Do you think it would be alright with the two of you if we did a bit of police work now?'

Beresford and Crane agreed that it would be alright and that, indeed, that was what they were there for.

'Let's start with motive,' Paniatowski suggested. 'Assuming, for the moment, that Mark Cotton *was* the intended victim, rather than Jerry Talbot, who would have wanted him dead?'

'The most obvious candidate is Jerry Talbot himself,' Beresford said. 'If he knew in advance that Cotton was planning to snatch the starring role off him on Monday night, he might well have been angry enough to decide to kill him. And since he's been under-studying the part, he'd know more about the rope and harness than the rest of the cast.'

'Who else?'

'Sarah Audley,' Meadows said. 'She was in love with Mark Cotton twenty years ago, and he rejected her. She thought she'd got over it, but then she saw him again and realized she hadn't.'

'And what made matters worse was that she saw Cotton going into the Royal Victoria with Lucy Cavendish,' Crane said.

'But surely she realized that if she killed him, she'd also be killing off her part in DCI Prince,' Paniatowski said.

'Love is blind, and so is hate,' Meadows said. 'Besides, remember what Sarah's sister Ruth said. It went something along the lines of, "Actors are self-confident. They have to be to survive – so some of them will automatically assume that, with a massive talent like theirs, they'll overcome any obstacle." In other words, losing the series might be a setback for her career, but it wouldn't neces-sarily destroy it.'

Beresford had been unsure what to do about Sergeant Parry, but now he reached a decision.

'I may have more on Sarah tomorrow, because – with your permission, boss – I'm going down to Sussex to interview an ex-police officer about her.'

'Is that really necessary?' Paniatowski asked.

Beresford told her about his conversation with Parry.

'It could be nothing,' he said in conclusion. 'It probably *is* nothing. But Parry truly believes he's on to something, and it's too risky to overlook the possibility that he might be right.'

'Do you intend to contact the Sussex Constabulary while you're down there?' Paniatowski asked.

'I don't think so – at least, not until after I've talked to Sergeant Parry,' Beresford replied. 'I get the feeling that there's no love lost between Parry and the local force, and I don't want to do anything to piss him off until I've heard what he has to say.'

'Fair enough,' Paniatowski agreed. She turned to the rest of the team. 'What other possibilities do we have?'

'Ruth Audley,' Meadows said.

'You'd pretty much dismissed her as a suspect this afternoon,' Paniatowski reminded her. 'What's made you drag her back into the frame?'

'Talking to her sister helped give me a more rounded picture of her. She's very protective of Sarah. She got her into the company when she was only seventeen, she took the burden of looking after their mother on her own shoulders, so Sarah could be free to pursue her career, and the only reason she's in Whitebridge at all is because Sarah asked her to come. I think it's perfectly possible that she saw how Cotton was making her little sister suffer, and decided to punish him for it.'

'Who else?' Paniatowski asked.

'Geoff Turnbull,' Crane said. 'He was bitterly disappointed that he was not allowed to direct, and may have decided to take his revenge in the appropriate theatrical manner. The same also applies to his wife, Joan.'

'Lucy Cavendish,' Meadows said. 'She's desperate to be back into the theatre, so there's a good chance she only slept with Cotton because he'd promised her the leading role if she'd spread her legs for him. But then he reneged on his promise. Besides, if she'd nothing to worry about, why did she bring her solicitor up from London?'

'True,' Paniatowski agreed.

'And then there's Tony Brown and Phil McCann,' Meadows said. 'There's no motive I can ascribe to either of them, but they both acted suspiciously. Brown clearly didn't want to be here, but he came – even though it cost him money. And McCann went to considerable effort to make sure everyone turned up, possibly because – as Jack suggested – he wanted the right audience for the murder.'

Beresford smiled. 'You've left out Bradley Quirk,' he said.

'Quirk is the only member of the cast who's pointed the finger at one of the others,' Meadows said. 'We were ready to eliminate Talbot as a suspect when Quirk told us about the play they'd once been in together, and how that might have given Talbot the idea of making it look like it was an attempt on *his* life. Besides, Quirk is far more relaxed about the investigation than anyone should be, which means – in my opinion – that what he's really doing is playing a part, and the question we have to ask ourselves is *why* he's playing that part.'

'I've suddenly realized this is just like *Murder on the Orient Express*,' Crane said, out of the blue.

The others looked at him blankly.

'*Murder on the Orient Express*!' he repeated. 'Written by Agatha Christie! You must have read it.'

None of them had.

'And I'm a little surprised that an intellectual giant like you has bothered to read it, Jack,' Meadows said.

'When I was up at Oxford, I once gave a paper on the way in which the detective genre can manipulate plausibility,' Crane explained. 'It was one of the books I used as an example.'

'So are you going to tell us why this is like *Murder on the Orient Express*?' Meadows asked.

'A man is killed on the Orient Express between stations, which means that the murderer still has to be on the train, just as our murderer still had to be in the theatre. There are twelve suspects and they all have a strong motive – just as our suspects have strong motives – and the victim died of twelve stab wounds.'

'They all did it together,' Beresford said.

'Exactly!' Crane said.

'You do *know* that's a completely made-up story, don't you, Jack?' Paniatowski asked.

Crane grinned. 'Of course, boss.'

'And you don't really think that all the actors conspired together to kill Mark Cotton, do you?'

'No, I don't,' Crane said, more serious now. 'From what I've seen of the Whitebridge Players on the documentary film, there was so much disagreement and backbiting going on that it's a miracle they managed to put on the play at all. So the idea that they'd ever be able to cooperate with each other long enough to stage a murder is laughable.'

Paniatowski smiled. 'Good,' she said. 'Now I'd like to move on. What you've all said about motive has been very sound, but I think there's one suspect we can at least move *towards* eliminating from the inquiry.'

'Who's that, boss?' Beresford asked.

'Jerry Talbot.'

'And you think you can eliminate him because . . .?'

'I think I can eliminate him because there was greasepaint on the metal steps that lead up to the platform.'

Paniatowski laid out her theory, the seeds of which had been planted by something Ruth Audley had said during her interview, and which had been slowly developing in her head for most of the afternoon.

When she'd finished, Meadows said, 'That makes complete sense to me, boss. I never was very keen on the idea that the killer had put the greasepaint on the step so that Cotton wouldn't have time to examine the harness properly.'

'But you'll need to get that confirmed by Talbot himself before you can be absolutely sure,' Beresford pointed out.

'I will – first thing in the morning,' Paniatowski said. 'And in the meantime, while we can't quite cross Jerry Talbot's name off our list, we can at least put a pencil mark through it. Are we in agreement on that?'

The rest of the team nodded.

'Right, moving on again,' Paniatowski continued. 'One of the crucial questions that we need to ask ourselves is why Mark Cotton was killed on *Monday* night. Jack thinks the murderer wanted an audience for his crime because that would make his revenge all the sweeter, and I think he's probably right about that. But it would have been a better audience – and hence an even sweeter revenge – on Tuesday night.'

'Better?' Beresford asked.

'More important,' Paniatowski clarified. 'No one famous was booked to watch on Monday night, because Jerry Talbot – who was a nobody in the acting world – was playing the main role. Tuesday was a different matter – Mark Cotton would have been centre stage. The critics were coming up from London, as were several well-known names in the entertainment world. If the murderer wanted to make a real splash, that would have been the night to do it. Yet instead, he chooses Monday night.'

'Which was a gamble, because even though he knew Cotton was an egomaniac, there was always a chance he'd allow Talbot to play Hieronimo on Monday, just as he'd promised he would,' Beresford said.

'I don't think it was a gamble at all,' Meadows said. 'It couldn't have been, because the murderer knew that he only had one chance to kill Mark Cotton in the way he *wanted* him to be killed, and given that everything else was so meticulously planned, I'm sure he also did something to make certain that Cotton *would* play Hieronimo.'

'Like what?' Crane asked.

'Well, there you've got me,' Meadows admitted.

'So why *did* the killer decide to strike on Monday night rather than waiting until Tuesday?' Crane asked. 'What made him decide he *had to* do it then?'

'If we knew that, it would probably be obvious who the killer was,' Paniatowski said.

She looked at her watch and saw it was eleven twenty. So it hadn't just felt like a long day – it had actually been one.

'Right, that's it,' she told her team. 'Kate, we'll start re-interviewing first thing in the morning. Jack, it's back to the monitors for you. And Colin – I'll see you when I see you.'

Paniatowski looked up and down the street. The mourning fans had started to drift away once darkness had begun to fall, and the police barriers had been removed shortly after seven. Now, everything was almost back to normal, with only the high mound of rapidly perishing flowers along the theatre wall to suggest that anything extraordinary had happened there.

She turned to the left, and when the constable on duty in front of the boarding house saw the bulky figure waddling towards him, he clicked his heels together and saluted smartly.

'Good evening, ma'am,' he said.

'Good evening, Constable . . .?'

'Johnson, ma'am.'

'Well, then, Constable Johnson, do you have anything to report?'

'Nothing of earth-shattering significance, ma'am. There were a few journalists sniffing round earlier, but when I made it plain to them that I could neither be bought nor charmed, they cleared off.'

'What have the actors been doing?'

The constable produced his notebook and moved to the edge of the pavement, where there was a street light.

'A couple of the women – Ruth and Sarah Audley – went out shopping in the late afternoon,' he said, 'and three of the men – Brown, Quirk and Talbot – went to the pub in the evening.'

'Together?'

'Quirk and Brown together, but Talbot went alone.'

'What state were they in when they got back?'

'You could tell they'd all been drinking, but only Talbot looked *really* the worse for wear.'

'And now they're all inside?'

'Yes, ma'am. The first bedroom light went off at ten fifteen, and by a quarter to eleven, all the rooms were in darkness. There's not much of the glamour of show business about that, is there, ma'am?'

No, there wasn't, Paniatowski agreed. She wondered if the murderer was lying awake in the darkness, bathed in sweat. It was perfectly possible. But she had also known killers who could sleep like a baby with their victims lying dead in the next room.

'When are you due to be relieved, Constable Johnson?' she asked

'At midnight, ma'am.'

'Then please tell your replacement that I want to see . . .'

Who *did* she want to see? Which one of the actors might actually have something useful to tell her?

'. . . tell him that I want to see Phil McCann, in the theatre, at nine o'clock sharp.'

'Will do, ma'am,' the constable promised, and she turned to walk away, he added, 'Good luck with the baby, ma'am.'

'Thank you,' Paniatowski said, realizing he'd meant well, but still wishing he hadn't spoken.

She *knew* she was pregnant – she was becoming more painfully aware of it every day – so why did nearly everyone she met feel a need to bloody well remind her of the fact?

EIGHTEEN

30th March 1977

I t was just after seven in the morning when Florrie Hodge left her kitchen – holding a tray on which she'd placed a small teapot, a cup, a milk jug, a soft-boiled egg and two rounds of toast – and began to ascend the stairs.

At the landing at the top of the first flight of stairs, Florrie stopped to catch her breath. Normally, she didn't offer her paying guests any room service – they all had their breakfast in the dining room, like civilized people – but she was making an exception for Bradley Quirk.

Bradley was such a *nice* boy. But he could be a *naughty* boy, too, and for the last two mornings he had missed breakfast completely – which was not good for him at all. Thus, Florrie was determined that that morning he would have a proper start to the day, even if it did entail her taking what was starting to feel like quite a heavy tray up two lots of stairs.

When she reached the second landing, Florrie put the tray down on a small table, and took her comb out of her nylon overall pocket.

It was silly for a woman of her age to care about how she looked in the eyes of a young man like him, she thought as she ran the comb through her hair, but you should always strive to make the best of yourself, and she was sure that he appreciated her making the effort.

She picked up the tray again, and knocked on the door.

'Breakfast, Mr Quirk,' she called out. 'Are you decent?'

She heard a giggle, and realized it came from her.

You daft old bat, she rebuked herself affectionately.

She knocked again.

'Mr Quirk?'

There was still no answer.

'Well, I'm coming in, ready or not.'

She turned the knob with her free hand, and pushed the door gently open with her left foot.

And then she dropped the tray and starting screaming.

Bradley Quirk was naked, lying face down on his bedroom floor. The back of his head had been smashed in, and the resultant mess was enough to put anyone not used to such displays of gore off their food for several days.

Dr Shastri *was* used to it. For her, this was just another day at the office, and as she looked down at the corpse she was even humming to herself.

'The attack will have occurred at least two feet from where he is lying now,' she told Monika Paniatowski. 'The force of the blow will have thrown his body forwards. With this amount of damage, I would be surprised if death was not instantaneous.'

'We think we have the murder weapon,' Paniatowski told her,

holding out a metal statue about eighteen inches long and pointing to the blood that was sticking to its base. 'Could this have done the job?'

'Indeed,' Shastri said. 'It would have been more than adequate. Do you think your murderer brought it with him, or was it already here?'

'It was here. It's called Oscar. Quirk's landlady says he takes it everywhere with him.'

'Oscar?' Shastri said. 'It does not look much like the one I expect to win for my screenplay about a simple Indian doctor who is forever being bullied by insensitive police officers.'

'It's Oscar Wilde,' Paniatowski explained.

'Ah!'

'Is a woman capable of striking a blow with that much force?' Paniatowski asked.

'It's unlikely, but not impossible. Women are capable of great feats of physical strength if they are driven by a strong enough emotion, and while I am not saying that is the case here, it is certainly evident that whoever killed Bradley Quirk was rather cross with him.'

'How long has he been dead?' Paniatowski asked.

'Not less than two hours, and not more than four.'

Paniatowski looked down at her watch.

'Listen, Doc,' she said, 'I—'

'You need the results of the postt-mortem as soon as possible?' Shastri interrupted her.

'Yes.'

Shastri smiled. 'Now that is something I do not think I have *ever* heard you say before.'

Jack Crane and Kate Meadows were standing out in the street, just in front of the boarding house.

'The boss was worried about the press gaining access during the night, so she had uniforms posted permanently on both the front door and the back door,' Meadows said.

'So it seems I was wrong,' Crane mused. 'This isn't *Murder on the Orient Express* at all – it's actually *And Then There Were None.*'

'That's another Agatha Christie, is it?'

'Yes, there are these ten people on an island, completely cut off from the world, and one of them is murdered. Then a second person is murdered, and then a third—'

'Fascinating,' Meadows interrupted him, 'but if I was you, I wouldn't mention your latest flight of fancy to the boss.'

And almost as if she'd been waiting for her cue, Paniatowski appeared in the doorway.

'Get on to Inspector Beresford, and tell him that what I want him to do, right away, is . . .' She stopped herself. 'Shit, Colin isn't here, is he?'

'No, boss.'

'Do we know when he'll be returning?'

'He's hoping it will be sometime today.'

'How can we contact him?'

'We could leave a message at this Sergeant Parry's house, I suppose, but he won't get that until he's in Sussex.'

'Damn, bugger, sod it!' Paniatowski said – and wished she had a cigarette. 'In that case, forget DI Beresford.' She turned to Crane. 'Jack, you're going to have to take over from me as Kate's sidekick in the interviews for a while.'

'But . . . but I've never been part of formal interrogation before,' Crane protested.

And if I could get hold of Colin Beresford, you wouldn't be part of one now, Paniatowski thought.

But aloud, she said, 'You'll be fine.'

'Wouldn't you rather do it yourself?' Crane asked, still unconvinced.

'Well, of course I'd rather do it myself,' Paniatowski said irritably. 'But now the shit's hit the fan, I'll be so busy fielding the flak that there'll be no time left over for doing proper police work.'

Beresford had studied the railway timetable with great care, and had been quietly proud of his efficiency in planning a route which was at least an hour shorter than any other he might have taken.

What he hadn't planned for – what no one could have planned for – was that a goods train would come off the rails somewhere between Crewe and Birmingham, and that, as a result, the train he was travelling on would be sent on a long country excursion. And it wasn't just long – it was slow. Even the sheep seemed to be moving faster than they were, and half the time the train was not even crawling along, but was waiting in railway sidings for other – luckier – trains to pass.

It had been a mistake to ever embark on this particular expedition, he fretted as the minutes ticked away. Sergeant Parry was probably no more than a nutty old man with a grudge, and he'd have been far better getting whatever he could out of the Sussex Constabulary over the phone, and leaving it at that. Yet having already wasted so much time, he supposed he might as well stick to his original plan.

If he had been Jack Crane, he might well have quoted directly from the 'Scottish Play': 'I am in blood stepp'd in so far that, should I wade no more, returning were as tedious as go o'er.'

But he wasn't Jack Crane, and he didn't.

The chief constable picked up a paper clip, examined it for a second, and then embarked on the task of straightening it out.

'This is a terrible mess that you've landed in, Monika,' he said. 'Really quite awful.'

Well, at least he hadn't said, This is a terrible mess you've landed *yourself* in, Monika, Paniatowski thought.

'No one went in or out of the boarding house during the night, sir,' she said. 'And that means that if we exclude the old landlady from our inquiries, the murderer can be only one of six people.'

'And is it your opinion that that person was also responsible for Mark Cotton's death?'

'It's more than likely,' Paniatowski said.

But it was also possible that either Geoff or Joan Turnbull killed Cotton, she thought. Or – even worse – that Bradley Quirk had killed him, in which case there would never be a satisfactory conclusion to the Mark Cotton case.

'I think I should bring in a second team to investigate the second murder,' Pickering said.

'I really don't think that's a very good idea, sir,' Paniatowski cautioned. 'Since both teams would be questioning the same people, we'd be constantly tripping over each other.'

'Then perhaps the new team could take over both murders,' Pickering suggested.

She had never wanted this case, and the chief constable was offering her a way out. But if she went now, she would forever be the woman who *didn't* solve the murder of the handsome DCI Prince.

'It would take me nearly all day to brief the new team, and that would be a day wasted,' she said.

Pickering wavered. 'Are you prepared to give a press conference in which you, as the officer in charge of the case, announce there has been a second murder?' he said finally.

He wasn't looking for a scapegoat – she was sure of that – but what he *was* doing was setting out his pieces on the board in such a way that if a scapegoat *did* eventually become necessary, she would be the logical choice.

She didn't like the idea much, but if that was his price – and clearly it was – then she was willing to pay it.

'Yes, I'll do the press conference,' she said.

'Excellent,' the chief constable replied – perhaps just a little *too* enthusiastically.

Meadows and Crane were sitting in the police canteen, and Meadows was examining the package she had just received from New Scotland Yard.

'How many of the Whitebridge Players do have criminal records?' Crane asked.

'Much to my disappointment, it seems to be just the one,' Meadows said, shaking the envelope as if hoping that something else would fall out.

'And which one is it?' Crane asked.

Meadows handed him the folder.

'Oh,' Crane said, 'that is a surprise.'

'You men!' Meadows said, in mock disgust. 'You're always such suckers for a pretty face, aren't you?' She stood up. 'Right, are you about ready to lose your virginity on the interview table, Jack?'

'Lose my . . .' Crane gasped. Then he smiled and said, 'Ah, now I see what you mean.'

'That's another thing about men,' Meadows said. 'The mention of virginity nearly always makes them break out into a hot flush.'

Paniatowski felt as if she was having a hot flush under the lights of the press conference, but she was not sure whether to put that down to the difficult position she now found herself in as a senior police officer, or to the child who was quite clearly trying to kick his way out of her womb.

She cleared her throat and switched on her microphone.

'Good morning, ladies and gentlemen,' she said. 'I am Detective Chief Inspector Monika Paniatowski of the Mid Lancs Police. The gentleman on my left is the chief constable, Mr Pickering, and the one on my right is Chief Superintendent Holmes. I will first make a formal statement, and then answer any questions you might care to put to me.'

She trotted out the usual clichés on the Mark Cotton murder – the police were following several strong leads, they could not promise an arrest in the next day or so, but they were certainly expecting to make one at some point in the future . . . blah, blah, blah.

And then she came to the big one.

'At seven o'clock this morning, the body of a forty-four-year-old man was discovered in the boarding establishment two houses down from the theatre. His skull had been crushed by a small metal statue, which has since been identified as being his own personal property. We are treating the death as murder, and an investigation has been opened.'

The assembled reporters sat in shocked silence for a moment, and then an almost-ecstatic expression came to most of their faces as they realized that a story which was already very meaty had just got juicier.

'I'll take questions now,' Paniatowski said.

'Are the two murders related?' someone asked.

'For the moment, we simply don't know,' Paniatowski replied. 'On the one hand, the two victims both knew each other well and worked together, but on the other, while the first murder was carefully planned, the second shows all the signs of being spontaneous.'

'Do you have a prime suspect?' another reporter asked.

We have six of them, Paniatowski thought.

'I'm afraid that I can't go into any of the operational details at this stage,' she said.

'I'm really rather worried about you, Chief Inspector Paniatowski,' said a third reporter, a woman called Claire Hitchens, who worked for one of the more sensational daily newspapers and was widely known as Hitch the Bitch.

'Worried about me, Miss Hitchens?' Paniatowski repeated, in a puzzled voice.

'Yes. This is clearly a very difficult case which requires the full attention of the person in charge, and to have assigned it to a woman who is on the verge of giving birth – and thus has many other things on her mind – is bizarre. Frankly speaking, it doesn't seem fair on you.'

It was a brilliant tactic, Paniatowski thought. If Hitchens had attacked her for being incompetent as a result of her pregnancy, public opinion – and the rest of the reporters – would have turned on her. But by *defending* the DCI's incompetence on the grounds that she was pregnant, she had got her message across without inviting any condemnation.

Paniatowski turned to the chief constable.

'Since that seems to be a direct criticism of you, sir, would you care to be the one to respond?' she said.

'I wasn't . . . I never intended to . . .' Claire Hitchens said, as she realized that though she'd planned to blast Paniatowski with both barrels, the chief inspector had managed to twist things around in such a way that she'd ended up shooting herself in the foot.

'DCI Paniatowski is one of the most outstanding detectives I have ever been fortunate enough to work with,' Pickering said. 'She is also one of the most disciplined. When she feels she can no longer handle her workload to her own exacting high standards, she will hand the case over to her highly-trained team, but in the meantime, she is giving it one hundred per cent of her attention.'

Louisa held her thumb up to the television screen in approval.

'Nicely handled, Mum,' she said.

She was at home because it was one of the perks of being in the Sixth Form that she needn't be in school if she didn't have classes scheduled – and, in her opinion, there was no point in having a perk if you didn't exercise it.

The implicit understanding behind the granting of this freedom had been that the students would use their time at home to study independently, and the two books on her lap were ample proof that Louisa was following the letter – if not quite the spirit – of the law.

She picked up one of the books now.

'If you intend to bottle-feed your child, then it is essential to purchase at least two bottles,' she read. 'It is most important that both these bottles be carefully sterilized . . .'

The baby would be arriving soon, she thought, and it was vital that at least one member of the family knew what to do, because her mother – for all that she might be an 'outstanding' detective, and had even got *a little* better at playing office politics – wouldn't have a clue.

*   *   *

The inhabitants of the boarding house could no longer be regarded as witnesses who might eventually be upgraded to suspects. They – and *only* they – had been in the establishment when Bradley Quirk had breathed his last, which meant that they had obtained an automatic upgrade, and henceforth would be interviewed in Whitebridge Police headquarters, where their interviews could be recorded and their reactions observed through a two-way mirror.

The first of the suspects to be interviewed was Lucy Cavendish, and when she was shown into Interview Room B, she was, as expected, accompanied by her solicitor. She also had her right arm in a sling, which *wasn't* expected, but, given the nature of her companion, *should have* been.

'What happened to your arm?' Meadows asked.

'My client suffered a fall in her room last night, and sprained her wrist as a result,' the solicitor said.

'When did this fall occur?'

'Around eight o'clock.'

'And did she receive medical treatment immediately?'

'No, it was only when I saw she was in obvious pain this morning that I advised her to go to the doctor.'

'It's all rather convenient, isn't it?' Meadows asked.

The solicitor tapped his briefcase. 'I have a medical certificate here. Would you like to see it?'

Meadows sighed. 'Since I'm sure you chose the *right* doctor, there wouldn't be much point, would there?'

'Just what are you suggesting when you say the *right* doctor?' the solicitor demanded.

'I mean the best available, of course,' Meadows said innocently. She turned her attention to Lucy Cavendish. 'I'm going to ask you some purely factual questions, and even though you have your expensive mouthpiece here, I'd appreciate it if you'd answer them yourself. All right?'

'We'll see how it goes,' Lucy Cavendish said.

'Could you give me some idea of the sleeping arrangements in the boarding house?'

'The old crone of a landlady lives on the ground floor,' Lucy Cavendish said. 'Ruth, Sarah, Tony and I have rooms on the first floor, and Jerry, Bradley, Phil and Mark were given rooms on the second. Not that Mark ever used his room – he was living it up in the Royal Victoria.'

'Was there any particular reason why the women were given rooms on the first floor?'

'The landlady thought that the "ladies" would like to be closer to the bathroom. Yes, I know it's disgusting that there's only one bathroom, and that we're all forced to share it, but, you see, we're here in Whitebridge to relive our glorious past.'

'One last question,' Meadows said. 'Did you hear anyone either going up, or coming down, the stairs that connect the second and third floors, between the hours of ten last night and five this morning?'

'No,' Lucy Cavendish replied. 'I didn't hear a thing. As a matter of fact, I slept like a log.'

'Which can have been no mean feat, considering.'

'Considering?' the solicitor repeated. 'What exactly are you implying this time?'

'My goodness, you're certainly earning your money today, aren't you, Mr Graves?' Meadows said. 'All I meant was that, considering the amount of pain she must have been in, it is quite amazing that Miss Cavendish slept so well.' She checked her watch. 'Interview concluded at eleven-oh-seven,' she told the microphone, and switched off the recorder.

'Is that it?' Lucy Cavendish asked, surprised.

'That's it,' Meadows agreed.

Lucy Cavendish and her solicitor stood up.

'I do have one more question before you go,' Meadows said, 'but it's more to do with my own curiosity than the murder case. And it's this – why do you always have your solicitor with you? He probably says he needs to be here – why wouldn't he, when he's making a small fortune out of you? – but I'm surprised that a smart girl like you allows herself to be taken for a mug.'

'I'm not being taken for a mug,' Lucy Cavendish said angrily. 'Maurice is here to stop me from being fitted up.'

'Shut up, Lucy,' the solicitor said.

'Why would you think we'd try to fit you up?' Meadows wondered. 'Have the police fitted you up before?'

'No comment,' Lucy Cavendish said.

'She must be referring to what happened down in London,' Meadows told Crane – who already knew. 'You see, Lucy runs this boarding house for young actresses. I call them "actresses" out of politeness, though none of them have an Equity card . . .'

'What's an Equity card?' asked Crane, slipping easily into the role of gormless sidekick.

'It's what the actors' trade union – Equity – issues to its members,' Meadows explained. 'You can't usually get an acting job without it. Fortunately for these young "actresses", they don't need that kind of work, because they are often visited by very generous gentlemen friends.'

'All charges were dropped!' Lucy Cavendish said.

'Yes, Maurice did a good job there,' Meadows agreed.

The solicitor opened the door.

'We're leaving, Lucy,' he said. 'We're leaving *now*!'

'I wonder how Equity would feel about having Lucy as a member if it knew she was running a brothel,' Meadows mused.

'You wouldn't tell them, would you?' Lucy Cavendish gasped.

'Me?' Meadows replied, shaking her head. 'No, of course I wouldn't. As much as I'd like to shop you to your union as payback for the way you've pissed us around in the course of this investigation, I'm a police officer who has gained the information from official sources, and hence I wouldn't be allowed to use it for any such purpose.'

'Thank God for that,' Lucy Cavendish said.

Meadows smiled. 'But it wouldn't *entirely* surprise me if someone else – somebody who couldn't possibly be traced back to me – did inform them anonymously.'

'I enjoyed that,' Meadows said, when Lucy Cavendish and her solicitor had gone. 'But it's a big step from running a brothel and trying to sleep your way into acting roles to becoming a killer, so while we can't entirely rule Lucy out, I really don't think she's guilty.'

'Neither do I,' Crane agreed.

'Who are we seeing next?'

'Phil McCann.'

'Well, unless he heard something last night, that will be a waste of time too,' Meadows said.

'Are you ruling him out as well?' Crane asked, surprised.

'Pretty much.'

'On what basis?'

'On the basis of the notes that Shagger Beresford took while he was talking to a chief inspector in the Herefordshire Police.'

Meadows slid a single sheet of paper across to Crane. 'Colin must be the most literal bobby in the whole of Lancashire, but that can be an advantage sometimes.'

Crane scanned the notes.

Assistant bank manager . . . plays very active role in the commu-nity . . . runs amateur theatre group in which his daughter is one of the stars . . . member of the Rotary Club . . .

'What does that tell you?' Meadows asked.

'Not much,' Crane admitted. 'What does it tell you?'

'It tells me that Phil McCann is far too boring to be a murderer, and what leads me to that conclusion is that I also think it tells me why he spent so much time and effort persuading all the others to attend this reunion,' Meadows said.

NINETEEN

To reach Sergeant Parry's house in deepest Sussex, Beresford had had to take three trains and hire two expensive taxis, but finally he was there, sitting in the sergeant's living room.

Parry did not look like the crank or weirdo that Beresford had been half-expecting to find. He was, in fact, a perfectly average-looking man in his late-fifties, living in a perfectly ordinary semi-detached house which was probably furnished in much the same way as every other house in the street.

But there was one thing which seemed to strike a slightly discordant note – his living room seemed to be overrun with felines.

'How many cats do you own?' Beresford asked.

Parry smiled. 'You don't own cats,' he said, 'they own you, but I suppose what you really meant is how many cats do I share my roof with, and the answer to that is seven.'

'It seems rather a lot,' Beresford said.

'My wife and I got a cat when we married,' Parry told him. 'We couldn't afford a washing machine or a fridge in those days, but we decided we'd get a little black kitten. We called her Suzie. Ellen – that was what my wife was called – loved that little kitten, and so did I.'

Beresford noticed the use of the past tense.

'Did your wife die?' he asked gently.

'She did. We'd only been married eighteen months when she got cancer. It wasn't an easy death.'

'I'm so sorry,' Beresford said.

Parry shrugged. 'These things happen,' he said. 'It still hurts, but it was a long time ago. Anyway, Suzie was a great comfort to me after Ellen died, and I've lived with cats ever since.'

'You never married again?'

Parry shook his head. 'I knew I'd never find another woman like Ellen, so there didn't seem much point.'

He stood up and walked around the room for a few seconds.

'Anyway,' he continued, 'you didn't come here to listen to my sorrows. You'd like to hear what I know about Sarah Audley, wouldn't you?'

'If you don't mind,' Beresford said.

'It all started with a rather major incident at Blackthorn Independent School,' Parry said.

The teacher on playground duty that day is called Miss Hobson. She is a conscientious young woman in her second year of teaching. She is well aware that she is lucky to have got a job at such a prestigious school and is determined to justify the headmistress's confidence in her, so when she hears what sounds like a serious disturbance behind the bike sheds, she immediately resolves to find out what is going on.

A group of pupils from the upper half of the school (both male and female – though mainly male) have formed a circle around some sort of event, and are cheering loudly.

It must be a fight, Miss Hobson tells herself. She is not daunted by the thought. Some of those forming the circle are taller than she is, but they are children and she is a teacher, and when they see her they will immediately yield to her authority.

She reaches the edge of the circle and taps on the shoulder of the boy nearest to her. He is still screaming wild encouragement as he turns, but the moment he sees her face, he falls silent.

It takes only seconds for an awareness of the fact that a teacher has arrived to communicate itself to the rest of the spectators.

The circle breaks up.

The human wall is gone.

And what is left is not two boys covered in snot and blood, but a boy and a girl.

*The girl is lying on the ground with her skirt up to her waist,
and the boy – his trousers pulled down well below his backside – is
lying on top of her.*

*Miss Hallam has been the headmistress of Blackthorn Inde-
pendent School for six years. She sits like a pharaoh at the pinnacle
of school life, and most of the children – quite wisely – live in fear of
her.*

*Now, in her study – her inner sanctum – she is looking across
her desk at a boy and a girl, who are, themselves, examining her
carpet.*

*'What you did was both immoral and disgusting,' she tells them,
'but since you have both reached the age of consent, what you do
in your own time is no concern of mine. What is my concern is that
you chose to carry out your vile act in my school – and in front of
other children, many of whom are much younger than you. So what
have you got to say for yourselves?'*

The two miscreants keep silent.

*'I asked you a question, Desmond Swift, and I expect an answer,'
Miss Hallam says severely.*

The boy raises his head. His eyes are full of tears.

*'I'm sorry, Miss Hallam,' he blubbers. 'I don't know why I did
it. I promise it will never happen again.'*

'And what about you, Sarah Audley?' the headmistress asks.

*Sarah raises her head, but there are no tears in her eyes, only
anger.*

'Screw you, you old bitch!' she says.

That didn't sound at all like the woman who had talked to Monika
about how she would approach her role as a chief inspector in DCI
Prince, Beresford thought. But maybe that had all been an act. After
all, she *was* an actress.

'How are you doing, today, Mr McCann?' Meadows asked.

'Considering that a man who I knew quite well was brutally
murdered only a few feet from where I was sleeping, I'm doing
comparatively well,' Phil McCann answered.

'Do you see what Phil just did?' Meadows asked Crane. 'He's
just told us, by implication, that he heard nothing last night.'

'It's the truth,' McCann said. 'When I go to bed, I put cotton wool in my ears. It's a habit I developed when my daughters were young and noisy.'

'Boring!' Meadows said, almost under her breath.

'What did you just say?' Phil McCann demanded.

'Have you *still* got cotton wool in your ears?' Meadows replied. 'I asked you if there was any good reason why we shouldn't make you our number one suspect in the murder of Bradley Quirk.'

'You said no such thing.'

'Well, did you kill him?'

'I did not. And I didn't kill Cotton, either.'

'Oh, I know that,' Meadows said airily. 'You had a very good reason for wanting Cotton to stay alive – at least for a little while.'

'As a normal caring human being, I like to think that I have a very good reason for wanting *everyone* I come into contact with to stay alive,' McCann said, slightly pompously.

Meadows chuckled. 'A normal caring human being?' she repeated. 'Oh, come on, Mr McCann, that's a little rich coming from someone who's used other people as much as you have, don't you think?'

'I have absolutely no idea at all what you're talking about,' McCann said stiffly.

'I hear your elder daughter's very interested in amateur dramatics. Is that right?'

'Yes,' McCann said – and it was clear from the expression on his face that he now had at least a suspicion of what was coming next.

'Is she planning to go to drama school?' Meadows asked.

'Yes.'

'And presumably you want her to go to one of the better ones. But competition for places is very fierce, so you start thinking about what you can do that will give her a head start over the other candidates. Dancing lessons? Yes, that might help – but almost all the little darlings will have had dancing lessons. Singing lessons, then? They certainly couldn't do any harm. But what would *really* help would be a recommendation from someone already in the business. If only you knew someone who was a big star! And, of course, you do! But the big star is – by all accounts – not a very nice man, and if he is going to help you, he wants something in return.'

'The big hook for the BBC was that it would be the same cast that had appeared in *The Spanish Tragedy* in 1957,' Phil McCann said, defeated. 'If it wasn't the same cast – and I mean *all* the same cast – then they weren't interested.'

'And Mark Cotton desperately wanted the documentary, because he hoped it would mean that people would take him more seriously?'

'Yes.'

'So that was the deal – you persuade everyone to come, and he writes the recommendation?'

'Yes.'

'Why didn't you tell us all this before?'

'Why do you think?' Phil McCann asked angrily. 'I didn't tell you because I was ashamed of myself for persuading some of the cast that coming up here was in their own best interests, when I didn't really believe it was.'

'And if you hadn't been so persuasive, it's more than likely that Mark Cotton and Bradley Quirk would still be alive,' Meadows said.

'You can't blame me for that!' McCann protested.

'*I* don't,' Meadows told him, 'but I think there's at least a small part of you that already has.'

On the other side of the two-way mirror, Paniatowski found herself nodding. She would not have handled the interview in the same way as Kate Meadows had done, but then there were very few aspects of police work that she and Meadows would approach from the same angle. That didn't matter as long as Meadows was effective – and she had been.

'You can't blame me for that!' Phil McCann had said, his face flooded with guilt.

But it had been the guilt of a man who thought he might have contributed to a death, rather than of a man who regretted taking a life.

There was a gentle tapping on the door, then the door itself opened and a WPC entered the observation room.

'Sorry to disturb you, ma'am, but you left instructions that you wanted to know the moment the doctors at Whitebridge General would agree to let you see Maggie Maitland,' she said.

'And they've agreed now?'

'Yes, ma'am.'

It was highly unlikely that Maggie Maitland would have anything useful to say about Mark Cotton's murder, and

Paniatowski really didn't want to go and see her. But the chief constable would expect her to talk to Maggie, and when you were fielding flak as she was, the last person you wanted to get on the wrong side of was the man who could take you off the case any time he felt like it.

And looking on the bright side, while seeing Maggie might be a waste of her time, it would at least be buying time for the rest of the team – and buying time for the rest of the team, she accepted, was something that she, and only she, could do.

'You look to me like a man who is suffering from the mother and father of hangovers, Mr Talbot,' Meadows said loudly. 'Am I right? Is there a blacksmith hammering away at an anvil somewhere inside your head?'

Talbot covered his ears with his hands.

'Yes,' he moaned.

'How much did you drink last night?'

'I don't know. I stopped counting after the ninth pint.'

'It was a celebration, was it?'

'More like a wake for my career. I was here when Mark Cotton died, and that makes me bad luck – it's like having the mark of Cain on me forever.'

'If I remember rightly, Cain got his mark because he was a murderer,' Meadows said. 'Are *you* a murderer, Mr Talbot?'

'God, no!'

'And yet you were seen to be hanging around the steps up to the platform, shortly before Cotton died.'

'I explained all that to you. I was just so angry I didn't really know what I was doing.'

'Bollocks,' Meadow said. 'You were clear-headed enough to notice that Ruth Audley was looking at you suspiciously, and then, because of that, to walk away. But not long after, you went back to the steps, didn't you? And this time you had a large jar of make-up with you.'

'I didn't . . .'

'There'll be no charges laid against you, Mr Talbot – not if you tell us the truth.'

'He'd taken my big chance away from me, and I wanted him to miss his cue,' Talbot said miserably. 'I wanted him to make a fool of himself in front of all those people.'

'Tell me what you did last night when you got back to the boarding house,' Meadows said.

'I nearly didn't make it back at all. I fell over twice. And once I was my room, I threw myself on to my bed and blacked out. The next thing I knew, it was morning and a bobby was waking me up.'

'Thank you very much, Mr Talbot, you can go for now,' Meadows said.

Talbot stood up very gingerly.

'I didn't kill Mark, you know.'

'I never said you did.'

'But if I'd known somebody had fixed the noose, I'd never have done that thing with the make-up. If I'd known he was going to his death, I'd probably have been standing by the steps in case he needed any help getting up them.'

'I take it Sarah Audley was expelled from Blackthorn Independent School,' Beresford said.

'Oh yes,' Parry agreed. 'Given the way she'd spoken, she'd left the headmistress very little choice. But it was what happened next – a few days after the expulsion – which is important.'

Though many of her younger pupils probably imagine that Miss Hallam lives in a dark tower guarded by vampire bats, she actually owns a rather nice bungalow on the outskirts of town, and it is to this bungalow that she is driving when she sees the column of smoke in the near distance. At first, she simply assumes that one of her neighbours is burning garden rubbish, but then she realizes that it is coming from her own garden.

She speeds up, then slams on the brakes as she reaches her back gate. Her garden shed is on fire, and though it has not yet been quite burned to the ground, she can see that it is already far too late to save it. Still, the responsible thing to do is to call the fire bridge as soon as possible, and she strides quickly up the garden path to the house.

And then, as she reaches the veranda, she sees her cat. It is hanging from a bracket designed to hold plant pots, and it is quite dead. A note, written in block capitals, has been fastened to the cat, and that note reads: 'SCREW YOU, YOU OLD BITCH.'

*   *   *

'Jesus!' Beresford said.

'I'll admit that the fact that a cat was involved gave me an extra incentive, but I would have been concerned anyway, because anybody who'll do that kind of thing is a danger to both the community and themselves,' Parry said.

'So what action did you take?'

'Based on the fact that the words on the note were exactly the same as the words that Sarah Audley had used to Miss Hallam only a few days earlier, I went to the Audley house to talk to Sarah.'

Maggie Maitland looked a mess. Her hair was tangled, her face was a mass of blotches, and she was wearing a straitjacket. But at least there was some comprehension – and possibly a little tranquillity – in her eyes.

'They say you're from the police,' she said.

'I am,' Paniatowski replied.

'They say if I can behave myself with you, they might let me out of this thing.'

'Let's hope so.'

'What is it you want to know?'

'How long were you hiding in the theatre, Maggie?'

'I don't know. I didn't count the days.'

'Were you there before the company arrived?'

'What do you mean?'

'Were you there before *Mark Cotton* arrived?'

'Yes. I had to be, because I knew that once his thugs turned up, they'd find a way to keep me out.'

'Would you like to tell me precisely *why* you were there in the theatre?' Paniatowski asked.

'You know why I was there.'

'Tell me, anyway.'

'I was there to kill Mark.'

'Then why didn't you? There were none of his security people inside the theatre, and he was there for over a week. You must have had numerous opportunities to do it.'

'You're wrong, there weren't any opportunities – because we were never *ever* alone. There were all those people there, talking to him, *touching* him,' Maggie said, and with every word her voice was getting louder and more out of control. 'He smiled at them sometimes – *he never smiled at me!*'

'You need to calm down, Maggie,' Paniatowski urged, glancing over her shoulder to see if the doctors, who she knew were watching them, were about to tell her that that was enough. 'If you want to get out of that straitjacket, you need to calm down. Do you understand?'

Maggie merely nodded, as if she didn't trust herself to speak.

'Take a few slow, deep breaths, Maggie,' Paniatowski said.

Maggie took some breaths.

'Is that better?' Paniatowski asked.

'Yes.'

'You were saying that you needed him to be alone. Why did you need him to be alone?'

'Because I couldn't just kill him like that, could I? I needed to follow the Plan, and I couldn't follow it if anybody else was there.'

'What was the plan, Maggie?'

'Look at me,' Maggie Maitland said. 'I'm beautiful, aren't I?'

'We're all beautiful – in our own way.'

'But not everybody's like me – I'm gorgeous. So why wouldn't Mark fall in love with me?'

'I don't know.'

'It's because he didn't believe that I really loved him. And that's where the Plan came in. I was going to give him a fatal wound, and as he lay there dying, I was going to kill myself right in front of him. Then he'd see, wouldn't he? In those last few moments of his life, he'd finally understand how much I loved him.'

'I can understand why you'd kill yourself to prove to him how much you loved him, but if you really *did* love him, why would you kill *him* as well?'

Maggie looked at her in a way which suggested she thought the wrong person was in the straitjacket.

'I'd have killed him so that nobody else could have him,' she said.

Sergeant Parry rings the bell, and the door is answered by a beautiful young woman. For a moment, he thinks this might be Sarah herself, but then he realizes that this woman is at least twenty-two or twenty-three.

He shows her his warrant card, and, in answer to his request, she tells him that her name is Ruth Audley.

'Do you live here, Miss Audley?' he asks.

'I used to,' she says. 'But at the moment, I'm living and working in Whitebridge, Lancashire.'

'So you're just visiting then?'

'Yes.'

'Are you here for some kind of family event?'

The question seems to confuse her.

Yes,' she says. 'Well no, not exactly. My sister's had a bit of a problem recently, and I've come down to advise her.'

Yes, he thinks, calling your headmistress a bitch and getting expelled from school could be called a problem, but Sarah has, in fact, more problems than her sister could ever imagine.

'It's your sister I've come to see,' he says. 'Is she in?'

More confusion.

'I think . . . I think it would be better if you talked to my mother,' Ruth says.

She leads Parry down the corridor and into a living room in which almost all the furniture is heavy, Edwardian and basically hideous.

Ruth reads the expression on his face, and laughs to cover her embarrassment.

'I know it's awful,' she says, 'but Mother inherited it from my grandparents, and she simply won't throw it out.'

She invites Parry to sit down and goes to look for her mother. When she returns, it is with a tall, rigid woman who has the coldest eyes Parry has ever seen.

'This is Sergeant Parry, Mother,' Ruth says nervously.

Parry stands up and holds out his hand.

Mrs Audley looks down at the hand as if he is offering her a piece of dog shit, and says, 'What do you want?'

No mention of his rank or evidence of any other social courtesy, he notes.

'I'd like to talk to your younger daughter,' he says.

'Concerning what?'

'There has been an incident. A cat was killed and a garden shed was set on fire . . .'

'That had nothing to do with Sarah,' Mrs Audley says firmly.

'There was a note pinned to the cat . . .'

There is emotion in Mrs Audley's eyes now – and that emotion is blazing anger.

'First that woman – who should never have been appointed headmistress – unfairly expels my daughter from school,' she said, 'and now she is accusing her of killing her cat. Well, that is just too much.' She paused. 'Since you seem to be completely ignorant

of the facts, I consider it no more than my duty to put you straight. What that so-called headmistress claims occurred behind the bicycle sheds never happened.'

'There were witnesses, Mrs Audley – quite a number of them.'

'It simply did not happen. I have my daughter's word on that. And now you may leave.'

'I need to talk to your daughter.'

'You will not talk to her. This is my house, and when I tell you to leave, you will leave.'

He really has no choice in the matter. He thanks her for her time, and she ignores him.

As he is walking down the path, he senses he is being watched. He turns around and see's a girl's face at one of the downstairs windows. He expects her to disappear now that she has been spotted. But she doesn't. She keeps on looking at him, and then slowly – very slowly – her face fills with a look of pure, malicious triumph.

'Of course, it's always possible she didn't kill the cat,' Beresford said. 'The lad she'd been screwing was there when she called the headmistress a bitch, and she might have told any number of her friends—'

'There's more,' Parry interrupted him. 'If there hadn't been more, I'd never have brought you all this way.'

TWENTY

'**D**id you notice anything unusual last night, Miss Audley?' Meadows asked, across the interview table.

'Well, yes,' Ruth Audley said. 'Except it was more like early morning than last night, and, at the time, I thought it was annoying, rather than strange.'

'Tell us about it,' Meadows suggested.

'I woke up at around about five o'clock this morning, absolutely bursting to go to the toilet, but as I was putting my dressing gown on, I heard footsteps on the stairs . . .'

'Were they coming up from the ground floor, or coming down from the second floor?'

'Coming down from the second floor.'

'You're sure of that?'

'Absolutely. The stairs from the ground floor to the first floor are solid oak, but the ones leading up to the second floor – which, I suppose, used to be the servants' quarters – are made of much thinner wood and creak. Really, the two sounds are quite distinct.'

'I see,' said Meadows – who, when she'd been in the house, had noticed the same phenomenon herself. 'Carry on.'

'The next thing I heard was the bathroom door clicking shut. I was really annoyed to have missed my chance, but then I told myself that since it had to be Jerry, Bradley or Phil, he wouldn't be long in there, because men never are. So I sat on the bed and tried to think of something else.'

'How long were you sitting there?'

'I don't know. Maybe two or three minutes. Anyway, since I hadn't heard him come out again, I stepped out on to the landing. And that was when I heard the sound of water, and realized he was running a bath. So I went up to the bathroom door, tapped lightly and whispered something like, "Could I just use the toilet before you have your bath"?'

'Why did you whisper it?' Meadows asked.

'I didn't want to disturb the others. But whoever was in there didn't open the door – I thought perhaps he couldn't hear me over the sound of running water – and I was getting fairly desperate by then. So I went downstairs to the kitchen and I . . . well, to be honest, I did what I had to do in a bucket.'

'And then you went back upstairs?'

'No, I was wide awake by then, and I thought that since I was in the kitchen, I might as well make myself a cup of tea. It was probably about fifteen minutes before I did go back upstairs again, and when I reached the first-floor landing, I saw the bathroom door was wide open.'

'So what did you think then?'

'I just thought that whoever had fancied an early bath had finished it and gone back to bed.'

'And what do you think now?'

Ruth Audley shuddered. 'I think the killer was in the bathroom, cleansing himself of Bradley Quirk's blood,' she said.

'That's what I think, too,' Meadows said.

*   *   *

'You saw Mark Cotton die, didn't you?' Paniatowski asked Maggie
Maitland.

'How do you know that?'

Because that's the only thing that would explain the state you
were in when we found you, Paniatowski thought.

'It's just a guess,' she said aloud.

'Yes, I saw him die. I was up in that place where there's all the
ropes and sandbags and stuff.'

'The fly loft.'

'Is that what it's called?' Maggie asked, uninterestedly. 'I'd been
there before. Once, there was somebody else there, and I nearly got
caught, but the rest of the time, there was nobody.'

That made sense, Paniatowski thought. After things were set up
for the production, there was no need for anyone to go into the fly
loft.

'Tell me what you saw on the night Mark Cotton died,' she said.

'I saw Mark step off the platform. I'd watched him do it before,
and he'd only fallen a little way, but this time he went much
further, and when he came to a stop, his head was at a funny angle.
And all I could think was – oh my God, he's dead, he's dead, and
now I'll never have the chance to show him just how much I really
love him.'

'So then you went back to the props room, which was where you
kept your supplies, to hide behind the scenery.'

'Did I?'

'Don't you remember?'

'I saw my darling – my wonderful angel – die, and then the next
thing I knew, I was in here.'

She had run blindly back to her den, like the wounded animal
she was, Paniatowski thought, and in the confusion, no one had
noticed her.

'Thank you for talking to me, Miss Maitland,' she said. 'You
should get some rest now.'

'What was the woman doing?' Maggie asked.

'What woman?'

'The one with the rope. The one I told you about, who nearly
caught me in that loft.'

'When was this?'

'I don't know.'

'What did she do?'

'She took the rope off the beam, and put another one in its place. What was wrong with the first one? Was it worn?'

Maggie Maitland was so obsessed with the fact that Mark Cotton *had* died that she hadn't even begun to think about *how* he died or *who* might have killed him, Paniatowski told herself.

'Are you sure it was a woman?' she asked.

'Yes, she had long hair.'

That wasn't much help, since all the women who could have killed Mark Cotton had long hair.

'What colour was her hair?' Paniatowski asked. 'Was it auburn? Platinum? Light blonde?'

'I didn't notice.'

'Could you describe her to me?'

'I've already told you – she had long hair,' Maggie said, getting a little irritated.

'Was she tall? Short? Fat? Thin?' Paniatowski pressed.

'I don't know. She was just a woman.'

Of course Maggie didn't know. The way other people looked was of no interest to her. All she cared about was Mark Cotton.

Sergeant Parry is walking down the High Street when, through a cafe window, he sees Ruth and Sarah Audley sitting at one of the tables and drinking coffee. Ruth is talking earnestly – with a great many hand gestures – and Sarah is listening to her with a bored, sullen look on her face.

Parry enters the cafe. He takes a seat behind a pillar, and waits.

The woman and the girl finish their coffees, and get up. Parry watches the table, praying that some overzealous waitress will not clear it before they leave the cafe.

None does, but it a close-run thing, and a waitress has almost reached the table when Parry steps in front of her, holding out his warrant card.

'I need to take one of those cups away,' he says.

Back at the police station, the cup is dusted for fingerprints, and those fingerprints match the ones found on the plant-pot holder from which the cat was dangling.

'So you filed a report, did you?' Beresford asked.

'No, I didn't.'

'Why not?'

'I used to talk to my Ellen,' Parry said, and his face became suffused with a grief so deep that it almost broke Beresford's heart. 'I mean, I knew she was dead, but I talked to her anyway, and sometimes – in my mind – it seemed as if she was talking back.' He sighed. 'That sounds crazy, doesn't it?'

'No,' Beresford assured him, 'it doesn't sound crazy at all.'

'So I asked Ellen what I should do about what I'd discovered, and she said, "What would be the point of getting the girl locked up? How would that help her?" So instead of filing a report, I went to see Mrs Audley again.'

This time, Mrs Audley doesn't even let him get past the front door.

'I consider this to be police harassment,' she says.

'This is important, so please listen to me,' he begs. 'Sarah has a real problem, and it should be dealt with now, before it gets any worse.'

'You're insane!' Mrs Audley tells him.

'She killed that cat, and I can prove it. I think she needs to see a psychiatrist, because what she did simply isn't normal.'

Mrs Audley slams the door in his face, and when he gets back to the station, he is summoned to the chief inspector's office.

'What were you doing causing trouble for Mrs Audley?' the chief inspector demands.

Parry explains about the cup and the fingerprints.

'It will never stand up in court,' the chief inspector tells him. 'The chain of evidence is corrupted. You could have produced that cup from anywhere.'

The chief inspector is an intelligent man, and Parry is surprised that he has not grasped the point.

'I don't want Sarah Audley to be charged, sir,' he explains. 'I want her to be helped.'

'No,' the chief inspector says angrily, 'what you want to do – for some twisted reason of your own – is to bring the Audley family down.'

'That's not true, sir,' Parry protests.

'I served under Lieutenant Colonel Audley in Italy,' the chief inspector says. 'He was a very brave soldier and a superb leader of men. He was killed in action, and awarded a posthumous Victoria Cross. Do you understand that, Sergeant Parry – he was awarded

the highest decoration that any soldier serving this country can ever be awarded.'

'But I don't see what that's got to do with—'

'And now that he's dead, now he can no longer protect his family, along come people like you – men who are not even worthy to lick his bootstraps – to try and exploit the situation. What does it matter to you if you destroy a family, as long as it results in another arrest being added to your record?'

'But I don't want her arrested. I just want—'

'Well, let me tell you this, Sergeant Parry. There are a number of men who served under Lieutenant Colonel Audley in this force, and as long as any of us are alive, his family will never go unprotected. That's all I've got to say on the subject. Now get out of my sight!'

'And that was it,' Parry said. 'I received an official reprimand and there was a black mark against my name from that day onwards. I suppose that in time – through hard work and extraordinary devotion to duty – I might have lived it down, but my heart just wasn't in it any more. I served out my time quietly, and when I'd got enough years in, I retired and – God knows why – took up golf.'

Beresford stood up and held out his hand.

'It's been a privilege to talk to you, Sergeant Parry,' he said. 'You're a good man – a *very* good man.'

'That's what I try to tell myself,' Parry replied, shaking Beresford's hand. 'But when I look back over everything I've done, I can't help feeling that I've been a bloody idiot.'

If she'd thought about it, Paniatowski would never have turned on her car radio on the journey back from the hospital, but it was a reflex action, and, with her mind firmly fixed on Maggie Maitland, she was not even aware of what the newsreader was saying until she heard her own name.

She listened, grimly, as the scant available details of Bradley Quirk's murder were milked for all they were worth, and though the newsreader did not actually say it was all her fault for not arresting the murderer before he could strike a second time, that was clearly what was being suggested.

'The man's a fool,' Paniatowski told the radio. 'We don't even know it *is* the same murderer.'

'Sir Charles Thurrock, the local Member of Parliament, had this to say,' the newsreader announced.

There was a slight pause, and then a richer – possibly port-laden – voice came through the speaker.

'I do not blame DCI Paniatowski for this failure,' the MP said. 'Rather, I blame her chief constable for putting her in a situation which is clearly beyond her current capability.'

After what Hitch the Bitch had said at the press conference, she should have been expecting this, Paniatowski thought, but it was still a shock.

And one thing she was certain of – if she hadn't made *significant* progress by the end of the day, she would be off the case.

There were three camera crews and a dozen reporters waiting for her in the police car park, but – she saw with some relief – there were also four constables to keep them at bay. Even so, the walk from her parking space to the back door of the station – under a barrage of questions – felt like an ordeal.

'Have you got any leads, Chief Inspector?'

'Will you be making an arrest soon?'

'Have you heard what your MP's been saying about you?'

Once she was safely inside the building, she found herself wondering if she still had the necessary strength to reach her office.

Maybe she should ask to be taken off the investigation before she was ejected from it, she told herself. Perhaps it really was too late in her pregnancy for her to be able to do a good job.

'Bollocks to that!' she said aloud – and headed for the lift.

Meadows and Crane were waiting for her in her office.

Meadows read the look of despondency in her eyes, and said cautiously, 'We think we might finally have some good news, boss.'

Paniatowski gingerly lowered herself into her chair.

'What kind of good news?' she asked.

'The post-mortem on Bradley Quirk,' Meadows said, handing the report across the desk to her.

Paniatowski quickly scanned the report, and then read it through a second time more carefully.

'It doesn't actually prove anything,' she said.

'No, but it tells us what the murderer was doing in Quirk's room

last night before the thought of murder even entered his head,'
Meadows replied.

'Unless Quirk had two visitors last night,' Paniatowski countered.
'That's not likely, is it?'

'No,' Paniatowski agreed. 'That's not likely.' She took a deep
breath. 'Now all we have to do is get him to confess.'

'Are you going to take over the interviewing again, boss?'
Meadows asked.

Paniatowski shook her head. 'No, I think we'll let DC Crane
conduct this particular one.'

Crane almost choked. 'Me, boss?' he said. 'But I . . . but I . . .'

'You'll do fine,' Paniatowski assured him.

It *had to be* Crane, she thought, because while the man being
interviewed might simply refuse to talk to her or Meadows, he
would find it much harder to resist a handsome boy like Jack.

Tony Brown was surprised to find that DCI Paniatowski was not
there to question him, and that the rather good-looking detective
constable had been the one selected to take her place.

The detective constable smiled at him.

'I'm DC Crane, I don't think we've ever been properly introduced,
Mr Brown,' he said. 'Would it be all right if I called you Tony?'

'That would be fine,' Brown said.

'You're a teacher, aren't you?' Crane asked.

'That's right.'

'I thought of going into teaching myself – I went to Oxford, you
know – but teaching is not that well-paid, is it, especially in private
schools like the one you work at?'

'I don't earn that much,' Brown admitted, 'but my needs are
simple, and there are compensations other than money.'

'I'll just bet there are – for somebody like you,' Crane said.

The expression on his face changed to one that Brown could
almost have mistaken for a leer, but it only lasted for a second, and
then Crane was once again the pleasant young policeman.

'We might have to question you for some time, Tony,' Crane
said. 'In fact, I can't guarantee we'll get through all we need to ask
you today, so . . .'

'Why should I have a longer interview than the others had?'
Brown demanded.

'Maybe you can be of more help to us than they were,' Crane

said. 'But what I was going to say, before I was interrupted, was that if you want us to contact anyone to explain that you're helping us, we'll be more than willing to do that.'

'There is nobody,' Brown said.

'Not a single person who'll care if you suddenly seem to have vanished into thin air.'

'No.'

'Not a wife?'

'No.'

'Not a girlfriend?'

'I've told you, there isn't anybody.'

'How strange,' Crane said. 'Oh well, let's get down to business.' He leaned back in his chair. 'So tell me, Tony, why did you kill Mark Cotton?'

'I . . . I thought I was being interviewed about Bradley Quirk's murder.'

'Just answer the question, please – why did you kill Mark Cotton?'

'Why would I want to kill *him*?'

'Oh, I don't know,' Crane said easily. 'Perhaps you were afraid he'd tell your headmaster your guilty little secret. It is quite a conservative school, isn't it? And while the law of the land may have changed a few years back, I'm sure the attitude of its board of governors hasn't.'

You're not an actor any more, are you? You're a schoolteacher – and, because of that, all I need to do to destroy you is to pick up the phone. Cotton had said.

But this young detective constable couldn't know that – it was all guesses and bluff.

'I don't know what you're talking about,' he said.

'I think in your situation, I'd have been inclined to ask what guilty little secret you thought I had,' Crane said. 'But we'll put that aside for the moment. Next question – if you didn't kill him, who did? Was it Bradley Quirk?'

'How would I know?'

'I thought he might have told you if he had. After all, you were very close, weren't you?'

'No, not particularly.'

'Oh, come on now,' Crane said. 'He's the only reason you came back. He's the only thing that would make you – a struggling teacher with leather patches on his elbows – take two weeks' *unpaid* leave.'

'You've got the wrong end of the stick,' Brown protested.

'Your nasty little friends may enjoy you employing sexual innuendo like that,' Crane said harshly, 'but I don't.'

'But . . . but it's just a common colloquial expression. I wasn't trying to imply anything.'

'We've read the pathologist's report on Bradley Quirk,' Crane said. 'She found recently ejaculated sperm in his anus. Now how do you think that got there? Was it a gift from the spunk fairy? And if it was, are you the spunk fairy in question?'

'Apart from Bradley, there were three men in this house last night,' Tony Brown said.

'Phil McCann is a married man with kids . . .'

'That doesn't necessarily preclude him from having homosexual affairs.'

'. . . and Jerry Talbot went out to the pub last night and got as drunk as a skunk. In fact, he was still a long way from sober this morning, so I think we can pretty much rule him out.' Crane paused. 'You went to the pub yourself, didn't you, Tony?'

'Yes.'

'Did you go alone?'

'You know I didn't.'

'So who went with you?'

'You know that, too.'

'Tell me anyway.'

'I went with Bradley.'

'So you did.' Crane paused again. 'We'll have no trouble proving you were in Bradley Quirk's bedroom – and Bradley Quirk's bed. There'll be hairs – from both on top and down below – which, of all the people locked in the house last night, could only have been shed by you.'

'Sleeping with him is one thing, and killing him is quite another,' Tony Brown said.

'I quite agree with you,' Crane conceded. 'But we've only to find a speck of Quirk's blood on your clothes and you're done for.'

'You won't find any blood on my clothes,' Tony Brown said firmly.

'Ah – of course – the reason you think that is because you were naked at the time.'

Crane reached down and picked up the cardboard box which had been at his feet. He opened it, and took out several pieces of doll's house furniture.

'I suppose these are what people in your line of work call visual aids,' he said with a smile.

He placed a doll's bed on the table, followed by a wardrobe, a dressing table and a chair. He arranged them in a pattern, frowned, then rearranged them a couple more times. Finally, he seemed happy with his work.

'This is roughly what Bradley Quirk's bedroom looked like, wouldn't you say, Tony?'

'I don't know.'

Crane reached into his pocket and produced a small doll, which he laid face down close to the wardrobe.

'So where were we?' he asked 'Oh yes, you were naked when you killed Quirk. But where were your clothes? On the floor? No, I didn't think so. You're a tidy person by nature, and before you surrendered yourself to passion, I'm sure you found time to fold them neatly over that chair.'

Tony Brown said nothing.

'Have you ever dropped a glass tumbler, Tony?' Crane asked.

'What are you talking about now?'

'You drop the tumbler, and it seems to shatter into a million pieces. You spend half an hour sweeping it up, and you're sure you've got it all. Yet for days afterwards you're finding tiny pieces of glass in places you're amazed they ever reached. Well, blood's a bit like that – especially when it's spurting out of a gaping wound in the head. You think you know where it's all gone, and then you're surprised to find the odd drop of it in the most unexpected places.'

'I don't—'

'Look at the chair, and look at the body,' Crane said, pointing. 'And then tell me just how unlikely you think it is that we'll find a speck of Bradley Quirk's blood on your clothes.'

'I want a lawyer,' Brown said.

'That's certainly your right,' Crane told him, 'but what would be the point? Come on, Tony,' he continued, in a much softer voice, 'we know you didn't plan to kill him, but, sooner or later, you're going to have to admit that that's exactly what you did do.'

'You're right,' Tony Brown said – because what *was* the point of pretending any more. 'I never planned to kill him. I thought things were going to turn out so very, very differently.'

*   *   *

They are lying in bed together.

'I almost didn't come back,' Tony says. 'I was afraid *to come back. But I'm so glad I managed to muster my courage in the end.'*

'So am I,' Bradley Quirk says, 'because if you hadn't, we'd never have had this jolly evening.'

'I want more than a jolly evening,' Tony says. 'I love you. I think I always have.'

Beside him, he feels the other man's leg tense.

'Oh dear,' Quirk exclaims.

'I've just opened my heart to you, Bradley, and that's all you can say?' Tony demands.

'Look, this is rather embarrassing . . .' Quirk begins.

'I don't expect you to be faithful to me – not all the time,' Tony says desperately. 'You can have affairs, as long as I know you'll come back to me in the end.'

'The problem is, you see, that you're almost an old man,' Quirk says.

'I'm the same age as you.'

'Yes, but I can still pull men who are much younger. Oh, don't get me wrong, it was quite pleasant, this evening, to relive old times, but once is quite enough. As the old joke has it, nostalgia isn't what it used to be.' Quirk pauses. 'I think you'd better go.'

'I won't go,' Tony says firmly. 'I'm going to stay here until I can talk some sense into you.'

Quirk gets out of bed. 'I'm going to open the door, and when I do, I'd like you to walk through it,' he says.

And suddenly, Tony is engulfed by a rage so fierce that it would terrify him if he stopped to think about it. But he doesn't *stop to think about it. Instead, he leaps out of bed, grabs the statue of Oscar Wilde, and pulverizes Bradley Quirk's skull.*

'I've been celibate ever since I left the Whitebridge Players,' Tony Brown said, 'and despite what you seemed to be suggesting earlier, I never touched any of the boys at school where I work. You have to believe that.'

'I do believe it,' Crane said. 'It's something a nice man wouldn't do, and everybody agrees you're a *very* nice man.'

TWENTY-ONE

Arresting Tony Brown had bought her a little time, Paniatowski thought, as she sat at her desk – but not that much. Bradley Quirk had never been more than a sideshow for the press, and what the hacks really wanted was the man or woman who had killed television's DCI Prince. And the irony of the whole situation was that Bradley Quirk's murder had not reduced her suspect list in the Mark Cotton case at all, because being dead didn't prove Quirk's innocence – it just proved he wasn't alive any more.

So what had she actually got to work with?

Both Lucy Cavendish and Maggie Maitland claimed to have seen a woman up in the fly loft. That might be a lead. But Lucy could have been lying to divert suspicion from herself and on to one of the Audley sisters or Joan Turnbull. And as for Maggie – well, when she looked into the mirror, she saw a beautiful woman staring back at her, so how credible was *anything* she said?

The phone rang, and Paniatowski picked it up.

'DCI Paniatowski?' asked the voice at the other end of the line.

'Yes?'

'This is Lew Wiseman speaking.'

Who?

'What can I do for you, Mr Wiseman?' Paniatowski asked.

There was a pause, then the caller said, 'Excuse me, Chief Inspector, but this is the point at which you're supposed to say, "Not *the* Lew Wiseman?" and I tell you that it is.'

'I take it from what you just said that you think I should have heard of you,' Paniatowski replied.

'I'm starting to get the idea here,' Wiseman said. 'You don't watch much television, do you?'

'No, I don't.'

'And you don't go to many variety shows, either.'

'I can't remember the last one I saw.'

Wiseman sighed. 'Life's always ready to kick you in the teeth, isn't it?' he asked. 'You've struggled for years to become a household

name, and just when you think you've made it, you talk to one
person who's never heard of you, and you feel a complete schmuck.'

Whoever had put this man through to her was due a good tongue-
lashing, Paniatowski thought.

'Listen, Mr Wiseman, I'm afraid I'm really rather busy just at
the moment—' she began.

'I know you are, darling. I've seen you on the telly. He's going to
be a giant, that baby of yours.'

'I'm sorry, but—'

'I'm the head of Midlands TV,' the caller said, before she
had time to cut him off. 'The television company that makes DCI
Prince.'

'Ah!' Paniatowski said.

'Ah, indeed,' Wiseman agreed. 'I've sent you something by special
courier that I think you ought to see, and the courier's just rung my
office to say he's delivered it.'

There was a knock on the door, and one of the clerical officers
stepped inside and placed an envelope on Paniatowski's desk.
Across the top of the envelope, in large black letters, were the
words: 'From the desk of Lew Wiseman'.

'It's arrived, hasn't it?' Wiseman asked.

'Yes,' Paniatowski agreed, 'it's arrived.'

'Timing,' Wiseman said, with obvious satisfaction. 'That's the
secret of success in my business.'

'Would you hang on while I open it?' Paniatowski asked.

'Be glad to.'

She slit open the envelope, and extracted a smaller envelope,
from which she took a single sheet of paper. It was a letter –
typewritten and brief – and it was clear, even at first glance, that
the writer was no expert typist.

> Daer Lew,
>   I've just heaRd that Sarah Audley has been offered a role
> as my co-star in Prince. I wish to make it per ectly clear that
> I will not tolerate this.

It was signed, 'Mark Cotton'.

'When did you get this?' Paniatowski asked.

'It arrived in the last post on Friday, but, as you can see for
yourself, it's in a plain envelope.'

'I'm sorry, but I don't think I quite see the significance of that,' Paniatowski admitted.

'Important people – and people who like to *think* they're important – make sure their name is prominently displayed on the envelope.'

Paniatowski glanced down at Wiseman's own envelope, which had his name displayed prominently in one corner.

'I see what you mean,' she said.

'If there's no name on the envelope, it means that even the person who *sent it* doesn't think he's got much clout, and it goes to the bottom of the pile – and since nobody looked at the mail over the weekend, that meant it went to the bottom of *Monday's* pile. Now Monday's a big day for mail – people like to give us the whole week to consider their proposals, and as a result, my secretary didn't get around to the letter until this morning.'

'It's genuine, is it?'

'If you're asking me if that's Mark Cotton's signature . . .'

'I am.'

'I'd say it's either a brilliant forgery or the real thing.'

'Did you anticipate this kind of reaction from him?'

'Let's just say I thought it was a possibility. But what choice did I have? Ratings for DCI Prince have been slipping, and the demographics are shifting from the viewers who have money to spend to the ones who don't. It's not a big change at the moment, but when the first small pebbles start rolling down the mountainside, you worry that an avalanche might follow.'

'Could you get to the point, Mr Wiseman?'

'So we began to wonder what we could do about it, and what with *The Bionic Woman* being so successful and Joanna Lumley really making a difference in *The New Avengers*, we thought a woman might be just what we needed. That's when somebody came up with DCI Mary Holland.'

'And you didn't think to tell Mark Cotton in advance about this new direction the show was taking?'

'We thought it might be easier face-to-face, but he wasn't in London, was he? He was somewhere out in the sticks.'

'He was in *Whitebridge*,' Paniatowski replied, feeling a small stab of local pride which instantly irritated her.

'That's what I said – out in the sticks.'

'And so was Sarah Audley.'

'Yes, but we didn't know that, did we? Mark's been keeping this whole little theatre project of his very quiet indeed, so we had no idea who was involved. But if it was Sarah who told him about Mary Holland, she's been a very bad girl, because she was supposed to keep it under her hat until we'd made the press announcement.'

'How would you have dealt with the situation if Mark Cotton hadn't been murdered?'

'I suppose we'd just have had to bite the bullet.'

'And what does that mean, exactly?'

'Mark's a known quantity and Sarah's still just a maybe. There would have to have been *someone* playing Mary Holland whether he liked it or not – and he wouldn't have liked it at all – but if he really hadn't wanted to work with Sarah, we'd have cancelled her contract and paid her off.'

And just how angry would Sarah have been if she'd found out about Mark's letter, Paniatowski wondered.

Would she have been angry enough to kill him?

'Thank you for calling, Mr Wiseman,' she said.

'Listen, before you hang up, there's something I have to ask you,' Wiseman said hurriedly. 'I've been very cooperative, haven't I?'

'Yes, you have.'

'And what I've just given you is a very good lead for your investigation.'

'It may or may not be a lead, but I couldn't possibly discuss that with you,' Paniatowski said cautiously.

'The thing is, if it doesn't take you anywhere – I mean, if it turns out that Sarah had nothing to do with Mark's death – then I'd really appreciate it if you'd let me know the second you know yourself.'

'I can't do that.'

'Look, cards on the table,' Wiseman said. 'Mark Cotton's death has left a big gap in the schedule, and we need something to plug it with pretty damn quick. We toyed with the idea of Prince having a brother, who's also a DCI, but while you can get most viewers to believe practically anything you put on the screen, we thought that was just—'

'As I said, I'm a busy woman, Mr Wiseman.'

'Anyway, one of my writers wondered why we couldn't take the character Sarah was going to play in DCI Prince, and give her a show of her own. Well, that would seem to tick all the right boxes and—'

'Would Sarah have known that possibility existed?'

'That's hard to say. When we signed her for DCI Prince, we did toss around the idea of her doing something else for us once that series had ended. But to get back to what I was saying – the new show would be moulded very much around Sarah, and, off the top of my head, I can't think of anyone else I'd rather have playing the role once we've developed the script in that particular direction. So if it was likely that she was about to be arrested for murder . . .'

'You'd like to know, so that you could drop the idea of DCI Mary Holland and try and come up with something else.'

'I knew you'd understand.'

'I can't treat you any differently to any other member of the public, Mr Wiseman,' Paniatowski said. She smiled. 'But I'll tell you what I will do – I'll try and arrest the murderer as quickly as possible, so you'll know one way or the other.'

'I'd appreciate it,' Wiseman said.

'That was a joke, Mr Wiseman.'

'Was it?' Wiseman asked, sounding puzzled. 'It must be northern humour, then.'

He was right, she realized – that was exactly what it was.

Paniatowski understood – better than most people – just how complex a murder investigation could be; how some strands of it overlapped other strands, sometimes hiding those other strands completely; and how strands which looked so very promising at first glance could wither and die under closer examination. She knew, and accepted, that waiting for a lead was a little like waiting for a bus – you stood there for ages, with no sign of one, and then two of them came along at once. So when she got Beresford's call, ten minutes after she finished talking to Lew Wiseman, she felt a great sense of relief – but couldn't honestly have said she was very surprised.

They found Sarah Audley in her room at the boarding house. She was packing her suitcase.

'I haven't given any of you permission to leave town, Miss Audley,' Paniatowski pointed out.

Sarah smiled. 'I wasn't planning to leave Whitebridge, Monika – just this house of horrors,' she said. 'And is it really necessary to sound so formal?' She noticed Meadows standing in the doorway. 'What's Sergeant Creepy doing here?'

'I'm going to examine your possessions,' Paniatowski told her. 'I do have a search warrant.'

'This is a joke, isn't it? It has to be a joke.'

'I'd appreciate it if you'd step out into the corridor while we conduct the search,' Paniatowski said.

'And if I refuse to?'

'Then I'll have you forcibly removed.'

'You *are* serious, aren't you?' Sarah asked.

'You'd better believe it,' Paniatowski told her.

The scissors were at the bottom of Sarah's suitcase. They were of a pre-war design, and the blades had serrated edges. One tiny piece of fabric – so small that only examination under a microscope would reveal its true nature – was clinging heroically to one of the blades.

Paniatowski took the scissors out into the corridor, where Sarah was being watched by a uniformed constable.

'Are these yours?' she asked.

'Yes, they are.'

'And do you always carry them with you?'

'I always carry *some* scissors with me, but I only acquired that particular set recently.'

'Aren't they rather large scissors for personal use?'

'Perhaps, but they have sentimental value. They belonged to my mother, you see.'

'I'd like you to come down to police headquarters with me, Miss Audley,' Paniatowski said.

'Am I under arrest?'

'No.'

'Then I must decline your kind invitation.'

Paniatowski wondered whether Sarah would make a run for it if she had the chance. Given her wilful nature, it was more than likely, and while she would be caught eventually, it could take a considerable time, during which a certain DCI Paniatowski would be ridiculed in the press for allowing Mark Cotton's murderer to slip through her fingers.

'It really would be easier all round if you came in voluntarily,' she said.

'No, it wouldn't,' Sarah contradicted her. 'It would be easier *for you.*'

Paniatowski sighed. 'Sarah Audley, I am arresting you on suspicion of murdering Mark Cotton,' she said. 'You do not have to say anything, but anything you do say may be taken down and used in evidence against you.'

Sarah Audley looked more defiant than shocked when the WPC led her into the interview room.

'This is a complete waste of time,' she said. 'I've phoned my solicitor, but he's based in London. He won't get here until tomorrow morning, and until he does, I'm saying nothing.'

'Why do you need a solicitor, if, as you claim, you're innocent?' Paniatowski wondered.

'No comment.'

'Because all you have to do is say you've changed your mind about having him present, and we can clear up what you're obviously convinced is nothing more than a misunderstanding.'

'No comment.'

'Otherwise, it *will* mean a night in the cells. You do realize that, don't you, Sarah?'

'No comment.'

So that was that.

It was getting harder and harder to squeeze her bloated body into her beloved MGA, Paniatowski thought as she walked across the car park, and before the baby was born in three weeks' time – or was it four weeks? – she was going to have to exchange the car for a more baby-friendly vehicle.

If she'd seen the woman as she was approaching the MGA, she'd have gone back into the station and asked for assistance. But the woman must have realized that was likely, and had been squatting down beside the passenger door, only to rise up like a spectre in the night as Paniatowski inserted her key.

'You shouldn't be here,' Paniatowski said.

'Is it true you've arrested my sister?' Ruth Audley asked.

'I can't talk about it – not to you.'

Ruth Audley came around the front of the car while Paniatowski was lowering herself into the driver's seat.

'You've made a mistake,' she said. 'Sarah really didn't kill Mark Cotton. It was me.'

'And why would you have done that?'

'I did it for her. She was still in love with him, and I could see how miserable he was making her.'

'So why didn't you kill him back in 1957, when he first rejected her? Why, instead, did you persuade her to stay with the company and tough it out?'

'I . . . I didn't know how *deeply* she was in love with him then. But when I saw that she still felt the same way after twenty years, I knew I had to do something about it.'

'So it was you who changed the ropes, and you who cut through the harness, was it?'

'Yes.'

'Who taught you how to make a hangman's knot?'

'I got a book out of the library.'

'What was it called?'

'I don't remember.'

'What about the knife you cut through the harness with? What did you do with that?'

'I threw it in the canal.'

Which was exactly what Sarah would have been wise to do with the *scissors* she'd used, Paniatowski thought.

'You didn't do it, Ruth,' she said.

She slipped her key into the ignition, and tried to close the door, but Ruth stood in the way.

'Please,' she begged, 'you have to understand. Now that Mother's dead, Sarah's the only person I've got left to live for – and how can I live for her if she's in prison?'

'How can you live for her if *you're* in prison?'

'At least then I'd have the consolation of knowing that she was free. And it wouldn't be so bad for me. I've got used to living within four walls this last ten years. In some ways, it's very comforting.'

'You're going to have to learn to live for yourself again, Ruth,' Paniatowski said.

'I'm not sure I could now.'

It was hopeless, Paniatowski thought.

She switched on the engine.

'Step away from the car, Ruth,' she said.

Ruth Audley took three steps back.

'Please arrest me and let Sarah go,' she pleaded. 'No one need know but the three of us.'

Paniatowski closed her door and slipped the MGA into gear. As

she left the car park she looked into her rear-view mirror and saw
that Ruth Audley had not moved.

When Paniatowski arrived home, the phone was ringing, and picking
it up, she found herself speaking to the chief constable.

'I missed seeing you at headquarters, and I just wanted you to
know how very proud of you I am,' he said. 'You've arrested *two*
different murderers in *one* day! That's got to be a record!'

'I haven't got a confession out of Sarah Audley yet, sir,'
Paniatowski cautioned. 'And given the nature of the evidence we
have against her, I really do need one to make my case.'

'You'll get it,' Pickering said confidently. 'DCI Monika
Paniatowski can do anything she sets her mind to.'

But it wasn't going to be as easy as that, Paniatowski thought,
as she put the phone down.

Given that the evidence *was* so circumstantial, she didn't dare leave
the interviewing to just Meadows. And yet, could she do it herself?

There was only one personality present in an interrogation room
– that of the man or woman being questioned. The interrogator was
a ghost – a godlike ghost, it was true, but a ghost nonetheless. He
had no back story. He had no weaknesses or worries that the suspect
knew about. And while he was asking that suspect to spread out his
whole life out on the table for inspection, he had to be careful to
keep his own hidden.

'But I won't be a ghost to Sarah Audley at all, will I?' she asked the
empty hallway.

Sarah Audley knew a great deal about her – and she had provided
that information herself, in the Drum and Monkey.

Was it possible that Sarah had planned for just this eventuality?
That she had intended to kill Mark Cotton long before he wrote the
letter, that she had calculated there was a chance she would be caught,
and it was possible that DCI Paniatowski would be the one to catch
her, and that if all these things *did* come to pass, it would be to her
advantage to know something about the woman who was attempting
to sweat a confession out of her?

Yes, given the cold, careful way Mark Cotton's murder had been
planned, it was possible.

Her head was aching and her legs throbbed with tiredness. She
would go straight to bed, she told herself, and maybe things would
be a little clearer in the morning.

TWENTY-TWO

The morning after Sarah Audley's arrest was cold and miserable. The wind blew in off the moors, and howled down the alleyways in the older parts of Whitebridge. The rain only fell intermittently, but *when* it fell, it was with a passion. It was not a morning which engendered hope. It was, rather, one which foreshadowed failure.

Thoughts of failure – lightly disguised, but all the more evident because of that – filled Paniatowski's office. And it was her fault that the team felt like that, she acknowledged. She had been too quick to arrest Sarah Audley. She should have waited until they had built up a stronger case. And she was still not quite sure *why* she had made the arrest then. Looking back, it almost felt as if Sarah herself had pushed her into it.

She became aware of the fact that her team were waiting for her to say something.

'Right from the start, Sarah Audley claimed that she wouldn't have killed Cotton because it would have damaged her career,' she began, 'but that argument doesn't hold water any more. If she killed him because he told her about the letter, then he'd *already* have damaged her career. And if she killed him out of jealousy, she'd have done so in the knowledge that even though that would be the end of DCI Prince, Lew Wiseman was already considering her for something else.'

'There's something about that letter that really bothers me,' Beresford mused.

'We've had the experts look at it, and they're certain that's Mark Cotton's signature,' Paniatowski told him. 'They've also established that it was written on a typewriter in the theatre.'

'It's not whether it's fake or real that's bothering me,' Beresford told her. 'It's that there's something not quite right about it.'

'In what way?'

'I don't know. There is a small part of my brain that knows the answer, but it's not talking.'

'Maybe it will come to you later,' Paniatowski said quickly, before Meadows had time to insert a witty barb into the conversation. 'Now here's what's going to happen. Kate and I will interview Sarah, but it's going to be a tough job, because she's no Tony Brown, who was already weighed down with guilt when Jack started questioning him. Do you agree with that, DS Meadows?'

'She's calm, she's cold and she's clever, which is not a good combination from our viewpoint,' Meadows said.

'The only way we're going to have any chance of breaking her down is to catch her out in a lie,' Paniatowski continued, 'which means that I need to know everything that went on in the theatre in the week prior to the murder. That's why I want you, Inspector Beresford, to go through every bit of documentation we have on the case, and you, DC Crane, to study the film again. Bring me something I can use, because if you don't, there's a good chance we'll have to let her go.'

Sarah Audley's solicitor was called Banks. He was in his late forties, smartly dressed, and as sharp as a razor. Paniatowski wondered how – even with her Kindly Witch from *Friday Corner* money – Sarah could afford such an obviously expensive lawyer, and then she saw a look pass between them, and realized that they either were – or once had been – lovers.

She found herself wondering whether that was just a coincidence, or if Sarah, knowing she might find herself in this situation – or, given her nature, a situation just like it – had selected her lover on the basis of his legal expertise.

She wouldn't put that past the woman, she decided. She wouldn't put *anything* past her.

For the first ten minutes of the interview, Paniatowski stuck to safe, uncontroversial matters. Then, judging the time was right, she hit Sarah with her first hard question.

'On the two occasions that we know you've taken a life, you've chosen to hang your victims,' she said. 'Should we attach any particular significance to that fact?'

'That is an improper question, and I strongly advise you not to answer it,' Banks said.

'But I want to answer it,' Sarah told him. 'Or, at least, I want to find out just what it is that she's talking about.' She turned her attention to Paniatowski. 'You say I've killed twice, Monika. Tell me more. I'd be really fascinated to find out who my victims are supposed to be.'

The previous evening, Sarah had been playing her cards very close to her chest. Now, with her solicitor there as a safety net if she needed him, she was being much more reckless. And it wasn't just the recklessness that was notable – there was a twinkle in her eye which suggested she was actually having fun!

'You know as well as I do who your victims were,' Paniatowski said. 'There was Mark Cotton . . .'

'I strongly deny having anything to do with his death.'

'. . . and there was the cat.'

Sarah seemed puzzled – or perhaps was just *acting* seeming puzzled.

'What cat?' she asked.

'Your headmistress's cat?'

'How did you know about that?' Sarah asked sharply. Then she shrugged. 'Oh well, I don't suppose it matters how you know.'

'Again, I advise you to say nothing, Sarah,' Banks counselled.

'I did not kill that cat,' Sarah Audley said firmly. 'I never even saw that cat. I didn't even know where that old bitch of a headmistress lived.'

'You left a note pinned to the cat.'

'I did not.'

'Your fingerprint was lifted from the plant pot bracket the cat was hanging from.'

'How do you know that? Have you checked the fingerprints you took yesterday with the ones on the bracket?'

Twenty years was a long time, and it was almost inconceivable that the fingerprints taken then still existed, Paniatowski thought – and Sarah would have guessed that.

'The note said, "Screw you, you old bitch." And that's not just how you described her a moment ago – it's also the same words you used when you were in your headmistress's study.'

Sarah threw back her head and laughed. 'You can't hold me responsible for what I said to her in her study. I was high at the time.'

'High?' Paniatowski repeated incredulously. 'In 1956? Nobody got high in 1956.'

'Well, of course, I didn't call it "being high" back then. It wasn't a term that anybody used. But do you really think I would have screwed a spotty schoolboy in front of a bunch of other spotty tossers if I *hadn't* been high?'

'How did you get high?'

'I took some pills. Don't ask me what they were called, because I don't know.'

'Where did you get these pills from?'

'From some Americans I knew.'

'What Americans?

'There was an American army base close to where I lived. The GIs were a bit older than the spotty youths at school, but they were equally as wet. Give them a hand job, and they'd get you anything.'

The date stamp told Crane that he was watching film that had been shot on the previous Monday, just a couple of hours before Mark Cotton had died.

Cotton himself was standing on the stage. He was wearing a light sports coat and sporting a cravat and a beret. He looked more like an actor playing the part of a theatre director than an actor preparing himself to play Hieronimo.

Ruth Audley walked on to the stage and started talking to him. It was difficult to say for certain at a distance – and without sound – but it looked as if whatever Ruth was telling him was of great interest to Cotton. Then Ruth pointed across the auditorium at one of the boxes, and Cotton nodded.

Was she indicating a technical problem – something to do with acoustics?

No sooner had Ruth left the stage than Sarah appeared. She stood chatting to Cotton for perhaps two minutes, but he did not seem as enthralled by her conversation as he had been by Ruth's. In fact, he seemed eager for her to be gone.

How cold do you have to be to chat like that with the man you intend to kill in two hours' time? Crane wondered. The woman must have ice in her veins.

Once Sarah had left, Cotton wandered over to one of the cameramen, and pointed into the auditorium, at roughly the same spot as Ruth had pointed.

The cameraman shook his head.

Cotton mimed moving the camera around, and the cameraman shook his head again, as if to say that it couldn't be done.

Then Cotton reached into his pocket and pulled out a wad of

bank notes. He held them up for the cameraman to see before stuffing them into the man's shirt pocket. And suddenly the cameraman seemed to be indicating that the impossible might just be possible after all.

Beresford was finding it hard to concentrate on the documentation, because every time he tried to read a report, he found himself thinking about the letter.

There was something wrong with it. He was sure there was. But how many things *could there* be wrong with a single sheet of paper?

The signature was genuine. The letter had been typed on a machine that Mark Cotton had access to.

There was nothing unusual about the paper itself, either. Admittedly, it wasn't the sort of posh pastel-coloured paper that an actor might use to make an impression. It was, in fact, just the ordinary plain white stuff.

But that was easily explained. When Mark Cotton had learned, in the theatre, that Sarah Audley was to co-star in his precious DCI Prince, he had flown into such a rage that he'd grabbed the first piece of paper he could find and typed the letter, not caring how many mistakes he made.

So if it wasn't the signature and it wasn't the typewriter and it wasn't the quality of the paper, then it simply had to be . . .

Beresford examined the letter again, then picked up the phone and dialled the clerical department.

'This is DI Beresford,' he said. 'I'd like a sample of every size of paper we have, please – and I'd like them now.'

'When did you learn about the letter that Mark Cotton wrote to Lew Wiseman, Sarah?' Paniatowski asked.

'What letter he wrote to Lew Wiseman?'

'The one in which he said he would refuse to have you as his co-star in DCI Prince?'

Sarah Audley shook her head.

'Mark wouldn't have done that.'

'Why? Are you saying he *liked* the idea of you co-starring in the show with him?'

'No, I'm certain that he hated the idea. He would have hated the idea of *any* woman co-starring with him, but the fact that the role would be played by a woman who saw stealing his limelight as just revenge for the way he'd treated her in the past would have really stuck in his craw.'

'And yet you say he wouldn't have written the letter?'

'That's right. Later on, he might have tried to persuade Lew to drop me, but he wouldn't have done it last week.'

'Why not?'

'You still don't get it, do you?' Sarah Audley said. 'What Mark wanted most in the world was to become the next Laurence Olivier.' She smiled. 'He'd never have made it, of course. He simply didn't have the talent.'

'What's that got to do with the letter?'

'Are you just pretending to be dense, Monika? Is this nothing more than some cleverly thought-out trap to try and trip me up?'

'No, I really don't know,' Paniatowski admitted.

'*The Spanish Tragedy* was supposed to be his springboard. It had to be a success. But just imagine that he did write a letter to Lew, and Lew rang me to say I was sacked even before I'd started. What do you think I would have done?'

Paniatowski had a sudden sinking feeling.

'Why don't you tell me what you think you would have done?' she said.

'There's no "think" about it – I would have walked out. And Ruth – because she's my dutiful older sister, and always does what I want her to do – would have come with me. Without us, there would have been no play, and without the play there would have been no springboard to thespian respectability. So tell me, Monika, do you really think Mark would have been prepared to take that chance?'

Paniatowski and Meadows were sitting in the canteen, shrouded in an air of despondency as thick as fog.

'Maybe Mark Cotton was so angry when he wrote the letter that he didn't even consider the consequences,' Meadows said half-heartedly.

'All he had to do was wait a week before contacting Wiseman, and then it wouldn't have mattered a toss to him what Sarah Audley thought,' Paniatowski pointed out.

'Perhaps he thought that if he *did* leave it a week, the project would be too far advanced for Wiseman to get rid of Sarah.'

'In that case, why didn't he just add a second paragraph to the letter – something along the lines of, "Please don't tell Sarah about this till next week." And if he was that angry, why write a letter at all? Why not just pick up the phone?'

Beresford strode purposefully – and triumphantly – into the canteen and sat down beside them.

'I know what was bothering me about the letter,' he said without preamble. 'It's the wrong size.'

'What do you mean?'

'Paper sizes aren't just random. There are international standards, and every piece of paper you buy matches one of them. The letter doesn't.'

'So what?'

'I took the letter up to the lab, and asked the technical people to examine the edges of it under a microscope. And what they say is that, from the way the fibres are torn, it's clear that it wasn't manufactured like that, but has been carefully cut down to that size using scissors.'

'Go on,' Paniatowski said.

'We've been working on the assumption that Cotton was so angry when he typed the letter that he didn't even bother to correct his mistakes. Would a man who wrote a letter in that frame of mind have taken the trouble to cut up the piece of paper so carefully that only the experts could tell he'd done it?'

'Perhaps he just found the piece of paper,' Meadows suggested.

'Why would *anybody* go to the trouble of cutting the paper up?' Beresford countered.

'You already have a theory,' Paniatowski guessed.

'Mark Cotton signed a much larger piece of paper, and whoever got their hands on that signature cut the paper down to make it roughly letter size.'

'Which means he didn't write the letter at all,' Paniatowski said. 'Then who did?'

'I think it's possible Sarah did it herself,' Meadows said.

'And why would she have done that?'

'She knew we'd think she had the strongest motive for killing Mark Cotton, she knew we'd probably find out about her hanging the cat, and she thought it was likely we'd arrest her. So she wanted to make sure that *when* she was arrested it was for the *wrong* reasons – and it's worked.'

Then she rushed me into arresting by refusing to cooperate,

Paniatowski thought. And she already had her fancy London lawyer standing by.

'The letter is the foundation stone to this case,' Meadows continued. 'It provides us with a motive. And when that letter turns out to be a fake, what are we left with? A lot of speculation, and a pair of scissors.'

'They *are* her scissors,' Beresford pointed out.

'Yes, they are. They're the scissors she used to cut through the harness. So why didn't she hide them – or throw them away? Because she wanted us to find them, to make sure we arrested her. My guess is that at some point in the future, she's going to tell us that she took the scissors into the theatre, and left them in a public place where anyone could have picked them up. And the rest of the cast will confirm it. So what are we left with then? Nothing! We'll have to let her go – and once we've done that, re-arresting her will be far from easy.'

'We've at least answered one question,' Paniatowski said, with a kind of gloomy satisfaction. 'We now know why she had to kill Mark Cotton on Monday night, rather than waiting until Tuesday.'

'Do we?' Beresford asked.

'Yes. As Sarah pointed out herself, Lew Wiseman would have either rung her or Cotton – or possibly both – once he got the letter, and the whole delicate plan would have fallen apart. So what she intended was that the letter would reach Lew Wiseman when Mark Cotton was already dead. But somehow she slipped up, and sent the letter too soon. And once she'd realized that mistake, she didn't dare wait until Tuesday night.'

'We have to find some way to connect that letter to Sarah Audley,' Beresford said.

'Yes,' Paniatowski agreed. 'We do. It's the only chance we have. I want you to show it to all the other members of the cast, and also to the landlady. Maybe they'll recognize it. Maybe they saw it in her hand.'

'But there's a pretty slim chance they did, isn't there?' Beresford asked pessimistically.

Neither Paniatowski nor Meadows bothered to answer him. There was no need to.

Crane was watching the staged conversation between Cotton and Sarah Audley that had been filmed after the Friday dress rehearsal.

'And with just a little bit of luck, we may get the chance to work together again,' Cotton says.

'Oh, there'll be no luck about it,' Sarah replies.

'No luck about it?' Cotton repeats.

'Well, we'll be co-starring in the next series of DCI Prince, won't we?'

She might be ice-cold most of the time, but she was being very human at that moment, Crane thought. In fact, she was really relishing it.

Cotton laughs uncertainly. 'You're joking, of course.'

A sudden look of concern came to Sarah's face. 'Oh dear,' she says, *'I have rather put my foot in it, haven't I? But you see, I thought they would have told you by now.'*

For a second, Cotton had gazed at her with pure hatred, Crane thought, and anyone who had seen that tape would not have been surprised if someone had told them that Sarah Audley had been murdered, and that Mark Cotton had been the murderer.

Suddenly, none of it made any sense to Crane.

Sarah was plotting the ultimate revenge. She was going to rob Mark Cotton of his life – and for her plan to work perfectly it was necessary that Cotton should not suspect that anything was wrong. Why then – for the sake of a much more petty revenge – would she risk throwing a spanner in the works on Friday?

As he reached for the phone to ring Bill Sikes, bits of the tapes he had watched earlier were playing in rapid sequence through Crane's mind.

'Do you remember ever having seen this envelope before, Mrs Hodge?' Beresford asked the landlady.

The old woman squinted at it. 'Yes, I have,' she said.

Beresford felt the briefest flicker of a flame of hope.

'You're sure,' he asked.

'I'm absolutely certain. As a matter of fact, Inspector, I was the one who posted it.'

The hope died as quickly as it had been born. There was no way on God's green earth that Sarah Audley would have given this woman the letter with which she hoped to run rings round the police, so it must be quite another letter Mrs Hodge was talking about.

'I think it was last Wednesday,' Mrs Hodge said. 'Yes, it was, because that's when I give the rooms on that floor a thorough cleaning. Anyway, I was in Miss Audley's room, and I happened to see the letter lying on the dressing table. And since I was already planning to go to the post office in the afternoon, I decided I might as well take it with me. I thought I was doing her a favour, you see – what with her being so busy with the play and everything – but that night, when I asked her for the money for the stamp, she gave me such a look that – well, I really don't want to say what it was like.'

'I want to make sure I've got this absolutely right,' Beresford said. 'You saw this letter on Sarah Audley's dressing table and—'

'No, not *Sarah* Audley's,' Mrs Hodge interrupted him. '*Ruth* Audley's.'

TWENTY-THREE

'**W**ell, this is certainly a turn-up for the books,' Ruth Audley said brightly. 'Last night, if you remember, I was confessing my little cotton socks off, and you quite simply didn't want to know anything about it.'

She was treating the whole thing as a game, Paniatowski thought, from the other side of the interview table. And that was understandable, because as long as she could keep things on a superficial level, she could avoid making the journey into the deep dark recesses of her own soul.

'Isn't that true?' Ruth said, sounding a little irritated now. 'You simply didn't want to know.'

'It's time to stop play acting, Ruth,' Paniatowski said quietly.

'You didn't want my confession then because you thought you could bring the real murderer – my sister Sarah – to justice,' Ruth said, ignoring her, 'but now that you've found out you can't make the charges stick against her, you've decided that I'm a much easier target. Well, sorry, but one chance of a confession from me is all you get.'

Paniatowski sighed. 'When you confessed last night, you never expected me to believe you,' she said. 'It was all part of playing the role of the loving sister. If you'd really been confessing, you'd have corrected me when I said the harness had been cut through with a knife, because you knew it had been cut with your mother's scissors.'

'How do you know Sarah *didn't* kill Mark?' Ruth demanded, as her emotional barometer swung towards anger. 'Is it because she told you she was innocent? I bet that's it! Sarah's so perfect, isn't she – and if she said she didn't do it, then she simply can't have.'

At some point in the tirade, Ruth had stopped speaking to *her*, Paniatowski realized, and was now addressing an invisible presence a few inches to her left.

'We know Sarah didn't do it because she didn't send the letter to Lew Wiseman,' Paniatowski said. '*You* wrote it – and Mrs Hodge posted it.'

'Even if I did write it – which I don't admit for a second – that doesn't prove I killed Mark,' Ruth said – and now it was Paniatowski, not the presence, that she was talking to. 'It could just have been my idea of a joke – a joke in bad taste, I now accept, but a joke nonetheless.'

'The letter's only the starting point,' Paniatowski told her. 'It does no more than identify our killer for us. But once we know – because of the letter – who killed Mark Cotton, we also know where to start looking for the proof.'

'What you really mean is that you know where to start doctoring the evidence.'

'Maggie Maitland saw you switching the ropes in the fly loft. You didn't know she was there, but she got a good look at you.'

'From what I've heard, Maggie Maitland is a real lunatic,' Ruth said.

'Only when she's not taking her medication,' Paniatowski lied. 'But she was taking it when she saw you, and she will be taking it when she stands in the witness box at your trial.'

'It'll be her word against mine,' Ruth said, 'and I'll look so distressed – and so wronged – that the jury will believe me.'

'We know you made the switch at half-past twelve on Monday,' Paniatowski said. 'The reason we can be so exact is because Lucy Cavendish was lying on the stage, playing dead, and saw you doing it. Every other member of the company – in other words, every other person who could have had the opportunity to engineer the murder – will have an alibi, and you won't. So why don't you just face the facts, Ruth – we've got you cold.'

Except they hadn't, she thought. Maggie would be useless as a witness, and a good QC could easily plant doubts in the jury's minds about when exactly the rope was switched.

'I didn't kill Mark Cotton,' Ruth Audley said firmly.

The interview was slipping away from her, Paniatowski told herself, and unless she took a gamble – a real leap into the dark – she was lost.

'I know why you won't confess,' she said. 'It's because of your mother.'

'My mother?' Ruth said, in a voice that was suddenly harsh and scarcely human – a voice which seemed to mingle fear with loathing and disgust. 'My mother!'

'Yes. She was the moral compass in your life, and even now she's dead you daren't admit you killed Cotton – because that would be the same as admitting that you'd let her down.'

'You don't know what you're talking about,' Ruth said. Her face had turned almost black, but now, as she made a determined effort to regulate her breathing, her normal colour began to return. 'You simply don't understand,' she continued, in a much calmer tone, 'but you will, when I've told you about my childhood.'

'I'd rather talk about Mark Cotton's murder,' Paniatowski said.

'I really don't care what you'd rather do,' Ruth countered. 'The spotlight's on me, now. It's my story that's being told, and for once – *for once* – I will have it told my way. So do you want to listen – or don't you?'

'I'm listening,' Paniatowski said, reassuringly. 'I *want* to hear what you have to say.'

'When Sarah was born, my mother made a great fuss of her,' Ruth began. 'That didn't bother me at first. I was old enough, you see, to know that mothers *did* make quite a fuss of new babies, and I loved Sarah, too. I assumed that I'd received the same love and attention when I was a baby, but as Sarah grew and reached an age that I could remember being myself, I began to see the differences. The four-year-old Sarah seemed to be getting much more affection than I had when I was four, and the eight-year-old Sarah had an infinitely happier life than the eight-year-old Ruth had had.'

'It must have been hard,' Paniatowski said sympathetically.

'It was *very* hard. Sarah could do no wrong as far as Mother was concerned, and so, of course, she did whatever she liked. She thought that nothing could touch her – and she was right. She actually screwed a boy behind the bike sheds – in broad daylight – you know.'

'Yes, I did know that.'

'After I left to pursue my career, Mother hardly contacted me at all, but as soon as Sarah got herself into that mess, I was summoned home.'

'It's not right that people are spreading these filthy disgusting lies about your sister,' Mrs Audley says. 'I won't have it. I'll take them to court – all of them!'

'Have you . . . have you spoken to any of these people?' Ruth asks.

'Of course not. I wouldn't lower myself.'

'I have *spoken to some of them, Mother, because I thought we needed to get the story clear.'*

'Who have *you spoken to?'*

'To the teacher who was on duty, and to some of the pupils. And it seems that while what Sarah did may have been exaggerated—'

'You've always been so jealous of her, haven't you? That's why you're so willing to accept their lies.'

'No, Mother, it's—'

'Sarah did not do those things, and I could not possibly love anyone who believed that she did. Is that clear?'

'Yes, Mother.'

'I had to make Mother see Sarah as she really was, even if it was by arranging things so that she got the blame for something she *hadn't* done,' Ruth said. 'And that's why I killed Sarah's headmistress's cat.'

'It was Sarah who did that – not you,' Paniatowski said. 'Her fingerprints were on the plant pot holder.'

'It was me,' Ruth said.

Sarah and Ruth are sitting in the Yew Tree Cafe when Ruth notices Sergeant Parry hiding behind one of the pillars.

For a moment, she wonders what he is doing there – and then it hits her.

She should have worn gloves when she went to the headmistress's house, but she had been so distressed at the thought of what she was about to do that she had forgotten. And that meant she must have left fingerprints – just like the fingerprints she will have left on the coffee cup she is holding now.

The threat of being exposed – of failing in her mission – terrifies her, and out of that terror comes a brilliant idea. She waits until Sarah has stood up, thus blocking Parry's view of the table, and then simply switches the coffee cups around.

Ruth shuddered. 'It was a terrible experience, killing that poor, helpless little cat. I really didn't want to do it. But I had to do *something*.'

'And the reason you had to do it was because you hated your sister so much?'

'No, I didn't hate her at all – not then. All I wanted was for Mother to love her a little less, so there might be some love left over for me.'

'I'm so sorry,' Paniatowski said – and she meant it.

'It didn't work, of course,' Ruth said, as a solitary tear trickled its way down her left cheek.

'Sarah is being made a scapegoat for everything vile or disgusting that happens in this town,' Mrs Audley said. 'She will have to go away. It will break my heart, but there is no choice in the matter. You will take her back to Whitebridge with you.'

'But Mother, I have my own life to lead, and—'

'You will take her back to Whitebridge with you, and that is the end of the matter.'

'I didn't want to bring her here,' Ruth told Paniatowski as she wiped away more tears with her sleeve. 'I can't say I was happy in Whitebridge – I don't think I've ever really been happy anywhere – it was just a little less painful than other periods of my life. But it was what Mother wanted and I didn't dare say no, in case I lost the little of her that I had.'

'Were you still having your affair with Mark Cotton at the time?'

'Yes, but I gave him up to save myself the humiliation.'

'What humiliation?'

'I knew Sarah would have him. Sarah always got everything that she wanted – everything that should have been mine – and I thought that at least this way it would look as if I didn't care.'

'After he broke up with her, you persuaded her to stay on. Was that so you could see her suffer?'

'No, it was because if I hadn't, she'd have gone back home, and Mother would have blamed me for things going wrong. But once the Whitebridge Players were disbanded, I couldn't be blamed any more, and we went our separate ways. Then, eventually, Mother fell ill.' Ruth paused. 'I told you I wanted to look after her, didn't I?'

'Yes, you did.'

'I wasn't lying. I really did want to look after her. I thought . . . I thought she might finally see for herself just how much I loved her.'

'And did she?'

Ruth laughed. 'Let me tell you about the day she died.'

There have been false alarms before, but Ruth can tell that this time it is the real thing, and that her mother is dying.

'Is that you, Sarah?' the old woman croaks.

And because she knows it is what her mother wants to hear, Ruth says, 'Yes, Mother.'

'I'm so happy you're here,' the old woman says. 'I love you so much, you know.'

'I know,' Ruth says.

'I've tried to love your sister, too, but it hasn't been easy. She was the reason I had to get married, you know. I'd had a lovely life up to then, and I didn't even like Arthur very much, but when I got pregnant, I married him. It was what you did in those days. But I resented Ruth for it – I really did.'

'It wasn't her fault,' Ruth says.

'No, it wasn't,' her mother agrees. 'But we can't help how we feel, can we? And then you came along, and it was the happiest day of my life. You were a child born out of love.'

'So you'd learned to love Father by then, had you?' Ruth asks.

And she is thinking, Why couldn't you have learned to love him before I was born. Why did you have to wait until you were making Sarah?

'I always loved your father,' the old woman says.

'I don't understand. You said you didn't . . .'

'Oh, I knew he was a rascal and that he'd probably let me down in the end. And he did. When I told him I was pregnant, he ran away, and when Ruth's father came home on leave from the army, I had to force myself to sleep with him again, so he'd believe the

baby was his. But I don't regret it, because I've got my memories
of your father – and I've got you.'

'You're wondering if I killed her, aren't you?' Ruth asked.
   'Did you?'
   'No. I might have done, if she'd lived a bit longer, but she died
almost as soon as she'd finishing telling me what a hollow mockery
my whole life had been. Then Sarah came down for the funeral.
And do you know what she said to me?'
   'No, I don't.'
   'She said, "It's almost as if Mother *chose* to die now, so you'd
be able to make it to Whitebridge after all. That would have been
so like her – she never wanted to be any trouble to anyone." She
had no idea of what I'd been through, you see. She had no idea
what an easy life *she'd* had. That was when I snapped. That was
when I knew what I had to do.'
   It was now or never, Paniatowski decided. She took a deep breath.
   'That was when you decided to kill Mark Cotton,' she said.
   Ruth shook her head. 'No, not then. That came later – and it was
never any more than a means to an end.'
   'But you *do* admit to killing him?'
   'Yes,' Ruth said – and seemed almost surprised to hear herself
confess.
   'You had no trouble making the noose, did you?'
   'None at all. I was a Girl Guide. I joined because I thought it
would make Mother proud of me. How pathetic is that?'
   'It's not pathetic at all,' Paniatowski said softly.
   'The day I was made a Queen's Guide – and there were only a
few hundred of those in the whole country – she didn't even come
to the ceremony. She said she wasn't feeling well enough.'
   'How did you manage to get Mark Cotton's signature?'
Paniatowski prodded.
   Ruth smiled. 'That was very clever. I dressed up as an old woman
and got him to sign my petition to stop the council poisoning pigeons.
Imagine that. We'd been working together only an hour earlier, but
even close up, he didn't recognize me. Now *that's* acting.'
   'It's very impressive,' Paniatowski agreed. 'And once you'd cut
down the paper to the right size, you wrote the letter. Why did you
do it sooner than you actually needed to?'
   'There was only one typewriter in the theatre, and Geoff and

Joan were always banging away on it, trying to look busy – trying to seem as if they had a *function*. And even when they weren't there, other people were, and I couldn't afford to let them see me typing the letter. So when I got my opportunity, I took it. My mistake was leaving the letter where Mrs Hodge would see it.'

'Because you'd planned to post it much later. But the moment you discovered it had gone, you realized you'd have to advance your plans if they were to have any chance of working. So why didn't you fix the rope for one of the rehearsals?'

'I couldn't have known for sure which of them would be playing Hieronimo in rehearsals. Mark was very unpredictable. Sometimes he'd want to do it himself, and at others he'd tell Jerry to do it. I needed to set it up for a time when it would definitely be Mark.'

'But at the same time, you needed to do it as soon as possible.'

'Exactly.'

'My clever young detective constable, Jack Crane, was watching the video tapes this morning, and it seemed to him that if Sarah had been going to kill Cotton, she'd never have bothered to piss him off beforehand,' Paniatowski said. 'And then it occurred to him that when the letter was sent, only two people in Whitebridge knew Sarah had got a part in DCI Prince – Sarah herself, and you. So he went back through some footage he'd been looking at earlier, and he saw you standing next to Cotton and pointing into the auditorium. There was also some other footage of Cotton in which he was pointing into the auditorium. Do you know what he was pointing at?'

'He was pointing at the box where Laurence Olivier would be sitting that night.'

'Olivier didn't come, did he?'

'Of course not. But I needed to get Mark to play the part that night, and I knew he'd be bound to if he thought Olivier was there.'

'Mark bribed the cameraman to make sure he took some shots of Olivier, and *because* he was bribed, the cameraman didn't put it in his statement.'

'I'm getting bored,' Ruth said. 'I don't want to talk about the cameraman.'

'Then let's talk about Mark Cotton,' Paniatowski suggested. 'Did you really hate him so much that you felt you had to kill him?'

'I didn't hate him at all,' Ruth said, as if she was surprised Paniatowski had even asked the question. 'He was a bit of a shit, but then you can say that about a lot of people. If he had been drowning, I might have thrown him a rope if I was standing on the pier, but if I'd had to cross the road to get to the pier, then I probably wouldn't have bothered. As I said before, Mark was no more than a means to an end.'

'And what end was that?' Paniatowski asked.

While she'd been talking about how she'd planned the murder, Ruth's expression had almost returned to normal. She had stopped crying, and there had been a certain flush of pride in her complexion. Now that all changed. Her cheeks were suddenly almost impossibly hollow, and her whole face became a bleak canvas of over forty years of misery and despair.

'I wanted Sarah to go to prison,' she said. 'I wanted her to find out for herself what it was like to be trapped between four walls year after year, and at the end of it come away with absolutely nothing. I wanted her to waste her life as I'd wasted mine. For the first time in my miserable existence, I wanted justice!'

TWENTY-FOUR

The charges had been laid. The prisoner had been taken down to the cells.

Paniatowski slowly and uncomfortably made her way back to her office. She was feeling neither a sense of satisfaction nor elation. Maybe those feelings would come later, when the team met up in the Drum and Monkey, but for the moment, it was mainly sadness and depression which held sway.

As in so many of her previous cases, she did not know who to blame – or how much to blame them.

Ruth Audley had murdered Mark Cotton. It was only proper she should go to prison for a long time, because no one had the right to rob anyone else of his life. But without excusing what she had done, it was almost impossible not to sympathize a little with a woman who had loved – and had worked hard all her life to be loved in return – only to have that love thrown back in her face.

As for Sarah, she had turned selfishness and lack of responsibility into almost an art form, but hadn't she been brought up to believe – encouraged to believe – that that was what she had been put on earth to do?

And then there was the mother. She had been wrong to deny Ruth love, but perhaps there was nothing she could do about it – perhaps she had really tried but could still feel nothing for the child who had led to her giving up a life she enjoyed and marrying a man she didn't love.

And perhaps that's how I will feel, Paniatowski thought – perhaps, however hard I try, I will feel nothing.

As she entered the CID suite she stopped, and grabbed the nearest desk for support.

'Colin!' she shouted. 'Colin! Get over here now!'

Beresford came running. 'What's the matter, boss?' he asked. 'She's never gone and retracted her confession, has she?'

'It's not retractions you need to worry about at the moment – it's bloody *contractions*,' Paniatowski told him.

'Are you sure?'

'Yes, I'm sure.'

'But you're not due for another three weeks, so it's probably no more than a false . . .'

'Look down at my feet, Colin,' Paniatowski said.

'You're standing in a puddle of water,' Beresford said. 'And that means – oh my God!'

'Exactly,' Paniatowski agreed.

'How long have I been here now?' Paniatowski demanded.

'Eight and a quarter hours,' Louisa replied.

'Eight and a quarter hours?' Paniatowski repeated. 'Then why haven't I given birth yet?'

'If you'd done the reading you should have, you'd know that first births usually take more than eight hours,' Louisa said. She paused for a moment. 'Sorry, Mum, that really wasn't helpful, was it?'

On the contrary, it was *very* helpful, Paniatowski thought. If Louisa hadn't been issuing her usual gentle rebukes, that would have shown that she was worried – and the last thing that was needed in this situation was *two* people who were shit scared.

And there was cause to be scared. There were two midwives and a student midwife in the delivery room with them, and, for most of the time, there was a doctor, too – because she was quite old to be having her first baby, she was having it prematurely, and the chances of things going wrong were high.

'I said I was sorry, Mum,' Louisa repeated softly.

Paniatowski squeezed her hand. 'There's no need to be, my little love. It's wonderful that you're here, and I don't know how I would have managed it without you.'

'You *haven't* managed it yet, but you're about to,' said the elder, sterner midwife after a quick glance under the sheet. 'It's time to start pushing.'

She pushed – and it hurt.

She pushed again – and it hurt more.

'I can see the head,' said the midwife.

And Paniatowski knew – with absolute certainty – that her vagina was on fire.

Her vagina is on fire, she has lost her shoes, her skirt is up around her waist, and her breasts feel as if they have been put through the mangle.

She groans.

'Can you hear me, bitch?' asks a disembodied voice.

She says nothing.

'Tell me you can hear me, or I'll hurt you again.'

'I . . . I can hear you.'

'Good, then listen carefully! You're probably thinking of going to the police, to report what's happened to you, but I wouldn't do that if I was you. And do you know why I wouldn't do that?'

She doesn't answer.

'Do you know why?'

'No, I . . .'

'Because they won't believe you. They'll think you came out here looking for a bit of fun, and that it was only when it got out of hand that you decided you didn't like it. They'll think that you're just a slag – no different to all the other slags we've screwed.'

'Yeah,' says another voice, 'and even if they do believe you, it won't get you anywhere. We weren't here at all, we were in the camp – and all the other Devil's Disciples will swear we were in the camp. So if I was you, bitch, I'd just put it down to experience.'

'And let's be honest,' says the first voice, 'you must have enjoyed being shagged by three real men for a change.'

* * *

'It's a boy – a little under-weight, but beautiful,' said the older, sterner midwife, whose face had been transformed by an almost angelic smile.

But the younger midwife was paying no attention to the baby, and instead was leaning over Paniatowski with her stethoscope.

'I can hear another heartbeat,' she said. 'I told you it was twins.'

The older midwife handed the baby over to the student, then took hold of Louisa by the shoulders, and began to edge her towards the door.

'But I want to stay!' Louisa protested. 'Mum needs me.'

'You can't stay,' the midwife. 'Things might turn very complicated, and you'll only be in the way.'

'What do you mean – turn complicated?' Louisa asked, almost hysterical now.

'You have to go,' the midwife said.

Paniatowski opened her eyes and discovered that she was in a room which was painted in gentle pastel shades. Then she heard someone cough discreetly, and when she turned her head she saw that Dr Shastri was sitting by her bed.

'What happened?' she asked.

'You gave birth to two boys, and then you haemorrhaged,' Shastri said. 'Haemorrhaged rather badly, as a matter of fact. But the kindly doctors pumped enough blood into you to float a battleship, and there does not appear to have been any permanent damage.'

'The boys?'

'They are fine, too. They were in intensive care for a while, but now they are in the nursery with all the other babies.' Shastri hesitated. 'It would be usual, at this point, for the mother to see the babies.'

'Then that's what should happen now, isn't it?'

'I'm not sure,' Shastri admitted. 'If you are considering putting them up for adoption, it might be better not to see them at all.'

'I'm not putting them up for adoption,' Paniatowski said.

'Please do not be so hasty,' Shastri said. 'If you keep the babies, you will be responsible for them for the next twenty or so years, and as you grow older, so it will get harder. You have vital work to do in the Mid Lancs police, and you might find that was no longer possible. And there are many loving, responsible couples who cannot have children of their own, but are yearning for a baby.'

She paused again. 'No one would blame you if you put them up for adoption, Monika. Everyone would understand.'

'I'm not doing it,' Paniatowski said.

Shastri sighed. 'Very well. Shall I ask the nurses to bring the babies to you?'

'If you wouldn't mind.'

Everything Dr Shastri had said made sense, Paniatowski thought, as she lay there, but she still could not put the babies up for adoption.

There had been times, over the previous few months, when she had blamed herself for the rape. She no longer did that, but she was still the one it had happened to, which meant that, since there was no one else to do it, she was the one who would have to carry the burden.

Her children were the seed of evil, violent men, and whilst it was possible that would have no effect on them, it was equally possible that the bad blood of the bikers would run through their veins. And as long as there was even the slightest chance that the boys had inherited their fathers' bad blood, she could not, in all conscience, foist them on to some poor unsuspecting party who only wanted to do good.

She could hear footsteps in the corridor and knew that soon she would be presented with her sons. She wondered if, when she looked on them for the first time, she would think of them as sweet, innocent babies, or whether she would read incipient evil into their small red faces.

Then the door opened and two nurses – each one carrying a baby – entered the room.